No Ghosts Need Apply

A Sebastian McCabe—Jeff Cody Mystery

Dan Andriacco

Paperback ISBN 978-1-78705-822-4
ePub ISBN 978-1-78705-823-1
PDF ISBN 978-1-78705-824-8

Published by MX Publishing
335 Princess Park Manor, Royal Drive,
London, N11 3GX
www.mxpublishing.com
Cover design by Brian Belanger

This book is dedicated
to my friend
Monica Schmidt, ASH, BSI
a force to be reckoned with

CONTENTS

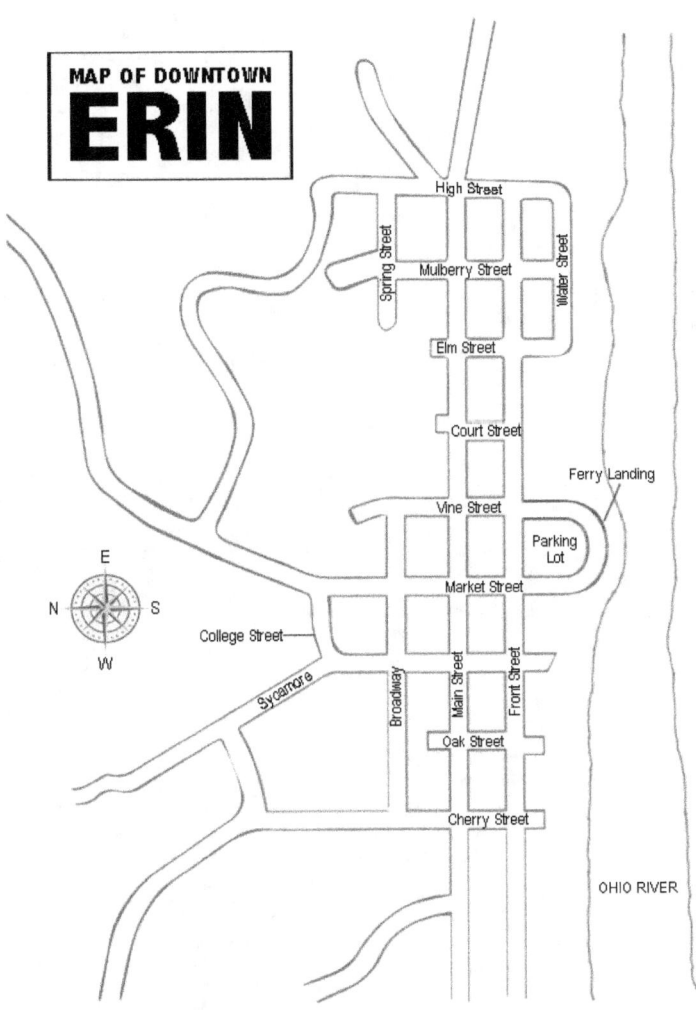

Chapter One
Ghost Story

"Believe in the supernatural?" Sebastian McCabe repeated, arching an eyebrow at my wife, Lynda. "Of course, I do! That is an inescapable part of my faith."

Tall, blonde Johanna Rawls wrinkled her Nordic brow and demonstrated the inquisitiveness that makes her such a good reporter. "I didn't know Catholics were into ghosts."

"Oh, ghosts!" Mac said. "I was thinking of God, Satan, angels, demons, the immortality of the soul—that sort of supernatural. Ghosts are another matter altogether, and a rather murky one, theologically speaking."

The broad, bearded McCabe phiz looked thoughtful. Being a professor in his day job, you can hardly blame the big guy for shifting into lecture mode, even though we were in a watering hole and not a classroom.

"The Bible mentions ghosts in both Testaments. In the First Book of Samuel, for example, the ghost of the prophet Samuel appears to King Saul—although the Church Fathers thought that to be a demonic apparition rather than a genuine specter. In St. Matthew's Gospel, the apostles mistake Jesus for a ghost when he walks on water, while in St. Luke's he calms their fears by assuring them he is not a ghost after the Resurrection. So, clearly, ghosts were known and feared in biblical times.

"Nevertheless, even the saints are divided on whether the souls of the dead can return. St. Augustine in the fourth century rejected the idea. St. Thomas Aquinas in the Middle Ages thought otherwise, however. The Divine Doctor believed that both saints and souls in purgatory could appear to the living."

Mac quaffed from his mug of Poltergeist Porter, brewed in the same building where we were drinking and yakking. "Myself, I think that spirits are real and nothing to trifle with, though perhaps the nomenclature 'ghosts' is best avoided as both prejudicial and overly dramatic."

"Well, ghosts are just what I had in mind when I asked about the supernatural," Lynda clarified. That's not the only kind of spirits she's interested in, as evidenced by the Manhattan cocktail in her hand.

"Whatever you call them, Father Juan says they're real," reported her gal pal, Sister Margaret Mary Malone— Sister Polly to most people; Triple M in my mind. "He told me he's blessed several houses that were disturbed by unquiet spirits. He's an exorcist, you know."

"No, I didn't know!" I said.

"Well, he doesn't talk about it a lot. Publicity for an exorcist is not necessarily a good thing. It can attract a lot of nutballs."

No surprise there.

I made a mental note to talk to the good father about his side gig in the ghostbusting line. As communications director for St. Benignus University, a small, Catholic institution in also-small Erin, Ohio, I'm always on the lookout for press release material concerning our faculty and staff. The Reverend Juan Diego Ortega—Father Juan—is our director of campus ministry, and thereby Triple M's boss.

We were gathered at The Speakeasy gastropub on that Martin Luther King Day, which was also the beginning of the last week of SBU's winter academic quarter, to celebrate Triple M's 41st birthday. With short black hair, parted in the middle, Triple M doesn't look her age to me. Maybe there's an aging portrait of her in Dorian Gray's attic.

Mac and Kate (his wife, my sister) were just back from Baker Street Irregulars Weekend in New York, where Mac hobnobs with his fellow Sherlockian wizards and whatnot, which provided a third reason to get together. Their oldest daughter, Rebecca, almost 21 and in the throes of a change in her major at SBU, was watching the three Cody offspring.

The Speakeasy features open rafters, visible pipes, and brewing vats that patrons can see from the bar and the dining tables. Starting with six varieties of beer from an India pale ale to a bourbon-barrel stout at its launch about four years earlier, the gastropub now serves up a brewer's dozen of malt and hop beverages. It also offers high-quality edibles, as indicated by the "gastro" on the front end of "pub." On a warm day we could be out on the sidewalk or the popular roof garden with its view of fireworks after Erin Eagles baseball games. In the waning days of January, that was a distant memory. Lynda wore a dark chocolate turtleneck sweater, so distractingly form-fitting it kept us both warm.

"Maybe Father Juan should bless this place to get rid of the ghost of Jackie O'Brien," she said, "but not too soon. There's a reason I brought up the supernatural. Tell them, Johanna."

Tall Rawls, looking even taller in after-hours attire of short skirt and three-inch heels, was Lynda's protégé back when Lynda was news editor of the *Erin Observer & News-Ledger*. My wife still keeps in touch with all of her former colleagues while not changing diapers, writing family saga novels, or handling the occasional freelance writing gig. As Mrs. Cody has no secrets from me, I knew what Johanna was going to say:

"We have a story in tomorrow's paper—well, it's actually in the *Online Observer* now—that the Wine & Spirits TV Channel is coming to Erin to make a Halloween episode about our local haunt. It's perfect because Jackie O'Brien became a ghost, if he did, when he was killed right here on Halloween night in 1920, when this was a real speakeasy."

I loved her journalistic qualifiers.

Mac's expressive visage expressed interest. By that I mean he arched an eyebrow.

"Isn't WSTV your favorite channel?" Kate asked Lynda.

"Yeah, I love it. I could watch it for hours." *You do watch it for hours.* The gold flecks in my beloved's deep brown eyes sparkled with enthusiasm. Or maybe it was just the lighting. No, she was jazzed.

"The show that's coming here is *Dining (Way) Out,*" Johanna went on, making the parentheses with her hands. "That's the one where these two brothers from Santa Fe, Stephen and Karl Lipinski, go to quirky bars and restaurants—ones that are shaped like a flying saucer, or underwater, or built as a movie set with low ceilings so the actors looked tall, or were once patronized by Albert Einstein, who ran up a tab and never remembered to settle up."

"You're making that up," I said. I never watch that stuff.

"She's not," Lynda informed me, brushing honey-colored curls off her lovely oval face. She wore it chin length at the time. "Those were all actual episodes, darling."

"So how does Jackie O'Brien's ghost fit into the format of that show?" wondered Kate. She's a no-nonsense woman for an artist, older than me by 18 months and with the same shade of red hair.

"Well, it is 'way out,'" Johanna said. Air quotes. "The gastropub having its own resident spook, I mean. Besides, this episode is a bit of an outlier by necessity. As you will read in my story, Karl Lipinski—"

"The funny brother," Lynda put in.

"—had a heart attack that's going to put him out of action for months." *Too many pastries; I've seen him on TV on my way out of the room.* "So, they brought in a kind of replacement, but not really. Stephen Lipinski's co-host on this segment is a guy named Stuart Diamond, who has his own YouTube show about weird and unexplainable happenings."

More proof that you can find YouTube channels on anything, from financial advice or looking good at 60-plus to conspiracy theories explained by guys in tin foil hats.

"*The Strange World of Stuart Diamond!*" Triple M said.

Her familiarity with such a thing was no surprise. The woman devours science fiction and horror novels, typically using holy cards for bookmarks when not reading the books on a screen.

"Well, if WSTV is looking for a haunted eatery and drinkery," I said, "this is as good a place as any. I've heard that Jackie O'Brien ghost story ever since I first got to Erin as a college student, and this building wasn't even a restaurant—excuse me, gastropub—back then."

Jackie O'Brien was a Prohibition-era speakeasy operator and bootlegger. You might say he was an early adapter because he went into business just months after the Volstead Act went into effect in January 1920. He ran liquor from Kentucky out of a big house in Erin that was once a stop on the Underground Railroad, welcoming escaped slaves who crossed the Ohio River by ferry to freedom. Such homes are not rare in Erin; Mac and Kate live in one.

You already know from Tall Rawls that on Halloween, 1920—exactly a century before the WSTV show was to air—O'Brien was shot to death at the bar of his speakeasy. No trick, and no treat. Taking no chances, the killer plugged him six times. The place quickly emptied out before the police arrived, and no witnesses came forward.

Pharmacist and attorney Franklin W. Galton a few years later succeeded O'Brien as Erin's leading bootlegger, remaining so until the end of Prohibition squashed his successful business plan. But O'Brien was not forgotten.

Over the years the building became a barber shop, a café, a hardware store, and a used bookstore called Pages Gone By until coming full circle as The Speakeasy with a photo of Jackie O'Brien on the wall behind the bar. And all through those decades there were stories of gunshots without guns, apparitions of a short man in a fedora hat (Jackie's preferred headgear), merchandise being toppled from shelves, and water faucets turning themselves on. On one occasion, during the bookstore years, Mac swore that a Sebastian McCabe novel was thrown at his back as he prowled the mystery section.

"I'm fuzzy on the details," Kate said. "Was the murder of Jackie O'Brien ever solved?"

"By thunder, it was not!" Mac said. "But then, I have never seriously looked into the case."

Uh-oh.

"Well, you solved the murder of Noah Bartlett, which was also in this building,"[1] Triple M said in a solemn voice. Noah owned the bookstore, though not the building. "Let's hope it was the last. I wonder why Noah doesn't haunt this place?"

"Maybe he's happy where he is, and therefore a quiet spirit," Kate suggested.

This was quickly getting too esoteric for me.

"Murders are such old hat for you, Mac," Lynda opined. "You should try ghost-hunting for a change of pace. That would be cool. As a magician, you should be good at it."

Don't encourage him.

"It is true that practitioners of the noble art of prestidigitation"—Mac-speak for stage magic—"have a long tradition of both engaging in the pseudo-supernatural in their acts and debunking fraudulent purveyors of the occult off stage. The former is harmless entertainment; the latter is a noble pursuit. The Great Houdini's efforts as an exposer of

---

[1] See *Bookmarked for Murder*, MX Publishing, 2015.

mediums spring readily to mind, although zealotry along that line destroyed his friendship with Sir Arthur Conan Doyle."

Mac, who now labors (if you can call it that) as a professor of literature and head of the small popular culture department at SBU while not cranking out mystery novels about magician Damon Devlin, misspent part of his youth doing street magic in Europe. He still does an occasional turn in that line, under the typically modest moniker of McCabe the Marvelous, Master of All Mysteries.[2]

"The classic ghost illusion on stage," he rumbled on, "is the one sometimes called Pepper's Ghost. It was first performed at the Royal Polytechnic Institution on Regent Street in London on December 24, 1862, during a theatrical performance of a scene from a Charles Dickens Christmas story."

Sebastian McCabe's memory and body shape are both elephantine.

Lynda bit her lip in thought. "I bet it was done with mirrors," she speculated.

"Clichés are nearly always based on reality, and that one is no exception. Several classical stage illusions do use mirrors. Not Pepper's Ghost, however. That one employed a large sheet of glass that reflected a concealed performer so that what the audience saw was a person who could be seen through, transparent like a ghost."

"That's almost a mirror," Johanna pointed out. "The principle is the same."

But Mac's train of thought would not be derailed as he continued to lecture about the stage and the supernatural:

"The audience of 1862 was delighted in being fooled as to the 'how' of the illusion, but contemporary accounts indicate that only a small percentage of dedicated spiritualists insisted that the ghost presented as entertainment was an authentic apparition. No injury to body or soul of anyone was

---

[2] See, for example, "Dead on the Fourth of July" in *Murderers' Row*, MX Publishing, 2020.

intended by the illusion. The same could be said for later stage magic evoking the supernatural, as well as countless books and films of the horror genre. Well and good!

"I must repeat, however, that genuine attempts to cross the boundary between the living and the dead are fraught with peril. The Church quite wisely condemns such efforts, even the use of the seemingly innocuous Ouija board and tarot cards as well as recourse to mediums."

"But why?" Johanna asked.

"Because when you open that door," Mac said quietly, "you never know who—or *what*—will walk through it."

The table went quiet for a while.

"Father Juan says demons can lie about who they are, so you don't know what you're really dealing with," Triple M said finally. "I agree with Mac that real ghosties and ghoulies and things that go bump in the night are not fun and games— far from it."

"You've got that right," came a voice behind me with a soft southern accent. I turned around as Mac boomed, "Ah, good evening, Nicholas!"

Nicholas Haldane, dressed like a cartoon chef except for the lack of one of those puffy hats, was co-owner of The Speakeasy, along with Charles Bexley. He'd operated the Hops & Hominy gastropub in Savannah as its owner and master chef for seven years before teaming up with Bexley, an Altiora Corp. engineer, to create the current enterprise out of the former bookstore. Actually, the teaming up came first; they were partners in life before they went into business together. I vaguely had the idea that they met in Savannah and that Bexley, who loves beer and is reasonably fond of good food, got the grand idea that what worked in Georgia would export well to downtown Erin.

Whether that's the way it worked or not, Nicholas Haldane now spends most of his time in Erin with Bexley and The Speakeasy. He's a slightly built man a little younger than me, say early 40s, with café-au-lait skin and a high forehead. Most of us at the table knew him, and Mac introduced him to the rest.

"I've been trying to get WSTV here for one of their shows since we signed the lease, just like I did with Hops & Hominy in Savannah," he said, picking up his point. "But not this way—exploiting the ghost for Halloween fun. I don't like it. It may be good publicity, but it's bad karma."

"So, you agree there's a ghost haunting this place?" Lynda asked.

Only later did it occur to me that Haldane should know a thing or two about such things, Savannah being reputedly the most haunted city in America.

He nodded. "Yes, ma'am. I've seen it. A man in a fedora. More than that, I've felt it."

Right then I felt something, too—like a centipede crawling down my spine.

"If you're so unhappy about the angle the show's taking, why are you letting them do it?" Kate asked.

Haldane seemed to choose his words carefully. "I'm not the only owner. Charles feels strongly that exposure like this will put The Speakeasy on the map and bring in some regional tourist business. Maybe he's right about that. We're right on the river and not that far from Cincinnati. So we may gain some trade, but at what cost? It's playing with fire to be so casual about what I am certain is a very troubled spirit."

"Indeed," said Mac. "I shall pray that you do not get burnt."

"Your prayers are appreciated, Professor. Charles doesn't really believe in anything beyond this life, so he doesn't see the danger. Nor has he seen the shade of Jackie O'Brien, as I have, or been in the room when the beer taps start flowing with no one near enough to turn them on. He thinks it's my imagination." This last was said in a tone of unmistakable bitterness.

"When does the TV crew get here?" I asked, to lighten the mood. "Halloween seems a long time away."

"They will have the show edited long before then, from what I understand," Haldane said. "They should be here on the fourth of March."

By then, the world would be different, though we had no clue at the time. Nobody did. On the day before Triple M's happy birthday in late January, a 35-year-old man in Snohomish County, Washington, went to an urgent care clinic with a four-day cough. He was the first confirmed case in the United States of a coronavirus so new that it didn't even have a name yet. Three weeks later, the World Health Organization dubbed it COVID-19.

Chapter Two
Coffee Talk

Lunch hour on the fourth of March found me at the Beans & Books coffee house on Main Street, contemplating my decaf cappuccino and wishing I hadn't given up Caffeine-Free Diet Coke for Lent. Maybe I could substitute Caffeine-Free Coke Zero, but somehow that seemed like cheating. The question was highly academic anyway, since Zero wasn't on the menu.

I'd popped into Erin's answer to Starbucks (which closed its local outlet in 2015) for a change of pace and a somewhat quieter ambience than my usual haunt, Daniel's Apothecary. The morning had been full, working with my essential assistant, Aneliese "Popcorn" Pokorny, on planning the next quarterly issue of the SBU alumni magazine, *Ben.* Things were changing fast at our little university under the dynamic leadership of Grant Kingsley, who had been inaugurated the year before after a solid run as interim president. A capital campaign was underway, new majors were being launched, our Davenport-Lattimore Bijou Theatre in downtown Erin was building new bridges between town and gown, and a new scholarship was set up to honor our revered president emeritus. Stuffing all that news—plus shamelessly promotional pictures of alums holding up copies of *Ben* while on vacation around the world—into the mag was a chore, though an enjoyable one. I needed a short break from campus. Hence, the ride into town on my bike.

Concern about something the media referred to as a "novel coronavirus" was much in the air, with talk of shutting down large gatherings already loud and getting louder. That was somewhere on my worry list, but not at the top as I leisurely sipped my cappuccino and read the titles of used mystery novels (the books part of Beans & Books) shelved on the wall opposite. More than a few carried the byline of Sebastian McCabe. I was musing with only slight regret on my own abandoned attempts at writing hard-boiled detective stories when I heard—

"Jeff Cody!"

I looked up to see the fair and willowy Mary Landfair, of the Sussex County Convention & Visitor's Bureau, with a young man in tow. By young man, I mean he looked like an underfed teenager who just rolled out of bed, but was probably in his early 20s. Mary is around my age, mid-forties, and high in gung-ho spirits and energy. Since I've been in meetings with her often enough to know her dynamism was caffeine-fueled, I wasn't surprised to encounter her in a coffee house. She works for Ralph Pendergast, my former boss and tormentor, which makes us siblings under the skin.

"Mind if we sit here?" she asked, pulling out a chair.

Would it matter?

"Be my guest."

I stood up, as one does when greeting new arrivals to the party.

"Jeff, this is Nuno Robles—he's assistant producer of *Dining (Way) Out*, which is going to make The Speakeasy's ghost famous and bring flocks of tourists to Erin. Nuno, this is Jeff Cody, media maestro at our local university, true crime writer, and general good guy. Plus, he's Sebastian McCabe's best friend, brother-in-law, and Boswell."

Thanks for not saying "factotum" or "dogsbody." And "Boswell" instead of "Watson" was a nice touch.

As we did the handshake-and-pleasantries bit, I took stock. Robles wore big glasses and an oversized Dartmouth sweatshirt, which probably added to my impression that he would be carded at The Speakeasy or Bobby McGee's Sports Bar.

"Welcome to Erin," I said as part of my share of the small talk.

"Thanks. I just got here this morning." He spoke with an almost-undetectable accent, the language of which I later learned was Portuguese.

"Where are you staying?"

"The Harridan."

I gave a thumbs up sign for one of our two classy downtown hotels, the other being the Winfield, and we all sat down. Nancy King, never without a smile even during the coffee house rush hours, made a perfectly timed appearance to hand Landfair a cup. Probably a standing order. She also gave me the grilled cheese sandwich I'd ordered with my cappuccino. "Do you need menus?" she asked. Most Beans & Books customers don't, but good servers always ask.

"He does," Landfair said, pointing at Nuno Robles. "And coffee."

"Right." She handed Robles the single sheet of paper, hand printed, and disappeared.

"Eat your sandwich, Jeff; don't wait for us," Landfair said. I tucked in while she gushed on without a pause: "Nuno parachuted in for two days to get the lay of the land before Lisa Carson, the producer, and what's-his-name, Stuart Diamond, come in to record interviews about the spook. Have you seen Diamond's YouTube show? It freaks me out." She gave a theatrical shudder. "And that guy seems familiar to me somehow. Maybe he looks like some actor."

He is an actor. All "reality show" stars are actors, even if they're only acting on YouTube.

By this time Lynda and I had watched a dozen or so episodes of *The Strange World of Stuart Diamond* on consecutive evenings after putting the kids to bed. Topics included a haunted trailer, the site of a man's spontaneous combustion (as in, just burst into flames for no reason), and a psychic barred from Las Vegas after winning more than a million of Uncle Sam's finest. Diamond wasn't a real ghost hunter, with electronic gizmos and all that; he was just a guy who interviewed people. He had a smooth "radio voice," and a delivery that reminded me of an attorney on a courtroom drama. At times the oddities he presented were a little questionable and the drama forced, but no worse than those home renovation shows on cable. Video quality was variable, however.

"Our videographer is local, from Cincinnati," Robles informed me, in response to my question about the rest of the team. "Lisa and Stuart are checking into the Harridan on Monday afternoon, then Stephen comes in later this week. Lisa and Stephen are married, you know."

"Yes, I know."

In fact, I knew more than I wanted to know, thanks to Lynda.

"There was a story about Stephen Lipinski—the serious brother—and their producer in *WSTV Magazine* a few months back," she informed me after we watched an old episode of *Dining (Way) Out.* This was my first full exposure to the show, and I must admit it didn't fulfill my worst fears of sappiness. At least the brothers didn't yell bleeped-out obscenities, like that one restaurant show guy on another network. "When the show started three years ago, Stephen was just coming off a bad breakup. A year or so later, Lisa's boyfriend was killed in a hit-and-run accident. She was devastated, of course, but Stephen was there for her to lean on. I would have said father figure, since he's in his fifties and she's early thirties, but apparently not. He told the magazine he's lucky she likes older men. Isn't that romantic?"

Since we were cozily watching TV in bed and not keeping what was already being called social distance, it wasn't somebody else's romance that was on my mind. I attempted to indicate this, with actions that spoke louder than words, but maybe I was too subtle. Lynda went on:

"They've only been married a year. He and his brother are the artists, but she makes the show tick as the producer. All her work is behind the scenes, even though she's gorgeous. You're not that interested, are you?"

"Not right now, no."

She leaned forward, treating me to the intoxicating fragrance of Cleopatra VII perfume and a view of her voluptuous figure best left unrecorded here. "You have something else on your mind, don't you, *tesoro mio?*" she said, her throaty voice at its throatiest.

"Now you're getting the idea."

Sitting at Beans & Books a few weeks later, I dragged my thoughts back from the smile-inducing memory of the pleasantness that followed.

"How did our local ghost come to the attention of you Wine & Spirits TV folks?" I asked Robles.

"Oh, it didn't. The way I get the story, Stuart—I don't really know the guy; we've barely met—suggested it to Lisa and she's like, 'Sounds good to me.' It fit right in with the idea for a Halloween special that she had when she approached the guy. I think she followed him on YouTube. Your ghost won't let us down, will he?"

"Of course not," Mary Landfair answered before I had a chance. She sent me a look that brooked no argument. I changed the subject.

"How's the format of the show going to work with Karl out and Stuart in?" I asked Robles, figuring I might as well play the first-name game; it seemed in the spirit of TV.

"Well, it won't be the same format, of course. Stuart will handle the spooky stuff, including interviewing the locals to tell their stories; that's in his wheelhouse. Stephen will be in the kitchen with the owners and their chefs as usual, learning about their special menu items. I understand there's something around here called 'goetta'?"

"I love goetta," said Landfair. "Everybody loves goetta."

"So, what's goetta?"

"It's German peasant food, a kind of sausage patty that's made with pork, beef, pinoats, and spices," I told Robles. "Very popular in this part of Ohio, especially downriver in Cincinnati. Cincinnatians eat a million pounds of it a year, no exaggeration, and everybody I've ever introduced it to loves it. That includes my parents, both from old Virginia families. I fed it to them when they were in Erin for my wedding. But goetta's not on that menu in your hand, so be sure to try it for breakfast at your hotel tomorrow. It's great with eggs, pancakes, waffles, any of that."

"I'll give it a shot. So, like I said, Stephen's part is the kitchen—that and sampling the pub's beer from the taps. He loves beer. Part of my job is scheduling Stuart's interviews. And this is literally my first time to do it. I've only had this job two weeks. So, I'm like, wow, what a place to start! Do you have any suggestions for who Stuart should talk to about this phantom bootlegger?"

Whom, not who.

"Who's already on your list?"

"Well, the owners, of course. Or one of them, at least. I talked to Charles Bexley on the phone. He said his partner is reluctant, so we'll see what happens there." Robles consulted a small notebook. "Bexley referred to a guy named Gulliver Mackie, who's the owner of the building. I haven't reached out to him yet."

Landlording is just a sideline for Gulliver Mackie. His main source of income is discreetly managing the investments of Erin's wealthiest families, including the Gambles and the Bainbridges, along with a few equally big-pocketed clients in Cincinnati and Louisville. He's also happily married to my uber-competent boss, Lesley Saylor-Mackie, SBU's executive vice president and provost.

"Gulliver could tell you about the history of the building," I said, "but I don't think he'll want to. He's a little sensitive about his former tenant being killed there when it was a bookstore."

"There was another murder there?"

"Right. That was five years ago this month. But the victim hasn't made any return appearances at the gastropub, so far as anybody knows. Noah Bartlett—he was the victim—wasn't much of a drinker." I argued with myself for a second. *Should I? Probably not.* But I did it anyway. "I may be able to fix you up with an exorcist."

Robles's eyes became almost as big as his glasses. "You have an exorcist in Erin? No fooling?"

I nodded. "No fooling."

"I didn't know that," Landfair said.

Neither did I until a few weeks ago.

"His name is Father Juan Diego Ortega and he's the head of campus ministry where I work. I just put out a press release on him earlier this year." *And it wasn't easy.* "He feels very strongly about what he says is a rise in demonic activity. Maybe I can convince him that a TV interview in which he warns the audience about that would be an act of mercy."

Landfair gave another shudder. "Do me a favor: Don't let him contact my first husband."

"Exorcists don't contact spirits," I said. "Mediums do that. Or so they say."

Accessing the Cody memory banks, I dimly recalled a grim story behind the bantering: Landfair's spouse had died some years ago by his own hand to escape the consequences of sticky fingers at a fairly high level.

Robles jumped back in, fired up once again. "Mediums! Do you have any of them in Erin?"

We came up empty on that one.

"But there's a palm reader over on College Street," Landfair said. "Would that help?"

"Not unless she can read the ghost's palm."

For one puzzled moment, I wondered how Robles knew that Madam Lena was a "she." But then I realized I'd never heard of a male palm-reader. I filed that factoid under, "Odd, but Irrelevant."

"You'll want to drop by The Speakeasy and see if any employees and patrons have Jackie O'Brien stories, of course," I said. "But you might go back to the days when the Pages Gone By bookstore was in that building. Mo Russert, who runs Mo's Mysteries & Marvels, worked there then. In fact, she found Noah's body. And Mac was a frequent customer—I know he had some unexplained experiences there in those days."

Robles's face turned quizzical. "Mac?"

"Sebastian McCabe," I elaborated.

"Mary mentioned that name earlier. Who is he?"

Landfair gaped. "You've never heard of Sebastian McCabe?"

"Not that I remember."

"He writes these cool mysteries about a magician." She glanced around at the used volumes on the shelves. "I'm sure you could pick up a few here to take back to your room."

"I don't read a lot. I'm more into gaming."

"Oh. Well, Mac would be a good interview. He's very erudite."

Only later did it strike me how apt it was to describe Sebastian McCabe in just the sort of multi-syllabic word in which he revels.

"And then there's Fred Gaffe," I soldiered on. "He writes a gossip column for the local paper called 'The Old Gaffer,' and he really gets around."

Landfair nodded. "Yeah, he knows everything about everybody."

"I keep joking that's going to get him killed one of these days. Lucky for him that only happens in mystery novels."

Chapter Three
Spirits

"Come on, Boss, spill," Popcorn said. "How did you talk Father Juan into being interviewed for *Dining (Way) Out*? He hates stuff like that."

"I just used charm."

My irreplaceable but sometimes rebellious assistant waxed dubious. I could see that in her big green eyes. Popcorn stands just under five feet tall, not quite as wide thanks to jogging and exercise, and has been dying her hair blond and reading steamy romance novels as long as I've known her.

"Not my charm—Father Joe's," I clarified. Nobody could resist Reverend Joseph F. Pirelli, SBU's president emeritus, when he pulled out his "for the good of the team" speech. "But I did remind Father Juan this was an opportunity to warn an attentive audience about the dangers of dabbling in the occult."

She nodded understanding. "The old 'what's in it for him' ploy. But I bet you really had to twist Mac's arm to get him to go in front of a camera."

We both burst out laughing.

This was March 10, almost a week after my Beans & Books encounter with Mary Landfair and the boy assistant producer from WSTV. Popcorn and I were beginning our workday together in the usual manner, with conversation and coffee (decaf for me) in my office. How else would I know what was going on at SBU? Her gossip network is second to none, and her loyalty to me is second only to her loyalty to the institution. Aneliese Pokorny and my smartphone enable me to play in Mac's sandbox and still do my job.

"Oscar thinks I'm crazy," she said, "but I really believe there's something to that ghost story. And speaking of Oscar—"

That would be Oscar Hummel, Erin's police chief. If they weren't both pushing sixty, I would say he and Popcorn are going steady.

"—I'm worried about his mother. Alma's ninety-one, you know, and she was moved to a rehab unit at Elysian Gardens after her hip replacement surgery."

"You should be worried about the nursing home." Oscar's mother is a force to be reckoned with, although Popcorn had won her over by years-long effort. Oscar moved Alma with him from Dayton when he took the job as Erin's top cop.

"Stop it," Popcorn said in a knuckles-rapping tone of voice. "This is serious, Boss. Dead serious. There were a bunch of cases of that awful new virus at nursing homes in the state of Washington. Apparently, it hits hardest at older people and those with certain other conditions. And now it's here in Ohio."

"Just three cases in the state as of now," I pointed out, "and no fatalities." I was up on it.

"As of now," she repeated. "So far as we know. But the governor declared a state of emergency yesterday and the World Health Organization just branded the virus a pandemic. The outlook gets worse every day. I'm very concerned about Alma, and I'm also worried about how it might affect SBU in a big way: Classrooms and dorms could become giant petri dishes."

"Take a deep breath," I advised. "I'm sure the Provost and GK are monitoring the situation and developing contingency plans. I'll give her a call right now."

Executive Vice President and Provost Lesley Saylor-Mackie was on another line, but she called me back within ten minutes.

"Good timing, Jeff," she said. "I was just about to pull you in. GK"—SBU's president, Grant Kingsley—"asked me to form a COVID-19 task force and, quote, 'light a fire under it.' We're meeting in a few hours. I've tapped Kelly Richards from legal, Janet Fischer from HR, and Aurelia Banfield from campus security." *Representing all the departments that need to be in the room when things go sideways.* "Sorry for the short notice, but I need you, too."

"Sure."

"But I don't want you to put out a news release about this. Not yet. Wait until the task force makes suggestions and GK acts on them. The way things are going, that could be soon."

"Probably the sooner the better," I said. The Cody brain had been working on the issue. "Our students think they're going to live forever, so they won't be too worried, but their parents will want to know what we're doing to protect their kids."

"I'm aware of that," the Provost said dryly. "I get emails and I see the social media postings. GK wants action fast. We all do."

She filled me in on the when and where of the first task force meeting. "Block out a few hours. I'm providing lunch."

My routine chores after we disconnected included writing a good-news release about SBU's baseball team, the Dragons. They came in first in the National Association of Intercollege Athletics (NAIA) baseball coach's poll of the top 25 teams. I was looking forward to the season ahead.

The Provost's confab later that morning and into the early afternoon was a "this is what we need to decide" affair that made reasonable progress under Saylor-Mackie's deft hand. We figured out what could be decided within a few days vs. what would take some time.

Aurelia Banfield, the young assistant chief of the St. Benignus University Police, more than pulled her weight in the meeting, with several spot-on observations. I would have expected the refrigerator-size chief, Ed Decker, or the head of the Department of Public Safety, Cal Daley, to represent the department on the task force. But Banfield is a smart up-and-comer, as was soon to be proved.

Later, Mac drove us downtown to The Speakeasy for his interview with Stuart Diamond. His 1959 Chevy with the 221B license plate number and fuzzy dice hanging from the rear-view mirror is the color of a fire engine, and almost as big. It has fins a shark would envy. Worst of all, it's one of the last places on earth Sebastian McCabe can fire up one of his $30 Antonio de la Cova cigars. The price of his smokes has increased as his opportunities to indulge in the vice have decreased, thus keeping his cigar budget roughly stable. That's my theory, anyway. I rolled down my window, it being a little too cool to ask Mac to put the top down.

Naturally, our talk turned to the ghost-themed production of *Dining (Way) Out*, which sent Mac off into full lecture mode as I gasped for air.

"I suppose a medium, if we had one in Erin, would bring some additional drama—or, rather, melodrama—to the production," he mused. "Sir Arthur Conan Doyle took part in séances in 1922 and 1923 in Cincinnati, with a woman named Laura Pruden. He called her 'one of the greatest mediums in the world.' Conan Doyle's profound belief in the ability to communicate with the dead is perhaps the best-known fact about him, other than the brilliance of his writing. When Houdini and others exposed the rather elementary tricks of mediums, he would either refuse to accept the evidence or make the excuse that the medium's powers must have failed on that occasion. He was a brave evangelist for his cause, but it is hard to acquit him of the charge that he was naïve. He even famously believed in fairies."

"How could the creator of Sherlock Holmes, who is like the epitome of logic, be so easily fooled?" I said. "Conan Doyle was a doctor, a man of science."

"Quite a few scientists of his day were spiritualists, including the chemist Sir William Crookes and the evolutionist Alfred Russel Wallace, who was an associate of Charles Darwin. From their point of view, I suppose they regarded the ectoplasm, ringing bells, messages on slate boards, and all the other trappings of mediums as empirical evidence of communication with the spirit world. Although it is true that Houdini and others demonstrated they could produce such phenomena by trickery, that did not by itself prove that—for example—Mrs. Pruden did so. Note, too, that from the standpoint of logic one cannot prove a negative, such as the impossibility of the dead communing with the living. In fact, I am as open as St. Thomas Aquinas on that point. As to mediums, however, I am skeptical."

"In that same spirit, some of my friends would say you also can't prove the existence of God, angels, the human soul, and the afterlife," I parried, just to keep myself awake.

"And I agree with them, Jefferson! For me, however, such proofs are quite unnecessary. That is why my spiritual beliefs are called faith."

By this time, we were pulling into The Speakeasy's parking lot. "When Stuart Diamond asks you questions on camera, try to keep the answers short," I advised. "He's not looking for an oration. Let me suggest a few soundbites."

I felt as though I already knew Diamond from watching him on screen at the Cody manse. But he didn't know Mac or me, so Nuno Robles introduced us a few minutes after I presented Mac to Robles. About fifty years old with suspiciously dark brown hair, Diamond sported a full beard and tortoise-shell glasses that made him look professorial. And I know professorial when I see it! Taller than Mac and not so big around, he was only slightly shorter than my six-one. I noticed that when he pumped my hand.

"I'm a big fan of your books," he said. *So, you're the one! I like you already.* "Oh, yours, too, Professor McCabe."

"When you're on camera," I told Diamond, "be sure to ask him the name of the book the ghost threw at him."

Diamond grinned appreciatively. "I'll do that."

He gave each of us a *Strange World of Stuart Diamond* pen, a reasonably cool tchotchke. The words lit up when you pushed on the end of the pen. It also doubled as a stylus.

The Speakeasy wasn't deserted, but the late-afternoon crowd was sparse enough to give the one-woman camera crew, Kerri Raines, space to set up her apparatus for the interviews. Charles Bexley and Nicholas Haldane hovered in the background, doing whatever pub owners do but also watching the TV types at work. Father Juan Diego Ortega, Fred Gaffe, and Mary Landfair mingled among themselves. The priest and the columnist were on deck to be interviewed. I found out later that Mo Russert took a pass on that honor.

"And this is our producer, Lisa Carson," Robles said. "Lisa, this is Sebastian McCabe and Jeff Cody—Mac has a ghost story." Robles had traded his sweatshirt for a sweater, but still hadn't found his comb. Carson, on the other hand, was quite well turned out with long black hair, deep blue eyes, jeans that cost more than my best suit, four-inch pumps, a cream-colored blouse, and a scarf the color of the sapphire surrounded by diamonds in her engagement ring.

"Pleasure." She held out her right hand in a business-like way for shaking. People still did that then. Before Mac or I could accept the gesture, the phone in her left hand rang. She answered swiftly. "Yes, Stephen. In the gastropub." She started walking rapidly away from us, handshakes forgotten, her scarf flying behind her. "Of course, Stuart's here. He's just about to…" Her voice faded out.

"Stephen calls her all the time," Robles reported. "He's at his restaurant in Santa Fe until Friday."

Mac and I were on the scene well before Mac's slotted interview time so that we could watch Father Juan take his turn. Mac just wanted to hear what he had to say, but I was on the job with my smartphone poised to take pictures of SBU's director of campus ministries in action so I could tweet them out. Kerri Raines sat him at a table, positioning the camera to take in the colorful mural of generic speakeasy customers *circa* 1920. Not the best background for a priest, I thought, but the options were limited. The MO was to record the answers, then splice in footage recorded separately of Diamond asking the questions or just looking wise.

After a few minutes of aimless chitchat to relax his victim, Diamond dove in:

"So, Father, are there such things as ghosts?"

Father Juan considered the question for a moment, his hands steepled almost in prayer. Don't let the ponytail fool you: He's a serious theologian as well as a worker in the vineyards of the Lord. Just under 40 years old, SBU is only his second assignment as a priest.

"That depends on what you mean by ghosts," he said finally, with more than a hint of Spanish in his pronunciation. "There are disembodied spirits, certainly—the souls of the dead that continue on after their bodies have died and decayed. We humans are all mortal in our bodies, destined to suffer death; but we are also immortal in our souls. Even in our secular age, polls show that most people believe this. Most people always have. Life after death in some form is a central belief of almost all religions dating back to ancient times in vastly different cultures everywhere in the world."

I took the priest's photo and tweeted it out with the words: *Spirits of the dead do live on, @Fr.Juan tells TV's "Dining (Way) Out" program.*

Diamond did the "I'm listening seriously" look behind his serious glasses, probably practicing up for when Raines turned her camera on him.

"But can these spirits make themselves known?" "Communicate with the living?"

Father Juan nodded. "I would say yes. There is no official Church teaching on this, but I believe so. Sometimes they come to ask for our prayers, sometimes they bring consolation or warnings. I have experienced this myself. Two years ago, I was driving to the hospital to visit a sick student when I heard my mother's voice in my head telling me, '*Adios, mi hijo,*' and telling me to take care of my brother. I hadn't been thinking of her and she wasn't sick. I noted the time on my dashboard clock—three-sixteen in the afternoon. Within half an hour my brother called from Miami to tell me that Mamá had died of a heart attack after being rushed to the hospital. The attending physician recorded the time of death: three-sixteen. May she rest in peace."

I'd heard the story before, but it still gave me goosebumps.

"I'm sure that was quite an experience, but a benign one," Diamond said. *Translation: Not what I was fishing for. I'll throw my line in again.* "We're sitting here in a restaurant, a gastropub, that has a reputation for being haunted by the ghost of a murdered gangster. What do you know about that?"

"Only what I have heard second-hand."

Diamond squirmed. Father Juan was making him work for it, but the YouTuber was up to the job. He tried again.

"You're an exorcist, Father. Doesn't that mean you've dealt with hauntings?"

"I prefer to speak in terms of unquiet spirits. The souls of the dead are usually not malevolent, just troubled. Sometimes the spirit has unfinished business, as in the case of a rectory disturbed by a pastor who died with many Mass intentions left unfulfilled. More commonly the location where a person has been murdered or committed suicide will be the site of manifestations, such as knocking or banging at the time of death. Occasionally a simple plea 'help me' is heard. When I am called into such a situation, as happens from time to time, I say a cycle of prayers called the Office for the Dead. The manifestations usually soon cease."

I tweeted: *Haunting is a cry for help, says @Fr.Juan.*

"That's fascinating," Diamond enthused. "I guess the effectiveness of the cure in those cases proves the diagnosis was correct. You are a real ghost-buster, Father!" Father looked pained. "But I gather you've never come here to The Speakeasy in that capacity?"

"I have not."

"Would you say this Office for the Dead right now and set the spirit of Jackie O'Brien free?"

I should have expected that.

Father Juan shook his head. "I'm sorry, no. For three reasons: It would take too long, I don't have the book with me, and—above all—this is not something I would do on camera for the entertainment of your audience."

Diamond didn't flinch at the implied rebuke, nor did he waste any time pressing the matter. "Is there anything else you'd like to add, Father?"

The exorcist leaned forward. "Just this: In my experience, troubled spirits tend to be souls who were already disturbed in life. The Lord tells us repeatedly, 'Be not afraid.' We all need faith in the sense of a belief system; that is a human necessity. But we also need faith in the sense of trust, the assurance that there is a God who loves us and will take care of us. We should never forget that."

"Good reminder, padre."

I tweeted: *@Fr.Juan urges: Have faith and trust.* Nobody reads long tweets.

Kerri Raines turned off the lights on her camera. Diamond and Father Juan stood up and shook hands.

"Good stuff," Lisa Carson commented.

"He's got me convinced," Raines said. She was a petite woman wearing a vest full of pockets. Having dated Lynda Teal during the years she smoked, I recognized the "I need a cigarette" expression on her face as she ducked out.

Carson's phone rang. "Yes, Stephen." She stalked off.

"How much of that do you think will be used, Jefferson?" Mac asked.

"Hard to say. On a news story, TV4 or Channel 11 will talk to me for fifteen minutes and use fifteen seconds. But all these cable reality shows tend to let people drone on. Not that Father Juan was droning."

Next up was Fred Gaffe, AKA "The Old Gaffer." Well into his eighties, he looked like the grandfather in a situation comedy—white-haired, a bit overweight, and slow moving. But nothing got past him. He'd been surveying the local scene in his free-lance column in the *Erin Observer & News-Ledger* ever since he retired, which he did well past the age at which I hope to hit the rocking chair.

"Jackie O'Brien's been haunting this building as long as I can remember," he told Diamond almost before the question was asked.

"And how long is that?"

"Oh, going all the way back to the forties, I guess. This was the Cricket Café in those days, owned by Hal Nash, who was mayor at the time. I was a young boy, but I used to come here for fish on Fridays with my parents. There were people still alive then who patronized the place when it was a speak, people who knew Jackie O'Brien. They always blamed old Jackie when the beer taps started flowing by themselves. I hear that's happening again now that the bar's back, although I haven't seen it myself. Jackie was killed right in front of the bar, you know. Not the bar that's here now, but it was in pretty much the same location as this one." He hiked a thumb in the appropriate direction behind him.

"Who do you think fired the shots that killed Jackie a hundred years ago this Halloween?"

The Old Gaffer shrugged. "No real idea. Lots of folks assume it was another bootlegger. But it could have been a jealous husband, for all I know. Still a mystery, isn't it?"

And so forth.

Diamond's interrogation of Mac started with the big guy's experiences as a frequent visitor to the former Pages Gone By.

"I understand this building was haunted even in bookstore days," Diamond said. "Tell us about what you saw and heard."

I tweeted: *@SMcCabe shares a real-life ghost story with "Dining (Way) Out" in place where it happened, now The Speakeasy.*

Mac adjusted himself in the chair, patently trying to get his corpulent corpus comfortable. He was dressed in a tweed suit, with a brown and orange bow tie. Halloween colors!

"As a consumer and collector of mystery literature, particularly from what is called the Golden Age period of the genre, one might say that I haunted the store myself." If you like that line, thank you. "Often, wandering near the area where I now know Mr. O'Brien was slain, I felt a distinct chill, as if someone had opened a door on a cold day, or even turned on the air conditioning. On one such occasion, after I turned my back on a particular bookcase, I felt a volume hurled at the back of my head. It proved to be one of my own Damon Devlin detective novels."

"And what was the title?" Diamond asked, right on cue.

"Ghost in the Graveyard."

Raines got a nice close-up of Mac saying that. I eventually saw the raw video, although the episode never aired. She later proclaimed the anecdote "creepy."

"To what do you attribute that rather extreme action?" Diamond asked.

Mac chuckled. "Perhaps Mr. O'Brien did not care for the book." *Everybody's a critic.* "It is not a genuine ghost story, as perhaps you will recall. Like all of my mysteries, it evokes the supernatural only to enliven the story and distract the reader's attention from the human agency and the all-too-human motive behind the crimes."

But Diamond wasn't interested in Mac flogging his old book. "Maybe the ghost was trying to get your attention because he wants you to solve his murder," he suggested.

"That would be a very cold case indeed after almost a century."

"Nevertheless, do you have any thoughts on it?"

"Well, just one." *Of course.* "In those far-off days before sophisticated money laundering schemes, it was credibly speculated that Mr. O'Brien had accumulated a large cash hoard. And yet his wife swore she knew nothing of it. I suggest it is a possibility that wherever that treasure wound up, there too is the murderer."

I tweeted: *Hundred-year-old Jackie O'Brien murder: Follow the money, says @SMcCabe.*

"Do you think solving O'Brien's murder would finally bring his ghost peace and cause the manifestations to stop?" Diamond asked.

That's called leading a horse to water, but Mac didn't drink. "Perhaps we shall someday find out," he said with a smile.

"Anything else you'd like to add?"

"I believe I have said enough."

That's never stopped you before.

Nicholas Haldane, next up in the interview chair despite his qualms about the show, reported encountering the late Mr. O'Brien only once. He didn't say that once was enough, possibly feeling the cliché unnecessary.

"It was shortly before we opened The Speakeasy," he recalled. "Walking near the bar, I suddenly felt a chill—like someone had opened the door of a big freezer. Then I saw this figure, saw right *through* this figure, of a man in a suit and a fedora standing right in front of me. He had a shocked look on his face—and it was the face of Jackie O'Brien."

He stopped.

"You recognized him?" Diamond prodded.

Haldane nodded. "That's his picture behind the bar." He pointed to a framed black-and-white photo of a broad-faced Irishman in said headgear. "The apparition only lasted a few seconds, I guess, and I never saw it again. But I was here once when the beer taps went crazy."

Diamond looked suitably impressed. "Do you think the spirit of Jackie O'Brien is malevolent?"

"I don't know, but he's certainly not resting in peace."

I wish I'd written that.

Mac and I didn't stay for the rest of the interviews. After a round of goodbye handshakes with Diamond, Carson, Robles, and Raines, we took off. But on the way out, I had a question for Diamond:

"How did you know about the haunting of this place?"

He gave me a TV (or YouTube) smile. "From you. I read about it in one of your books. The one about the murder when this was a bookstore."

"Most curious," Mac rumbled when we were out of Diamond's listening range. "You realize, of course, that what he just said could not possibly be true."

"That did occur to me. He's either mistaken or trying to flatter me."

Diamond couldn't have read about Jackie O'Brien's ghost in *Bookmarked for Murder*, my book about the Noah Bartlett case. Mac talked me out of including any reference to the bootlegger's demise in that account because he thought it would be cheating to introduce a mystery without a solution into a true crime book. So, whatever Diamond's source of information, it wasn't my deathless prose.

Chapter Four

Bad Times, Hard Times

That was the last I thought of ghosts for several days, although death was much on my mind. COVID-19 was a wave, and it was about to wash over us. I wasn't surprised when Lesley Saylor-Mackie summoned me on Thursday of that week to a confab with Grant Kingsley in his fifth-floor quarters, up one flight of stairs from me in the Gamble Building. Crisis was in the air.

"Wish me luck," I told Popcorn on my way out.

"Better than that, I'll send up a prayer."

"Much appreciated."

Exercising the right of communication directors everywhere, I nodded at GK's executive assistant and walked right into the presidential corner office. Saylor-Mackie was already there, a formidable woman in her early sixties who sees no need to dye her impeccably coiffed sandy-gray hair.

"Ah, Jeff, good, thanks for coming," said GK. *As if I had a choice.* He waved with his hand toward the open chair in front of him, alongside Saylor-Mackie's. *The Wall Street Journal* was open on his desk. "Lesley's been filling me in on the task force's recommendations."

"I was just about to say there is really not much of a choice," she said as I took my seat. "For the health and safety of students, faculty, and staff, we have to suspend on-campus classes for the rest of the semester and go completely to an online teaching model," she said. "Everything needs to be canceled—from sports to commencement." *There goes the ninth annual "Investigating Arthur Conan Doyle and Sherlock Holmes" conference scheduled for April. Mac's baby is about to be thrown out with the bath water.* "That will cause us a lot of pain in almost every conceivable way in the short run, but all members of the task force agree the only real decisions to be made are when and how."

I knew all this, of course, being one of those members myself. We had to do something, and on that day in March there was nothing else to do.

With a background that included 27 years of teaching the science of leadership at the Air Force Academy in Colorado, followed by a stint as senior vice president of the Altiora Corp. in Erin, GK knows a thing or two about decision-making. And one of those things is that how decisions are communicated matters. But he also knows that if you try making a silk purse out of a sow's ear, you come up with a really funny-looking purse.

"What do you think, Jeff?" he asked.

Good thing I was listening. For some reason I'm always distracted by the painting of Air Force jets flying in formation that GK installed behind his desk shortly after being appointed interim president. Also, I still expected Father Joe to be sitting there, not this taller man with military posture and closely cropped steel-wool hair.

"I think we announce the closing of the campus as soon as all those decisions get made, but not before," I said. "We need to be able to answer all the questions students and parents will have, or at least most, not just hit them with the bad news and then flounder when pressed for the details. They'll want to know when they have to leave the dorms, whether they get a refund on tuition or room and board, things like that. I'll put out a comprehensive Q&A to go with the basic press release when all that gets figured out."

GK nodded. "Copy that."

"I hope we can get all the specifics ironed out at today's task force meeting, or at least begin the process,"

Saylor-Mackie said. "But I'm sure you can see that no matter what we do, the financial impact of the pandemic on St. Benignus will be devastating. Every source of funding is compromised. If states start imposing restrictions that cause businesses to close, some students may have to drop out because they or their parents can no longer afford tuition. The capital campaign may be crippled by the inability of donors to meet their commitments. With sports canceled, there will be no ticket revenue. And if the stock market tanks, so will our endowment.

"Looking ahead, those hundreds of international students that my predecessor so successfully courted may not be willing or able to come here in the fall. And perhaps we should only offer online classes in the fall in any case—there are widespread fears of a second wave of the virus then. That's something to consider." A noted historian, Saylor-Mackie always takes the long view. "We're fortunate that we already have a solid infrastructure for that since we pushed strongly into long-distance learning several years ago. The major investment Ralph made then will pay off."

"But as Kelly Richards"—the university's top legal eagle—"pointed out at our meeting, somebody unhappy about all classes going virtual is bound to sue, probably sooner rather than later," I said. "They'll argue that classes without the chance to mingle with their prof or other students isn't what they signed up for."

"No doubt." The Provost sighed. "Even if we win, litigation is expensive."

"Always," G.K. said. "Do you have any good news for me, Lesley?"

She emitted a grim smile. "A little. I've already spoken to some of my counterparts at similar-sized institutions around the country, and we are in better shape to weather this storm than a lot of them. Last month a book came out by a University of Pennsylvania professor predicting that about 100 private, liberal arts colleges—a tenth of the total—will close over the next five years. And now this."

"That means that ninety percent will survive," GK countered, "but the policy we make over the next twenty-four hours will have a lot to do with whether SBU is among them. Lesley, I need you to bust your— I mean, go all out. I want the task force's recommendations no later than 10 A.M. tomorrow so that Jeff can be prepared to announce everything tomorrow afternoon. I know that's impossible, but I also know that you can do it."

If Saylor-Mackie realized the appropriateness of the next day being Friday the 13th, she didn't show it. She just looked determined, in her elegant sort of way. "All right. I'll grab as many members as I can to start the meeting early."

"Good! And ask your team to consider the wisdom of letting students defer fall tuition payments. That's counter-intuitive from a financial point of view, I know, but consider this: Students would get breathing room so they wouldn't have to drop out for a semester or maybe forever. Meanwhile, we still get tuition money from federal loans and grants.

"Oh, and another thing: Over the next several weeks, we should have faculty and staff call every single student to check on how they're doing. Make it a priority."

The man was an idea machine! As the sign on his desk says, **LEADERS LEAD**.

"Nothing like this has ever happened in our lifetimes," he went on. "It can be overwhelming. But it doesn't have to be. We have to remember that we're not just hapless victims of fate. Even though we can't make COVID-19 go away, what we can do will make a difference. One of my favorite quotes says: 'Bad times, hard times, this is what people keep saying; but let us live well, and times shall be good. We are the times: Such as we are, such are the times.' St. Augustine said that about sixteen hundred years ago."

Didn't he also say there was no such thing as ghosts?

Later that day, the governor of Ohio and the state health director ordered the closing of all schools K-12, prohibited mass gatherings of more than 100 people, and banned visitors to state psychiatric hospitals. Beyond our state, the NBA canceled the basketball season, and Broadway shut down. All of that was background noise to me as I took part in the six-hour task force meeting and then slogged away in my office for several more hours.

On Friday the 13th, we put out the press release and Q&A about the campus closing, accompanied by a video of GK that was posted on our YouTube channel and the whole range of social media. We were a few days behind Miami University of Ohio with our shutdown, but right on track with other universities in the state. I served up sound bites for TV4 Action News in Cincinnati and spent some quality time on the phone with Hadley Reams, recent SBU graduate and now the education reporter for *The Erin Observer & News-Ledger*.

"What would you say to students who object to paying full tuition when they aren't getting the full campus experience?" Reams asked.

I would say I hate "what would you say to . . ." questions, even when they're about as predictable as rain on Good Friday.

"We aren't closing the university or canceling classes, Hadley; we are merely moving online. We believe that video technology will enable our faculty to deliver the same quality education that our students expect and deserve, while at the same time assuring their health and safety. Room and board are entirely different, of course, and we will be refunding some of that on a prorated basis." *As it says in the Q&A.*

"Your announcement says that online learning will continue for the summer semester. How about the fall? Graduating high school seniors are expecting to hear from college admission offices by the end of the month and start making their choices."

"It's too soon to make a decision on that because the medical situation is still evolving. We hope to be able to say within a few weeks, as I'm sure other institutions do as well."

I hung up 20 minutes later impressed that Hadley Reams had turned out to be a worthy successor to education beat veteran Maggie Barton. But I missed jousting with the old gal. Lynda is still watching her cats, Binkie and Bunkie, which I'm afraid is going to be a life-time appointment.

Later I got a call from Cindy Weller, a reporter for *The Spectator*, the SBU student newspaper that Reams and I had both edited in our separate generations.

"I was wondering, Mr. Cody, what would you say to…"

And so forth.

But apparently the show would go on at WSTV, from what I read in the *Observer* the next morning. The banner headline at the top of the page was **SBU HALTS IN-PERSON CLASSES**. But claiming a big amount of real estate on the center of the page, including a photo, was a feature by our leggy friend Johanna Rawls: ***Searching for Spirits at Erin's Gastropub***. The photo was of Stephen Lipinski decked out in a white chef's coat and one of those chef's scarves, a red one. I guess you could say blood red.

That much I could see from a casual glance while Lynda exercised a recovering journalist's right to read the local paper first as she drank caffeine-laced coffee out of a cup touting "*The Erin Observer & News-Ledger* – Your Source for Local News." I ingested the weekend *Wall Street Journal* along with my cereal, as per usual.

"We should have gone to The Speakeasy last night," she announced a little while later, turning to the horoscopes at the back of the paper. "Sounds like it was fun."

"More fun than giving the twins a bath while preventing Donata from whacking off her own hair with a pair of scissors? Surely you jest."

It was 8 A.M. and all three of the little darlings were covered with remnants of Cheerios.

I tossed aside the first section of the *WSJ*, with its depressing news of stocks falling, the president declaring a national emergency, and Disney shutting its U.S. and Paris parks. Leaving the other three sections for later, I picked up the *Observer* to read Tall Rawls's story.

> Celebrity chef Stephen Lipinski visited The Speakeasy at Front and High Streets last night in search of spirits, but not the kind behind the bar.
>
> Lipinski, co-host of the reality show *Dining (Way) Out* on the Wine & Spirits TV Channel, and guest co-host Stuart Diamond of YouTube fame are in Erin to record an episode based around the gastropub and its resident ghost. The episode is expected to be released on Halloween as the program begins its third season.
>
> "We always try to bring our viewers a backstage view of a unique bar or restaurant, something really different," said Lipinski, who owns a popular eatery in Santa Fe. "This is our first haunted gastropub. Unfortunately, my brother is out of action for a while recovering from a heart attack, but our producer had a great idea for a replacement."
>
> Lipinski's producer on the show is his partner in life, wife Lisa Carson. He stood near her all evening at The Speakeasy, often holding her hand.
>
> "She was familiar with Stuart Diamond's work as a psychic investigator of sorts, and she thought maybe he could find us a haunted bar,"

Lipinski said. "He not only did that, he agreed to come aboard as co-host for the episode."

Diamond, host of *The Strange World of Stuart Diamond* on YouTube, arrived earlier in the week to talk to Erin residents about their experiences with the uncanny phenomena said to be related to the ghost of Prohibition-era bootlegger Jackie O'Brien. O'Brien died in what is now The Speakeasy, a name that hearkens back to its history.

By most accounts, the O'Brien shade is a poltergeist who makes noises and turns on beer taps, but ghostly apparitions have been reported over the years as well.

Lipinski spent much of Friday in the kitchen recording with Charles Bexley and Nicholas Haldane, owners of the four-year-old gastropub. But as the cocktail hour crowd began to gather on Friday, he emerged to shake hands and chat with customers. One of them was Fred Gaffe, long-time author of "The Old Gaffer" column in the *Observer*. Diamond interviewed him earlier in the week about Jackie O'Brien.

"Jackie's been haunting this building for a hundred years, even when it was a bookstore," Gaffe said. "The guy never gives up."

Patron Holly Burdette, 24, pronounced the ghost of the gastropub "really cool." She said she has never seen the spirit in action but hopes to.

Civic leaders, meanwhile, are excited at the attention from *Dining (Way) Out*.

"This is a great boon for our area," said Mary Landfair, of Sussex County Convention & Visitors Bureau. She stopped by Friday with husband Rowan. "We expect this episode of a popular cable show to bring visitors from nearby towns in Ohio and Kentucky who otherwise might not have thought of Erin. And once here, they'll patronize our unique shops, ride the bike trail along the river, and maybe take in a play at the Davenport-Lattimore Bijou Theatre."

But the COVID-19 pandemic has put the immediate future of all retail businesses, especially bars and restaurants, in doubt.

"With social distancing, I'm wondering how long it will be before the governor says we have to close up," said Speakeasy co-owner Charles Bexley.

(Please see "Ghost Story: Murdered Bootlegger Lingers On," p. 8A.)

"Not long" was the answer to Bexley's question. The state ordered restaurants and bars to close their dining rooms until further notice as of 9 P.M. Sunday, March 15. The WSTV team filmed at the gastropub right up to the mandated closing time. They also planned to stay around town for a few more days to conduct some final interviews from a social distance. This I learned later.

The Speakeasy is always closed on Mondays, like a lot of eateries that serve on Sundays. So the first day it was affected by the state order was Tuesday. Charles Bexley entered the deserted building that morning, St. Patrick's Day, to do some paperwork. And that's when he found the bullet-riddled body of Stuart Diamond lying in front of the bar.

Chapter Five
The Body at the Bar

"Nice tie, Boss," Popcorn told me that morning when I arrived at the office. "Love the shamrocks."

"That's about as celebratory as it's going to get today," I said gloomily. "No St. Patrick's Day Parade—in Erin or anywhere." They'd been canceled all over America, and even in Ireland. Erin's parade is a big deal by our standards, so much so that a controversy over marching in it once split the town.[3] "No keggers with breakfast at Bobbie McGee's Sports Bar and no party at Luther's house tonight."

"I'm bummed, too. But, hey, at least Joyful Noise will be livestreaming Irish music on their Facebook page."

The performance by the three holy tenors—a priest, a rabbi, and a minister—was one of the highlights of the annual shindig put on by Luther Kressel, SBU professor of history and economics.

"It won't be the same," I grumbled, refusing to be cheered up. "Nothing will be the same."

Would it ever be? Popcorn and I were keeping our distance from each other, six feet, and talking about working from home. (A wordless glare greeted my gentle suggestion that she should distance herself from Oscar as well.) Students were moving off campus. The NAIA had canceled the spring sports season, meaning the top-rated St. Benignus Dragons wouldn't be taking to the baseball diamond. And with 50 confirmed cases of COVID-19 now in the state, though no

---

[3] See *Erin Go Bloody*, MX Publishing, 2016.

known deaths yet, Ohio's governor and health director had ordered bowling alleys, movie theaters, fitness centers, gyms, and recreation centers to close. Lynda and I had found it hard enough finding the time to work out at the Nouveau Shape gym since the birth of the twins; now it would be impossible. No taekwondo for Lynda and Triple M, either.

"Things are going to be really dead," I said.

"I am not sure whether to call that choice of wording apt or ironic, old boy."

For a huge man, almost as tall as me and tipping the scale a hundred pounds or so more than he should, Sebastian McCabe occasionally demonstrates a surprising ability to sneak up on me. There he stood in the doorway of my office, wearing a bow tie in a pattern of the mostly green McCabe clan tartan and carrying his walking stick with the top carved in the shape of a hound dog's head

"You mean—" I stopped. Clearly, somebody was dead. "Who is it?"

"YouTube's aficionado of the arcane, Stuart Diamond. Oscar called me just a few moments ago. He thought we would be interested in Mr. Diamond's demise because of the unusual circumstances."

Mac filled me in on said circumstances on the way to the scene. In creating The Speakeasy, architect Jonah Whittle had carefully placed the bar in the same location as the original in Jackie O'Brien's 1920 establishment. That meant that if Stuart Diamond's body didn't fall exactly where O'Brien's had almost a century earlier, it was close enough.

The Speakeasy was closed—*really* closed, with the yellow crime scene tape up—but the food truck parked across the street seemed to be doing a landmark business. About a dozen patrons, not all of them keeping their distance, waited to be served by a wiry guy with dark, curly hair, glasses, and a light blue paper mask that hid a good deal of his face. Even though the Centers for Disease Control and Prevention hadn't yet recommended face masks as protection against the COVID-19 virus, masking up was becoming more common every day. (Eventually nobody would even be permitted to enter Gamble Bank without wearing a mask, which still seems weird to me.) Kate kept busy sewing up artistically decorated face coverings for her friends and for clients of the Serenity House social service agency. I wasn't there yet, and neither was Mac, but the food truck guy was. I was pretty sure his mask hid an impressive handlebar mustache, because I thought I recognized him as a former bartender at The Speakeasy with that particular form of facial hair.

"Hungry, Jefferson?"

"No. Why do you ask?"

"You are staring at that vehicle."

"I was just admiring the name: 'Tony's Cal-Zone.' That's a cute moniker for a vendor of Italian fast food."

"I prefer slow food, especially when it comes to Italian cuisine. Lynda's cooking skills are quite adept in that particular gastronomic arena, by the way."

"I'll say!"

Now I am hungry.

At the entrance to the gastropub we told Officer Lehmann, new to the force, who we were and why we were there. He logged us in to the crime scene. Inside, we immediately heard Oscar Hummel loudly muttering, as is his wont on such occasions, "Hell's bells!" Sixty pounds or so overweight and hiding his bald head beneath a blue and yellow peaked cap, the Chief looked like a man in desperate need of a cigarette—or, rather, a vape. Instead, he pulled out a stick of gum.

Standing in the main room of The Speakeasy, Oscar formed a tableau with his assistant chief, the imperturbable Lt. Col. L. Jack Gibbons; a seasoned officer named Mentzel, who was dusting for prints; and the two horror-struck owners of the business. If you can call it a tableau when most of the people are trying to stand six feet apart from the others.

"Where's the corpse?" I asked, slightly disappointed. There was blood, but no body. I had the callous thought that the cops and the Sussex County coroner fussing around the corpse would have made great video for WSTV.

"At the morgue," Oscar informed us. "Where else?" *That was a rhetorical question on my part, Oscar.* "I apologize for not calling you guys in sooner." *And that was sarcasm on yours.*

But he was just being grumpy to stay in practice. It's a measure of how our relationship with the Chief has changed that he would call us in at all. In our first case together, he resented Mac and suspected me.[4] That has morphed over the years into a reluctant admission that in certain crimes—a small percentage of the total—the unique perspective of Sebastian McCabe is an invaluable addition to standard police resources. At times, Oscar has even referred to us in unguarded moments as unofficial (i.e., unpaid) deputies. The fact is, Mac can solve murders, while Oscar's attempt to write a mystery novel floundered in the early pages.

"It would be fascinating, Oscar, if the weapon used proved to be a Smith & Wesson Model 10, a .38 Special," Mac said.

"Eh? How's that?"

"Because that is the type of weapon that slew Mr. O'Brien, and it was never found. The model was a favorite of Prohibition-era gangsters and lawmen alike, by the way."

Only Sebastian McCabe would use the word "slew" in a spoken sentence. Or call Jackie O'Brien "Mr."

"So maybe the same gun was used here? That idea is so screwy it could be true," Oscar allowed. "We'll see what the ballistics report from the BCI[5] turns up. They'll have plenty to work with."

Okay, I'll bite. "What do you mean?" I asked.

---

[4] See *No Police Like Holmes*, MX Publishing, 2011.

[5] The Ohio Bureau of Criminal Investigation, the state's crime lab, serves local, state, and federal law enforcement agencies 24/7. Sussex County, in which Erin is located, has no ballistics laboratory of its own.

"It didn't take an autopsy for Arly"—Dr. Arlene Eppensteiner, our county coroner—"to see that he was shot six times."

"I just can't believe this crap," Charles Bexley exploded. "First the lockdown, now murder! What's next, the seven plagues of Egypt? Do you have any idea how razor-thin our margins are in the restaurant business? How little it would take to ruin us?" This wasn't the upbeat Bexley that I knew. The brawny beer fancier hadn't given up his successful career as an Altiora Corp. engineer to start a gastropub without a degree of optimism. But now, even his thick walrus mustache seemed to droop. His slighter partner, Haldane, put an affectionate and comforting arm around him. They weren't social distancing. But then, they lived together.

"Chief Hummel said there were no signs of a break-in and a key to this establishment was found in the victim's pocket," Mac noted. "How did that come about?"

"I was about to ask that question," Oscar said.

"At Diamond's request, I left the key for him and told him how to disable the alarm and reset it when he left," Bexley explained. "He said they wanted to do some filming when the pub was empty—B-roll he called it."

"You had no hesitation in turning over the key to this YouTube personality?" Mac said.

"No. I assumed I could trust the guy. I've lived in Erin long enough to pick up that habit. This is a real kick in the balls."

I'm sure Diamond would apologize for staining the floor with his blood, if he could.

"What time was this?" Mac asked.

"He called me about five o'clock yesterday and said the crew would be here later in the evening, about nine o'clock. He made it clear he didn't need us around this time, which was fine by me. So, I put the key in a flowerpot. I know that's a cliché, but this is Erin."

Mac looked around, maybe wondering why the TV types had to come back for more video. "Presumably, the videographer and the producer or assistant producer were here at nine o'clock or shortly thereafter. However, they must have left some time later, while Stuart Diamond stayed behind and subsequently was shot to death."

Nobody needed to point out that we would learn later whether the coroner's time-of-death estimate lined up with that scenario.

"And while the TV people were here you were— where?" Oscar asked, with a "just for the record" air.

"At home with Nicholas, as I am on most Monday nights. It's our off day."

"We were watching the Food Channel," Haldane said in his hint-of-Savannah drawl. "A bit of a busman's holiday."

"Was the door locked when you arrived this morning?" Mac asked Bexley.

"Yes. It didn't require any special knowledge for anyone to do that. It was just a standard lock. But the alarm wasn't set."

"Mentzel found no fingerprints at all on the back door," Gibbons offered. "The killer must have wiped it off on the way out."

"Don't burglars always do that?" said Bexley.

"So, you figure it was a burglar," Oscar stated unnecessarily. "Anything missing?"

"Not that we could tell right off, but we haven't had much of a look yet."

"If this was not a burglary," Mac said, "have either of you any idea at all, however fanciful or tentative, as to what happened here?"

Bexley's response was vigorously negative, in words my genteel poet mother wouldn't want to read in this report. He clearly favored the burglar theory, so much so that I wondered why. Haldane, however, hesitated.

"I wonder." He paused. "I've been worried that something bad would happen since we agreed to that Halloween show. Call it a presentiment. It can hardly be a coincidence that this murder is virtually a replay of what happened here, in this building, a hundred years ago—six shots, the body falling right in front of the bar. Stuart Diamond made a minor career out of meddling with the supernatural. It's no surprise to me that there were consequences."

The look on Bexley's face made me think he would have something to say about that when the two of them were alone, with nobody else around to be cut by the sharp words.

"If the supernatural is truly involved, then the official police and I are out of our depth here," Mac pontificated. "As Sherlock Holmes famously said in 'The Adventure of the Sussex Vampire,' 'This agency stands flat-footed upon the ground and there it must remain. The world is big enough for us. No ghosts need apply.' Whether ghosts exist or not is a different question, and one well outside our purview. We are criminal investigators, not psychic ones. The supernatural is Father Juan's domain. You have no living suspects in mind, Mr. Haldane?"

"Suspects? How would I have suspects? I didn't really know the man. Probably no one in Erin did. He was only here, what, a week maybe?"

"You're making this too complicated," Bexley said. "Diamond was just in the wrong place at the wrong time. Some waste of perfectly good DNA jiggled the door, found it unlocked, and thought he could help himself to some cash. Diamond interrupted him and got shot for his efforts."

"Six times?" Haldane's voice dripped with skepticism.

Bexley shrugged his broad shoulders. "He panicked."

A few minutes later we left the gastropub and stood on the sidewalk with the Chief.

"What say you, Oscar?" Mac asked.

"I say I like simple explanations, but Bexley's isn't working for me. Why would Diamond be here alone? Why would a burglar assume the place was empty if the door was unlocked and the lights on? And why would that burglar carry a gun? They usually don't, you know."

"Bravo, Oscar!"

Oscar tried not to look pleased at the plaudit. "I'll tell you something else: If it wasn't a burglary the motive must have been personal, directed at Diamond in particular rather than at a guy who just happened to be standing there. It doesn't take a"—*Don't say it!*—"Sherlock Holmes to figure that out."

"The six bullets, you mean?" I said.

"That and the fact that I can't think of any *im*personal reason to kill him. I can't imagine he had a load of money on him, for instance—nobody does anymore. It's all credit and debit cards."

"Then Diamond must have moved awfully fast to get somebody so hacked at him in such a short time in town."

"Don't overlook the obvious, Watson," Oscar said with a smirk. "Maybe the hatred wasn't home-grown in Erin."

"You mean someone from the television crew might have developed animus for him?" Mac asked.

"That's my bet."

"That is certainly a line of investigation that needs to be pursued. Why do you suppose the killer struck in Erin, if he or she is not a resident?"

Oscar shrugged. "It had to be somewhere. When I get them in for an interview today, I'm going to advise the TV people not to leave town until we get this sorted out."

Chapter Six
Grilling the Chef

That afternoon, between fielding media calls about issues related to closing the campus and another task force meeting, I was back in the president's office for a pow-wow about a news release on SBU's new chair of the board of trustees.

Grace Langley, founder and CEO of a medium-sized advertising agency in Chillicothe, had just been elected to the volunteer post held by GK before the board appointed him interim president in a crisis.[6] The timing was not great for her, what with the lockdown challenging her own business and the university, but GK was enthusiastic about the choice.

In the Father Pirelli era, I would have drafted a comment for the president to approve. I still do some ghostwriting for GK, notably speeches, but he most often puts words into his own mouth for me to tweak and then disseminate. He did so this time. The release had him saying:

"Grace Langley is the perfect person to lead the trustees of her alma mater in this time of turmoil. At her firm of Langley, Stratton, & Griggs, launched at the height of the Great Recession in 2009, she has demonstrated not only entrepreneurial drive, but a commitment to quality, integrity, and community service—three core values shared by St. Benignus University. She is not afraid to make difficult decisions and to stand by them in the face of criticism, which is one of the hallmarks of a true leader."

---

[6] See *Too Many Clues*, MX Publishing, 2019.

Not for quotation, he told me more: "She'll have my back as long as I deserve it. I can't ask for anything more than that."

Talk turned to other matters.

"I'm worried about the impact our closing will have on Erin," GK said. "I don't have to tell you that in a college town, the college is the 500-pound gorilla. Without the students, trade will dry up for all kinds of small businesses. And there's nothing SBU can do about it."

He drummed his fingers distractedly.

I had a fleeting thought that Bexley and Haldane would not be well positioned to pay their landlord, Gulliver Mackie.

"Look at the bright side," I said, with a weak attempt at gallows humor. "It looks like the governor and the health director are going to effectively close a lot of businesses sometime soon anyway."

Popcorn was monitoring coronavirus shutdown news for me, including whatever came out of the governor's 2 P.M. briefing every day.

"Just today the state ordered elective surgeries and procedures"—*what's the difference between a surgery and a procedure, by the way?*—"delayed to save on use of personal protective equipment for health workers, so it can be available for those dealing with COVID cases," I reported, in case GK wasn't keeping up. "For minor illnesses, they're encouraging the use of telemedicine instead of office visits. That's going to hurt the bottom line at St. Hildegarde, because that's where the hospital makes money."

"And even non-profits need to make money, universities included, or they go out of business," GK said. He suddenly switched gears, maybe to cheer himself up. "Meanwhile, what does Mac think about the murder at our local gastropub? Don't look so surprised that I heard about it. I had five calls this morning from people who each wanted to be the first to tell me."

Grant Kingsley takes a childish interest in Mac's amateur sleuthing and his mystery novels in equal measure. Childish is a word I often associate with Sebastian McCabe.

"I don't know what he's thinking yet," I said. "He's at the inscrutable stage, which will last approximately until the end of the case." A slight exaggeration, I admit. "But I went to the murder scene with him."

I filled GK in on our morning's activity, hoping he wouldn't notice that we went to The Speakeasy during what might be considered "company time." He listened with rapt attention, almost as if he didn't have a university to run in the midst of a pandemic. He's a great multi-tasker.

"All this social distancing should make talking to suspects an interesting challenge," he observed when I'd finished.

"At this point *finding* suspects looks like a challenge. Oscar's giving a hard look at the WSTV people, but that's about all he's got right now."

"Well, keep me posted. I don't want to disappoint my board members who think I'm plugged in." He switched back into president mode. "Speaking of social distancing, Jeff, I want you and Popcorn to work from home as much as possible. She's a tad over sixty and a few pounds north of ideal, which puts her in the vulnerable category. You both need to stay safe. That won't present any problems, will it?"

"Not at all. We can work together apart. My office is wherever I am. Everybody in SBU administration has my cell phone number, and so do all the local media. If they want an on-camera interview, I have the Zoom app on my laptop. After you approve the final draft of the Langley release, Popcorn can send it out from home first thing in the morning."

"Then that's the plan."

When I got back to the office, Popcorn fired off a double-barreled update:

"The Vegas casinos are closing, and the Catholic bishops of Ohio have suspended public Masses."

"Times are tough for everybody," I said, not entirely sure how these two news items got coupled.

I quickly briefed her on the plan to move our base of operations to our separate haciendas. Then I went to work on finishing the Grace Langley press release, much of which was recycled from an earlier release when she joined the board. Two of my favorite words are "cut" and "paste."

I'd sent the completed release up the food chain to Saylor-Mackie and GK for final approval and turned my thoughts to an interview with Langley for the alumni mag when Mac called my smartphone.

"Good afternoon, Jefferson," he boomed. "Are you still in the office?"

"Yeah. You caught me."

And just barely! It was 4:30, time to wind down the day and get home for cocktail hour.

"Ah, good. Ms. Carson and Mr. Lipinski are here with me. I thought you might wish to stop by."

"Do I have a choice?"

"Excellent! I knew that you would. We will see you shortly, then."

At least it was on my way home. Mac's quarters as the Lorrenzo Smythe Professor of English Literature and head of SBU's minuscule popular culture program are located across campus in Herbert Hall. His office is crammed with books, papers, and bagpipes. The place was a firetrap before Saylor-Mackie wheedled and cajoled his promise to remember this is a smoke-free campus. (The sign on his desk, "Thank You for Not Breathing While I Smoke," is but a sad remnant of days gone by.) Actually, I still expect it to spontaneously combust any day.

Lipinski wore a bolo tie with a silver and turquoise slide instead of the regulation chef's outfit of white coat and scarf. He was about a foot shorter than his wife, as well as a generation older and distinctly wider. She was casually dressed in jeans and a simple white blouse that accentuated her long, black hair. We skipped the handshake thing, one of the least damaging side-effects of the pandemic, and I was just as happy. I had the distinct impression Lipinski might have crippled my hand by accident.

"Mr. Lipinski and Ms. Carson have appealed for my help," Mac explained.

"I need to get back to my restaurant in Santa Fe," Lipinski said. "Restaurants all over the country are being closed except for carry-out, not just in Ohio. It's only a matter of time before New Mexico gets on the bandwagon. Maybe tomorrow. I have sixty-five employees at the Cactus Flower whose jobs are threatened if we don't change our business model pronto. I need to get back there to oversee that. From what I've read, the plane to get there should be practically empty. But your police chief won't let us leave town while this Stuart Diamond murder investigation is ongoing. And who knows how long that could take!"

"So you want Mac to solve the murder," I interjected, cutting to the chase. I figured that if he kept talking, Lipinski would either cry or punch a wall. Maybe both.

"What?" Carson said. "Solve the murder? Not at all. That would be very nice, of course, but that's not what we had in mind." *Is that a glower behind Mac's beard?*

"Oh."

"We understand that Professor McCabe is close to Chief Hummel from working with him on previous cases. We were hoping that he could use his influence to get us and my assistant producer—you met Nuno—out of here. The idea that we could have had anything to do with the murder of a man we barely knew is laughable."

I didn't laugh, but I did notice there was no social distancing between reality star and producer as Lipinski put an arm around his wife. That was kind of sweet.

"What possible reason could we have for offing the guy?" the chef asked. I think he was just putting Carson's point into different words, not expecting an answer.

"Possible or plausible?" Mac asked.

"Either, damn it! What difference does it make?"

"Quite a bit." Far from rattled by the duo's angst, Mac was in his element as he gave his imagination full reign.

"Let us say possible, then, since only the impossible can be eliminated. Surely it is possible that you murdered Mr. Diamond to boost the ratings of your program. The publicity would be enormous and the loss to you small. By your own admission you barely knew the man and he was not a regular element of the program. His portion of the one episode in which he was to appear was already recorded, meaning that it could still be broadcast to incredibly high ratings."

Not bad, considering that I could tell he was just riffing off the top of his head. And speaking of heads, Lipinski looked like his was about to explode.

"What a crock!" he said. "I mean, I see where you're coming from in your ignorance, and it probably makes sense to you. But there's one gigantic problem with that fairy tale."

"That being that it doesn't make real-world sense," Carson explained coolly, running a hand through her dark tresses. "We're not desperate to pump up ratings. Most other shows on the WSTV Channel would kill to get the ratings we already have. You'll have to do better than that."

Mac pivoted.

"Perhaps Mr. Diamond spotted some financial malfeasance in connection with the production of the program," he said.

Carson shook her head, while her husband just fumed. "Even worse," she said, with a hint of a smile. "WSTV is the tightest outfit in the business. I can't spend a nickel without the money crunchers knowing it. We produce this show for half of what the Food Channel and HGTV spend on theirs."

"Then perhaps," Mac steamed on, "you attempted to suborn Mr. Diamond into a plan to simulate a timely appearance of Jackie O'Brien's ghost in order to make the episode more exciting and promotable. In response, he not only refused to go along but made it clear that he would expose the fraud."

Sounds like a Scooby-Doo *plot.*

"First of all, there was no such plan," Lipinski said. "And secondly, even if there was and Diamond threatened to expose us, we'd yawn in his face. There are about 50 reality shows on TV that have survived worse scandals than that, from tax evasion by a *Survivor* contestant to sexual harassment allegations against a *Great American Baking Show* judge. It would take more than a little fakery to sink *Dining (Way) Out.*"

"And all those home shows on other networks are fake," Carson chipped in. That depends on what your definition of fake is, I suppose, but I was in her corner. When you think the young couple with three kids are trying to decide which house to buy at some outrageously high price, they've already bought it. "Is that all you've got?"

"At the moment. I was extemporizing. Perhaps something else will occur to me later."

"Bring it on," Lipinski said, "and we'll knock that down, too. Meanwhile, maybe if you tell Chief Hummel the best you can come up with goes nowhere, he'll let us be about our business."

Mac approximated an air of regret as he shook his leonine head. "I fear that friend Oscar, once convinced of a notion, is not so easily unconvinced. And right now, his attentions are turned in your direction. He is not likely to easily give up a search for evidence to support his scenario. His force is small, so that will take a while. The Erin police will investigate your alibi—"

"We already told him we were together in our hotel room," Carson said.

"I won't say what we were doing, but we were doing it together." Lipinski didn't waggle his eyebrows, but his tone of voice gave that impression. The expression on his wife's face said she was unamused by this exercise in TMI.

"—and finances of the program, if they think of that," Mac added, "and certainly any possible connection to Mr. Diamond that you have concealed."

"There is none!" Lipinski blasted, giving his beefy arms a good workout.

"Forgive my husband's impatience," Carson said. "That's his artistic temperament."

"I understand," Mac assured her. "All of this is by way of saying it was only natural that Chief Hummel asked you to remain in town while he and his team go about the painstaking business of turning over every metaphorical rock. Your best hope of getting out of Erin and back to your restaurant in New Mexico is detection of the real murderer, assuming that neither of you is that person."

"Assume it," Lipinski snapped. "Is that your way of saying you'll look into it, do more than just spin a few theories out of whole cloth?"

I would have asked more politely if I were in his fix, but Mac didn't seem to mind.

"As a practical matter, Chef, I am already involved in the matter. Chief Hummel called me to the scene of the murder this morning. Although he has not specifically asked for my help, he acknowledged that this is 'my kind of case.' That gives me no authority, no carte blanche, but it does indicate that the Chief will not block my efforts, nor will he be uninterested in whatever I turn up."

With the situation clear, Mac put on his metaphorical deerstalker.

"Since you two were in your hotel room at the time Mr. Diamond was killed, I presume you were not part of the shooting—the video shooting, that is—at The Speakeasy that night."

"Nobody was," Lipinski said. "There was no video shoot. We already told Hummel that."

Mac lifted an eyebrow.

"We didn't need any more B-roll of the empty bar," added Carson, who should know. "We got plenty of that on Sunday night after 9 P.M., when the place closed by state order. Before that, we also got lots of sad patrons bemoaning the shutdown before they were kicked out, which was great stuff. The only thing we didn't get was video of the ghost. I was really hoping for that, but the spook didn't even have the courtesy to turn on the beer taps or make noise."

She spoke ironically, or whimsically, or something— I think.

"That doesn't mean it's not real," her husband said. "It could be."

"Since when did you become a believer?" Carson demanded. "You were the biggest skeptic on the team!"

"Since Diamond died exactly the same way as the other guy. I mean, that's pretty uncanny. It can't be a coincidence, can it? What do you think, McCabe?"

"Coincidences do happen, although in this instance the possibility does seem rather remote. At the moment, however, I am more interested in the startling news that you had no lack of B-roll. Stuart Diamond procured a key from one of the owners of The Speakeasy by telling him there was to be new video obtained that night."

"Hummel told us that during our interrogation," Lipinski said. "He called it an interview, but it was an interrogation. I can't explain what Diamond said. It makes no sense. I can only repeat, there was to be no more video at the gastropub."

"It appears, then, that the late Mr. Diamond wanted to get into The Speakeasy for reasons of his own and fabricated a reason for Charles Bexley to hand over a key. That is the simplest explanation. Do you have any idea what

Mr. Diamond might have been up to? It had to have been something to cause him to lie about his true intentions."

That earned a shrug of Lipinski's sizeable shoulders. "Maybe he met with somebody, say a married woman, for romantic purposes and the tryst went south. Lisa knew him better than I did, since I only met him for the first time on Friday, but he seemed to me like the type."

His wife didn't comment on that theory, but she offered a different one. "It could be that he wasn't lying, that he really thought we were going to meet him there. The last we saw of him was yesterday afternoon, when we did some outside shots—Diamond walking down High Street, standing in front of The Speakeasy, that kind of stuff. Maybe somebody sent him a message that seemed to come from us."

That's not half-bad!

"You had some regular channel of communication?"

Carson nodded. "As the producer, I occasionally called him on his cell or sent him a text."

"The 'spoofing' of phone numbers in calls is a rather common occurrence," Mac noted. "I presume that could be done for text messages as well. Therefore, Mr. Diamond could have received a text from the murderer that appeared to come from you. I will ask Oscar if any such appeared on the victim's phone." He paused, signaling a shift in the line of inquiry. "How well did you know Stuart Diamond?"

"On a personal level, not very well," said Carson. "I was familiar with his YouTube show, which I thought was goofy fun."

And possibly highly profitable, which means that Diamond may have had a pile for somebody to inherit. I filed that thought away for future reference. I remembered reading a *Wall Street Journal* story a few months before about college kids making tens and even hundreds of thousands of dollars on their YouTube channels. None of them were SBU students, but the size of the numbers stuck with me.

"Goofy is the word," Lipinski said. "At least, that's what I thought when Lisa forced me to watch it. Now I'm not so sure. Maybe some of it's true."

"True or not, Stuart really thought The Speakeasy was haunted," Carson said. "I'm sure of that."

I had a flashback to Diamond telling me he knew about the Jackie O'Brien ghost story from reading *Bookmarked for Murder*, which could not have been true.

"He also thought the gangster's missing money was around somewhere," Carson added, as if an afterthought.

"Indeed!" Mac said. "He talked about that, did he?"

"More than once. He said O'Brien must have taken in millions in cash from bootlegging, but it never turned up."

Again, the raised eyebrow. "That opens an intriguing possibility. If Mr. Diamond prevaricated about the reason he wanted the key" —back to that theory—"it could be that he wanted to explore the premises in solitude to search for the rumored O'Brien cash hoard."

"And then what?" I asked Mac. "How did get dead?"

"Perhaps Mr. Diamond and an accomplice found the money and the accomplice was dissatisfied with settling for half of the treasure."

"Let me get this straight." My voice dripped sarcasm. "A stranger to Erin and some hypothesized co-conspirator managed to find this pile of cash after just a few hours of looking? In a building that's been torn apart and reconfigured multiple times over the past hundred years, most recently less than five years ago?"

"That is a stretch, undeniably," Mac allowed. "Still, one does wonder who killed Jackie O'Brien and where his money went."

"I don't," said Lipinski. "I just want to get back to my restaurant. You're not helping."

"What did you think?" I asked Mac after the couple stalked out, non-too-happily.

"Chef Lipinski's bolo tie was not to my taste."

Give me strength! Sebastian McCabe, seldom seen without a bow tie beneath his multiple chins, is poorly positioned to criticize anybody else's neckwear.

"He's from Santa Fe," I pointed out.

"Ah, yes, of course. That explains it. The late John Bennet Shaw, a legendary Sherlockian and also a Santa Fe resident, was much addicted to the same sartorial habit. In fact, it is the official tie of the state of New Mexico."

How does he know this stuff?

"Can we get back to the murder at hand?"

"The means is clear and will be somewhat more specific after the ballistics report. Motive and opportunity remain uncertain."

"Money is always a good motive," I pointed out, "and Diamond may have had plenty of it if his YouTube program was that big a hit."

Mac nodded. "A fertile field for investigation, to be sure. As for opportunity, you will have noted four weak alibis, Jefferson."

This was a test, and I passed:

"Lipinski and Carson alibi each other, as do Bexley and Haldane. But here's no third-party confirmation in either case."

"Precisely, old boy! And that is certainly worth noting. Whether it is significant is another matter altogether."

Chapter Seven
Home Office

We didn't forget about Nuno Robles, the assistant producer, and Kerri Raines, the videographer.

"Maybe they'll have better alibis," I said.

Never mind that even the inventive mind of Sebastian McCabe couldn't come up with anything better in the way of motive for either of them than a hypothetical unwelcome advance (to either one or both of them) spurned with extreme prejudice.

"I trust that Oscar's troops, meaning Colonel Gibbons, will have looked into that, Jefferson."

And there the case rested, at least for us.

At home I caught Mandy Peters on TV4 Action News reporting from in front of The Speakeasy wearing a cute tie-dyed protective face mask. Unable to connect with anybody who knew anything, she interviewed the equally masked food truck maven Tony Ranieri of Tony's Cal-Zone across the street.

"I used to work at The Speakeasy until I was let go," Ranieri said. "That could have been me killed! I'm just shocked, gutted that this happened in downtown Erin." I took his muffled word for that, but I wondered how he remained ignorant of all the other local homicides in the city center. I made a mental note to give him a few of my books.

After dinner, Lynda and I watched the livestreamed St. Patrick's Day performance of the tenor trio Joyful Noise—Rabbi David Goldman, Reverend Mayor Fred

Sutterlee, and Father Francis Xavier O'Boyle. Irish music, which really isn't all that joyful, failed to take my mind off the day's activity on Wall Street—the worst one-day plunge for the market since 1987, when I was thirteen years old and just starting to pay attention.

"If I were a stock picker instead of an index investor," I told Lynda in mid-concert, "I'd be buying Netflix and Clorox, selling airlines and cosmetics."

"Why cosmetics?"

"Because working at home will soon be massive. How often have you put on make-up since you've been working at home?"

"Every day."

I took that as an invitation to investigate my beloved's olive complexion, beautiful oval face, and cutely crooked nose close-up. Which I did.

My own first day of working from home began the next morning with the usual chaos of attempting to feed three children age four and under, plus ourselves, while glancing at the *Observer* and *The Wall Street Journal*. **YOUTUBE STAR SLAIN AT PUB**, the former informed readers. Tall Rawls shared the byline with news editor Ben Silverstein. On a small town daily even the boss writes stories, and crime had been one of Ben's four beats when he was a reporter. The story began:

> Stuart Diamond, whose *Strange World of Stuart Diamond* YouTube program became a hit with thousands of subscribers, was found shot to death at The Speakeasy gastropub at Front and High Streets—a murder eerily similar to that of bootlegger Jackie O'Brien in the same place 100 years ago.
>
> The Speakeasy co-owner Charles Bexley discovered the body Tuesday morning. Dr. Arlene Eppensteiner, Sussex County coroner,

estimated the time of death at between 8 P.M. and midnight on Monday. Diamond had been shot six times.

"This is hard to wrap my head around," said Bexley. "It's surreal."

He discarded any possible supernatural element.

"No ghost did this," he said. "There was a human killer, if you can call that human."

Diamond came to Erin last week to co-host an episode of *Dining (Way) Out*, a popular program on the Wine & Spirts TV Channel.

"I didn't know the man well, but his murder shocks me to the core," said celebrity chef Stephen Lipinski, one of a pair of brothers who normally host the program.

The tenth paragraph reported a quote from Oscar: "If anyone has any knowledge…," etc. He said there was "no person of interest at this time."

Most of the rest of the story was background on Diamond. He hung his hat (if he owned one) in Indianapolis, but little else was known about him except that he had built a steady audience for *The Strange World of Stuart Diamond* over the past two years.

"You and Mac should check into that YouTube angle," Lynda said.

"Jake looked at me!" announced Donata, our oldest.

"Jake, don't look at Donata," I said.

Jake laughed wickedly, egged on by his evil twin brother, Sam. There's a reason they call that age "the "terrible twos."

"What YouTube angle?" I asked Lynda.

"How should I know? You guys are the sleuths." She bit her lip in thought. "Maybe he had a rival or offended somebody"—she lowered her husky voice—"or some*thing*."

Cue the spooky music.

Lower on the *Observer*'s front page was a story that began: "Today's City Council meeting may be the last open to the public for some time if the governor issues a shelter-in-place order, as other states have done, although Council will continue to broadcast on cable and livestream the weekly sessions." Other pandemic-related stories from near and far filled the paper. That would go on for weeks. I read enough of it to feel informed on the big picture. I turned my mind to domestic implications.

"How are we stocked on toilet paper and tissues?" I asked Lynda.

People were starting to hoard the stuff.

"We're good there—but a little low on paper towels."

I made a mental note of that.

"Well, I guess I'd better go to the office now," I said, meaning a stroll down the hallway.

"Um, let's talk about that, darling."

Uh, oh! Incoming!

"Talk?"

"My home office is a bit of a mess."

I wasn't going to bring that up.

My wife's business card reads "Lynda Teal, *Storyteller*" because of what she does in that office while the kids nap or are otherwise out of her hair. (In the other rooms, she's Mrs. Cody.) She completed a Kentucky family saga *Bluegrass*, now awaiting publication by a mid-sized publisher, and was working on another multi-generational novel called *Ink*, about a newspaper family. Lynda also sometimes toils there on freelance projects for Megan Whitlock of the Grier Newspaper Group North Central Division, her former employer. One such gig was a recently completed true crime podcast called *Murder in Paradise*, based on a case Mac solved in Barbados a few years back.[7]

---

[7] See "A Destination Murder" in *Murderers' Row*, MX Publishing, 2020.

"But I know where everything is in that mess," she continued. "If you get in there, you'll organize everything and then I'll never find it."

"Well, that is a knotty problem," I conceded. "What's your solution?"

"You can take your laptop out to the porch."

"The porch?"

"Sure. Just set up your laptop on the table and spread out. It's screened-in to keep the bugs out, and there's a heater for cool days. If it rains, pull down the shades. It'll be perfect!"

That's not the word I'd use.

"If it's so perfect," I said, "you should relocate there. I'd feel guilty getting the better office."

"Don't be silly, darling. I'm all situated here."

Just then, Sam spit a mouthful of Cheerios at Donata, Jake laughed, Donata screamed, and the phone in my pocket jangled.

"Good morning," I yelled to Popcorn above the din. I gave Lynda a hit-and-run kiss as I ran to my new office, grabbing the SBU laptop on the way.

Chapter Eight
Virtual Sleuthing

Phone calls (some of them redirected from my office phone), email, social media chores, a GoToMeeting online gathering of the coronavirus task force, two press releases, and chasing the occasional screaming child kept me too busy to wonder whether this home office thing was going to work. Which meant that it was working. The only thing I missed was Popcorn popping in with decaf and gossip.

Ashley Crutcher, fellow member of the Poison Pens mystery writers' group and paralegal at the Slade Law Firm, interrupted the workflow in mid-morning.

"Hi, Jeff! I want to put a bug in your ear," she said.

"Just what I need—an insect in my auricle."

She didn't even pause to appreciate the witticism.

"This Stuart Diamond murder is a big deal. When Mac catches the murderer, they'll need a good attorney. Remember your friends, okay?" Erica Slade, ex-wife of Sussex County prosecuting attorney Marvin Slade, is the leading defense lawyer in town.

"You're chasing an ambulance that hasn't even been called to the scene yet, metaphorically speaking," I pointed out. "Is that even ethical?"

"Hey, how are Lynda and those adorable kids of yours?"

And so forth.

About an hour later Mac called with a cheery, "How goes the battle, old boy?"

"Same old, same old, except different. I'm on the porch. Don't ask. What's up?"

"I have spoken with Jonah Wittle."

"The architect who designed The Speakeasy? Why?"

"Just a little notion I had. I reasoned that, in order to turn a bookstore into a gastropub, Mr. Wittle must have spent some time on the scene to get a clear grasp of the realities of the situation. Ergo, he could assess for me the likelihood that a secret panel or some such hiding place—perhaps a remnant of the building's days as a stop on the Underground Railroad—might conceal Jackie O'Brien's rumored and never-found fortune in cash."

"You really think Diamond was looking for that when he was killed?"

"It was, at least, a possibility. Alas, Mr. Wittle assures me that the building was gutted, right down to the four exterior walls, at the time of its transformation from a bookstore. There was nothing left of the original illegal speakeasy, and had not been for decades, although there was some attempt to create the gastropub in its image based on a few faded photos."

"Didn't you know all that from being a customer of Pages Gone By?"

"I thought as much, but I needed to be sure."

"Well, that's that, then. I guess Wittle didn't have much to tell the WSTV crew."

"*Au contraire*, Jefferson! Our television friends are interested in how the architect worked with Mr. Haldane to redesign the building in a way that balanced aesthetics and practicality. Mr. Wittle was unable to speak with Chef Lipinski earlier because of a scheduling conflict, but he told me that Oscar has granted permission for the WSTV crew to travel to Cincinnati to speak with him in his office. They preferred to do so there as a visual change of pace from The Speakeasy and for ease of him showing them models of some other projects on which he worked."

Wittle lives in Erin but operates his highly successful practice out of a high-rise office building downriver.

"Oscar must not be too worried the happy couple will go on the run if he's giving them that long a leash," I said.

"That possibility does seem remote. Speaking of Oscar, he has requested that we join him in a Zoom meeting in about an hour to discuss the case and compare notes."

"Why not just do a conference call on the phone?"

"I gather that Miss Burdette has persuaded Oscar to test out the video technology."

Holly Burdette, quoted in Tall Rawls's story about the Friday night goings-on at The Speakeasy, is Oscar's savvy executive assistant, which he thinks sounds better than admin. And, truth to tell, the title is appropriate. Holly holds a degree in business from Murray State University and is finishing a master's in criminal justice at SBU.

Her face was the first one I saw on my laptop screen at the appointed hour. And a cute young face it is, framed by copper-colored hair in a pixie cut that showed off her pearl earrings. She always looks like she just stepped out of a shower ready to take on the day.

"Hi, Jeff! I hear birds singing. Are you outside on the porch?"

"I prefer to think of it as my office away from office."

Mac Zoomed in a few seconds later from his man cave. He calls it a study, but it's a man cave: books on all four walls, a handsome computer desk where Mac writes his own novels, leather chairs, a love seat, and a rarely watched wide flat-screen TV over the small wet bar with a beer tap.

Having accepted Mac in, Holly moved aside and Oscar's big head with its balding noggin took over a third of the screen. Because of the camera angle, he appeared to have three chins instead of two. I didn't think he'd thank me for bringing that up, so I didn't. I could see his coffee mug within easy reach.

"This isn't exactly like Dick Tracy's wrist TV," he said, "but it's pretty neat."

"You'll get over the thrill in three or four meetings," I assured him. "By the way, why aren't you vaping?"

He looked grim. "Popcorn says it's not good for me. Cigarettes apparently are also not good for me. Caffeine—well, I had to draw the line somewhere."

Mac filled him in on our conversation with Lipinski and Carson.

"I still don't see any better suspects," Oscar said.

"And yet you gave them permission to interview Jonah Wittle at his office in Cincinnati?" Mac said.

Oscar shrugged. "It sounded legit. And I don't think they're motivated to run. They underestimate me."

He was probably right. It was easy to do. Oscar has his strengths, and one of them is that he knows his weaknesses. That's why he has Holly Burdette and Lt. Col. L. Jack Gibbons at his side, with Sebastian McCabe at his back.

"Were there any recent texts on the victim's cell phone?" Mac asked.

"No. The latest was some very boring 'see you at four o'clock' kind of stuff with Carson, Robles, and Raines from Friday. Strictly business."

"So if the killer lured Mr. Diamond to The Speakeasy after hours on a pretext of video recording, he must have done so in person. I say 'he' only for convenience, not assuming the sex of the perpetrator—or perpetrators. You have spoken with Mr. Robles and Ms. Raines about the night of the murder, I trust?"

"Yeah. They were together, playing miniature golf."

Again with the mutual alibi!

"Is that the best they can do?" I said.

He swigged his java, which I knew to be black.

"Actually, it's pretty solid, as alibis go. For one thing, the attendant at Putters remembers them because Raines was the taller of the two and she paid the bill. Secondly, she paid by credit card and she still had the receipt, which gives the time as nine o'clock. They played for an hour or so, which would line up pretty well with the time of the murder."

"I suppose they spent the night together." Call me cynical.

"They didn't say so," Oscar reported.

"Then they probably didn't, which means their alibi isn't perfect," I pointed out.

"And all the more credible for that," Mac retorted. "If they were lying, they would swear they never took their eyes off each other all night." *Even while they were sleeping.* He pivoted: "Perhaps the motive for this crime is unrelated to Stuart Diamond's involvement with the television program and its team. It is axiomatic that most murder victims know their killers intimately. Have you identified the next of kin?"

Oscar got an odd look on his face, which in retrospect may have been a *"holy crap, I should have started with this"* kind of look, considering what came next.

"Funny thing about that," he said. "Gibbons ran a complete background check, and you know he never misses anything. Not only couldn't he come up with any next of kin, he couldn't find any records of Diamond that go back more than about a decade ago."

"A stage name, perhaps," Mac speculated.

"If so, it's the only name he used. It was on all the paperwork in his wallet. But the Indiana driver's license and the Social Security card both date to 2011. Gibbons figures Diamond hired a teenager to apply in person for the card so there would be no question as to why a man in his forties at the time didn't have a social. That's an old scam. And get this." Oscar leaned forward. "Those glasses of his? They were phony, too. Clear glass. So Gibbons got a big lightbulb over his head and asked the coroner to check on the victim's hair."

Mac arched an eyebrow.

Okay, I'll bite.

"His hair?" I repeated.

Oscar nodded. "Yeah. And, just like Gibbons guessed, it was dyed. Both the hair on his head and the beard. And not just to get rid of gray. His natural color was light, like straw, not dark brown."

"Excellent work!" Mac praised.

Oscar looked like a proud father. "Gibbons is top shelf. That's all off the record, by the way. I'm not going to announce who the victim *isn't* until we know who he *is*. BCI's running his fingerprints, which we didn't ask for before because we thought we knew who he was."

"Perhaps you could request that they make the procedure a priority in deference to Chef Lipinski and the others marooned in Erin."

"I already asked them to put some speed on it. Opioid cases have fallen off a bit lately, so that will help."

"Excellent! What do you have on the fatal bullet?"

"Bullets. There were six, remember? The killer took no chances."

"Or didn't like the victim, whoever he was," I hazarded.

"Or intended to echo the murder of Jackie O'Brien," Mac said.

Or is a ghost, proving that messing with the supernatural is not a longevity plan. Not that I really believed that, but it did pop into my head.

"Whatever," Oscar said. "BCI reports that the bullets were .45s, probably from a Sig Sauer. The weapon for sure wasn't the S&W .38 that dispatched our own late, lamented Jackie O. Sorry your brainstorm about that didn't work out, Mac."

He didn't sound sorry.

"Hardly a brainstorm," Mac chided. "It was just a happy thought that perhaps the never-found murder weapon in the O'Brien murder had emerged at last. No matter. We still have several lines of investigation to pursue."

We do?

Mac's phone pinged. He looked down at it and punched in a response.

"Well, have at it," Oscar said. "I have a home-grown, pandemic-inspired crime to deal with."

"Toilet paper theft?" I joshed.

He gave me a *"what the hell"* look. "How did you know?"

"Are you kidding me?"

"I wish. Some asshole in a protective mask walked out of Lawrence's IGA Foodliner with two big packages of the stuff—eighteen mega-rolls each, which is the equivalent of seventy-two regular rolls. Bob Lawrence yelled at him to stop, but the guy just walked faster. The two elderly ladies in the store at the time were not exactly built to stop him. By the time Bob got to the sidewalk, the master thief was nowhere in sight."

"That is intolerable!" Mac exclaimed. "At a time when Americans are increasingly donning masks, primarily to protect not so much themselves as their fellow citizens, this malefactor adopted one to hide his identity while committing a brazen theft."

"It's just toilet paper," I said. "I don't exactly think Morrie Kindle at the AP will be all over the story." (I was wrong about that.)

Mac ignored my objection.

"How goes the investigation?" he asked Oscar.

"We're just about to study the surveillance tape. Wanna see it?"

Mac paused only a moment to give that a think. "Thank you, but no. That course of action has never been particularly helpful in our previous inquiries. In the murder of Warren Burch, in fact, it was a positive distraction.[8] I think Jefferson and I need to visit the scene of the crime."

---

[8] See *Too Many Clues*, MX Publishing, 2019.

Chapter Nine
The Man Behind the Mask

"I hope you can tear yourself away from your office to join me on this field trip to Lawrence's IGA Foodliner," Mac said after Oscar had left the Zoom meeting.

"I'll make the sacrifice." I thought: *It will be nice to get out of the four walls, even though they're porch screens.* "But what about those 'several lines of investigation to pursue' in the Diamond murder? Shouldn't we be pursuing them?"

"This should not take long. And that rather inexact term 'several' may have been a slight exaggeration, Jefferson, at least until we find out more about the pseudonymous Stuart Diamond. However, I am happy to say that the good Lynda is on the case, so I feel free to engage in this other matter in good conscience."

What the—

"Did you say Lynda? *My* Lynda? The Lynda who's a few yards away from me?"

"None other, old boy! She texted me a few moments ago and offered to pursue what she called 'the YouTube angle,' which she further characterized rather colorfully as 'taking a deep dive' into the public history of the YouTube phenomenon who called himself Stuart Diamond. It would have been churlish of me to discourage so generous an offer."

"You could have talked to me about it, you know," I told Lynda a few minutes later as she was in the process of grabbing one of the twins.

"And what would you have said?"

"Well, uh, I would have asked Mac, in case he was already working that end."

"Well, there you are! I cut out the middleman and saved you the trouble. You're welcome. Grab a diaper, will you, darling? Wait a minute, make that two."

Lawrence's IGA Foodliner is on Spring Street, not in the heart of downtown but not far from it. It's small, but ideal for picking up the necessities of life in a quick trip. Toilet paper, for instance. Mac drove us there, with me attempting to social distance by sitting in the back of the mammoth vehicle on the passenger side—not six feet away, but almost. Besides, he was facing away from me.

With protective masks on my mind, I noticed when we walked into the store that about half of the two dozen or so patrons were wearing one.

We found Bob Lawrence in the cereal aisle, stacking boxes. I wondered whether we had enough Cheerios at home. Lawrence wore one of those blue paper masks, but it was looped around his chin like a beard as he talked to us.

"I still can't get over it," he said. "Once in a while we catch a kid trying to walk off with something, sure. But the loss to shoplifting here is minor compared to what you'd find at a supermarket."

In his mid-fifties with thinning hair and a sunny disposition, Lawrence would know. He managed Erin's Kroger store before he gambled all his savings at mid-life to save the local IGA when the previous owner retired.

"And this creep stole toilet paper!" he raged on. "It's crazy. But I hear that people are stockpiling the stuff all over the country. They're making a big deal out of nothing. This virus is no worse than the flu. In a month everything will be back to normal and we'll laugh about this pandemic panic."

If only he'd been right.

"How is it that the robber managed to escape in broad daylight?" Mac asked.

"I was over in the back room when I heard Martha yelling at the jerk to stop," Lawrence said. "She was stuck behind the counter, and I couldn't exactly run after the guy." Lawrence is built more for waddling than for running. "Everybody else in the store at the time just stared. I think they were all stunned."

Or they didn't want to get involved. Even in Erin that happens.

Lawrence went on to note that the perp was white, male, about five-seven, neither fat nor skinny, and old enough to know better. In short, he was an average sort of guy and there was nothing about him to remind Lawrence of anyone he knew. But he only had a quick glimpse.

"Did you see what his mask looked like?" I asked.

"No, I only saw him from the back. Maybe Martha noticed."

We would have seen for ourselves on the surveillance tape if Mac hadn't—

"Surely the design of the mask is irrelevant," Mac said. "It strains credulity to think that the scoundrel is so witless as to wear a mask that might be associated with him or to retain and use afterwards the same mask employed in the commission of a crime."

We aren't talking Moriarty here, Mac.

"Maybe this was more a crime of opportunity than something well planned," I speculated.

"Well, Martha said the guy came in, made a bee-line for the TP, and scooted out with it," Lawrence reported.

"You mentioned 'stockpiling,'" Mac said. "I gather that the stolen product is a commodity much in demand these days."

"You bet! I can't keep rolls in stock. People are filling their shopping carts with them. I should set limits on how many packages customers can buy. We were out of all brands, from the most expensive to the cheapest, for four days. A new shipment arrived just an hour before the thieving magpie showed up."

A McCabe eyebrow shot up.

"This would have been the first opportunity in some time, then, for anyone to have bought or stolen toilet paper in this store?"

Lawrence looked at Mac like he was thinking, *"Hello, Captain Obvious!"*

"Yes, that's right."

"Perhaps that is revealing. You indicated a moment ago that Martha said the thief entered the store in a determined way, as with a goal in mind. Presumably only an employee of the store would know that the desired item had arrived. Therefore, one of them is an accomplice who alerted the thief."

Lawrence shook his head. "No way!"

Just as a Mac opened his mouth to respond, a thirtyish brunette in a flowered dress and no mask sneezed about four feet away from us. She'd been pretending not to listen to our conversation as she studied the oatmeal.

"Bless you," Mac said reflexively.

The three of us stared at her. Heads turned our way from around the store.

"It's an allergy," the woman said. "I mean, I'm not sick. Don't look at me like that!"

She grabbed a package of Quaker Oats without looking at it, threw it in her cart, and moved quickly on. I made a mental note to get one of Kate's masks and cajole Mac into doing likewise as long as we were with each other. It couldn't hurt, and it might help protect the people around us if we got the coronavirus without knowing it.

Mac turned back to Bob Lawrence and picked up where he left off:

"This would not be the first time in my experience that an employee has been involved in a larceny." He no doubt had in mind that Santa Claus robbery, around the same time as the Warren Burch murder.

"I don't care about your experience," Lawrence shot back. "I know my own. Look, Martha's been with me from the beginning. Randy Sherwood's one of the most responsible young men I know—he handles social media for me along with stocking shelves, and he's been picking up extra hours since the high schools closed. And then there's Sherry Roth, who's my wife's cousin. None of these people is so desperate they have to steal toilet paper, for crap's sake!"

Maybe not the best turn of phrase in this case.

"The truth is sometimes hard to accept," Mac platitudinized. "If you are unwilling to consider that one of that trio is involved, then there is nothing more I can do."

"Yeah, well, do me a favor and don't do me any favors."

I picked up a large box of multi-grain Cheerios on the way out.

Mac's usual ebullience was AWOL during lunch at Daniel's, and my efforts to cheer him up fell mostly on deaf ears. Afterwards, he decided to convey to Oscar in person the disappointing outcome of his exertions in the toilet paper caper. We walked the short distance to the police station, an old Art Deco building on Court Street that was once home to the long-defunct Fifth National Bank of Erin.

You know how in a dream sometimes people from different times or places in your life show up together in a mash-up, maybe an old boss and somebody you went to college with? It felt a little like that to see Aurelia Banfield, assistant chief of the St. Benignus University Police (SBUP), in Oscar's office. Not that she and Oscar don't know each other, but I wasn't expecting to see her there when Holly Burdette waved us in as usual. But L. Jack Gibbons, with whom Banfield is smitten, was also present, so it added up: She probably stopped in to see her beau from time to time.

The nondescript Gibbons faded into the background next to his boss and his honey, which no doubt is the way he likes it.

Oscar looked happy. In fact, I would go so far as to say he chortled. "While you guys have been wearing out your shoe leather, Banfield here solved the case."

Mac lifted both eyebrows, looking shocked as he said to Banfield: "You have identified the murderer of the man known as Stuart Diamond?"

She shook her head of brown hair pinned back in a bun. Was that impatience I detected in the gesture? "No, Seb, not that case—the robbery at the IGA."

Gibbons almost smiled. I wish I had photographic evidence of that. Nobody else on Earth could get by with calling Sebastian McCabe "Seb." Maybe he's afraid of her. More likely, it's just that she's not afraid of him. The woman only stands five-foot-six and has a leg made of plastic and metal, but she's muscular and battle-hardened tough from her taxpayer-financed visit to Afghanistan. She wore her Ohio National Guard uniform rather than SBUP togs this morning. I later found out the Guard had been mobilized to help deliver food because of the pandemic.

"Please expound," Mac requested.

Banfield shrugged in a manner a novelist might call studied nonchalance. "Piece of cake, really. I just looked at the surveillance video of the robbery." *The surveillance video! Oh, this is so much fun.* "What happened was, I popped in to say hi to Jack and found him going over the video of the robbery and I recognized the guy wearing mask who walked out with the TP."

"How so, given that he was wearing a mask?"

"Well, when masks started being a thing, I knew there was a potential big problem for law enforcement. I mean, if everybody is going to be wearing a mask, how are you going to tell which ones are the bad guys? And how are you going to know who's behind the mask? That's not always obvious, even if you know the person and that person's distinctive features are obscured. So, I've been making it a point to ask myself whenever I see a mask—something other than paper or a solid color, anyway—whether I can identify the person behind it in case I encounter them in a situation where they'd rather not be ID'd, if you see what I mean. And how often do you see a protective mask in a cow print design, like in the TP robbery? But I had, and I knew who was behind it."

"Who?" I asked.

"Glen Monroe, from the maintenance staff at SBU. I see him in the parking lot all the time." Banfield's office in Public Safety (AKA campus security) is located on the lower level of the Physical Plant, not a part of campus that Mac or I visit often. "He's a bit of a health nut, and he has a great six-pack, let me tell you."

But she also noticed the mask. What a pro!

"Are you quite sure he is guilty?" Mac asked.

"He confessed over the phone," Gibbons said in his customary just-the-facts delivery. "He said he has an over-the-top credit card bill from gambling at the Forty Thieves Casino and an exasperated neighbor who said he'd pay a hundred dollars for a big packet of toilet paper."

"He said all that?"

"I may have given him the impression we have more evidence than we do. But it probably also helped that Bob Lawrence isn't interested in pressing charges. Monroe promised to come in and make a statement at three o'clock."

"He'll have to resign from the University, of course," Banfield added.

"I'm not looking forward to the news story," I said.

Armed with Banfield's identification of Monroe, Gibbons had squeezed a confession out of the robber in not much more elapsed time than it had taken us to do nothing more useful than buying a big box of cereal. Banfield and Gibbons certainly made a formidable team. I'm sure that had occurred to Banfield, who eyed the imperturbable lawman adoringly as he spoke. But she got the major credit on this.

"SBUP Assistant Chief Solves Robbery" would make a great press release—except for the embarrassing fact that the TP robber was a university employee. Maybe I could bury that in the 17th paragraph.

In the three seconds that it took all this to zip through my head, Mac recovered. "I confess myself to be utterly confounded," he said. "How could anyone but an employee know of the freshly arrived consignment of toilet paper? On that point my logic seemed eminently sound."

"Not quite," Banfield said. "Randy Sherwood posted that info on Facebook and Twitter. I could have told you that. Lawrence IGA's Facebook page has about three thousand followers, and I'm one of them."

"Oh. I see." He looked like a man facing the hangman on an empty stomach, the latter part being the hardest for him. "I applaud you, Aurelia, and I indict myself for a colossal error in reasoning. It would be a vast understatement to say that this was not my finest hour."

"Copy that, Seb."

"Please assure me that embarrassing episode will not go unrecorded, Jefferson."

Oh, don't worry. "I promise. Since you asked."

"That was my Norbury moment, and I am chastened by it."[9]

"Well, I hope it will teach you not to overcomplicate things. So, what are you going to do about this humiliation?"

"Solve the murder of Stuart Diamond, of course! It is the only way to regain my self-regard. But that may not be possible until we find out who the man really was."

---

[9] At the end of "The Yellow Face," Sherlock Holmes says: "Watson, if it should ever strike you that I am getting a little overconfident in my powers, or giving less pains to a case than it deserves, kindly whisper 'Norbury' in my ear, and I shall be infinitely obliged to you." It is of some slight comfort to know that even Holmes, like Homer, nodded on occasion. – *S. McC.*

Chapter Ten
YouTuber

Lynda's deep funk was clear to the keen Cody eye as soon as I arrived home at our arts and crafts bungalow on Campion Lane that afternoon. The lady of the house stared listlessly at Donata, who apparently was designing a dress, while the boys buzzed around the two of them like a swarm of bees.

"What's wrong?" I asked, certain that if something truly awful had happened she would have texted me. But in that I was in error. Catastrophe had struck.

"The state shut down barber shops, hair styling salons, and nail salons after the end of business today," she said, barely able to get out the words without crying, "and I have an appointment with Myrtle for next week."

Her honey-colored curls did wilt a bit, but she was no less lovely for that.

"You look great!" I said.

"You're just saying that." *Only because it's true. Well, no; I'm saying it to make you feel better. But it is true.* "You might feel differently if you were affected."

Lynda has been cutting my hair since we walked down the aisle, sometimes better than at other times, at a savings of well over a thousand dollars so far. Since the clippers cost less than fifty bucks, and the price of the scissors was negligible, that's a tremendous return on investment. But I knew better than to tell my volunteer barber that while she was glumping. What I said instead was:

"It's almost five o'clock. I'll fix you a Manhattan."

"You're a darling."

The boys having settled down for the moment, Lynda followed me into the kitchen, where I built her favorite cocktail just the way she likes it.

"So, how was your day?" she asked as I worked my magic.

"Mine was fine. Mac's, not so much."

I gave it to her in chronological order, from the Zoom call where Oscar unloaded about the mystery of Stuart Diamond's real identity to Mac's brilliantly wrong solution to the toilet paper robbery and how it was solved by Aurelia Banfield.

"That Banfield's a keeper!" Lynda said.

I resisted the temptation to crack wise about L. Jack Gibbons's intentions along those lines. "What did you find out about Stuart Diamond?"

"Plenty! Especially since he doesn't exist! Maybe we could call him 'Pseudonymous Diamond.' Anyway, I wrote it all out in a report which I sent to Mac and copied to you. You'll see it when you look at your email."

"Thanks, but why don't you just give me the gist of it?"

"Okay."

And that's what I've decided to share here, rather than the report she prepared for Mac.

"Some of this is based on internet research," Lynda said, "and some comes from calling a reporter in Indianapolis and presenting myself as a journalist from the *Observer*. Well, it's almost true. It used to be true. And besides, I'll share what I learned with Johanna. So, it's almost like I'm still working for the paper, but not getting paid. Remind me to send her a copy of my report."

"I'm sure even Mac would say you weren't lying."

"Anyway, whoever Mr. Diamond was, it looks like he did okay for himself financially. He was quite the YouTuber.

He monetized his *Strange World* channel with ads, mostly for all kinds of occult products—books, videos, psychic hotlines, the works. He also picked up sponsorships from viewers via the Patreon membership platform. All of that must have added up to more than pin money."

"I've read stories about college students or college dropouts making a mint on YouTube," I said. "I think *Forbes* magazine said the top earner is an eight-year-old reviewing toys. Some of these people have a couple of hundred thousand subscribers and over a million views."

"Diamond wasn't quite there, but he was heading in that direction. This wasn't his first YouTube channel, by the way. He had earlier and less successful ones dealing with such varied subjects as gambling, legal advice, and travel. It's pretty clear that he kept experimenting until he hit the right topic, the one he could make real money on. But where there's success, there's envy and controversy, right?"

"I wouldn't know."

"Cute. So, I checked out Diamond's Facebook, Instagram, and Twitter accounts, both his personal ones and his *Strange World of Stuart Diamond* accounts. Bingo!"

"A controversy?"

"A rival. Jake, don't throw things at your sister. Stop it! Okay, time out for you, young man."

What with one thing and another, I didn't get the rest of the story until everybody was in bed. Including us. In between, I initiated or fielded five calls related to our errant maintenance worker with the sticky fingers for toilet paper.

"Where was I?" Lynda asked as we settled into the marital sack for a quiet conversation at last.

"Diamond had a rival, you said."

"Antagonist might be a better word. A small-time radio personality named Conrad Starshak, who calls himself a paranormal investigator, was constantly ragging Diamond on social media for what he called shoddy work and overdramatizing. He'd get really specific about what he objected to in particular episodes of the show."

"How was it any skin off of his scam?"

Lynda shrugged her admirable shoulders. "I don't know. Professional pride maybe—the idea that if Diamond didn't do it well, he would reflect poorly on anybody else in the same sandbox. Or maybe Starshak's radio show competes with Diamond for psychic advertising or something."

"I don't think Oscar would find either possibility much of a motive."

"Not for the average person, but this Starshak is a bit of an oddball." *Only a bit?* "I mean, he doesn't seem to have much of a life outside of his obsession with the paranormal. He doesn't post about anything else on social media, for instance. But I didn't spend a lot of time on his background, so he may or may not have a family and a day job in some other field."

"But you think he's a good suspect?"

She shook her head. The curls didn't look so bad in the bedroom light. "Sorry, but no. I was just playing out the possibility on the motive thing. His alibi for the night of the murder is tighter than a drum. Starshak lives in Clinton, Iowa, where he hosts his call-in radio show on the psychic and the supernatural for two hours every Monday evening, starting at seven o'clock. To get here from Clinton would mean driving two and a half hours just to get to the airport in Chicago. I didn't bother to check on flight times. The timing just wouldn't work."

"Maybe he owns a helicopter."

"Only if he's a bazillionaire, and I see no indication of that. No, the only reason I mentioned Starshak is that he's the one person I could find who was in a public conflict with Diamond, not counting the occasional know-it-all posting a rude comment on the YouTube page. Also, I thought it would impress Mac to put him in my written report."

"Noted. What did you find out about Diamond?"

"He rented a modest house in a small town called Zionsville in suburban Indianapolis. I talked to one of the neighbors, Mrs. Alice Fortenberry. She somehow thought I was doing a security check for a government agency. Don't look at me like that. Anyway, she said Diamond lived alone and mostly kept to himself. But he got into a shouting match two weeks ago with a neighbor over the neighbor's dog making a deposit in Diamond's garden."

"That sounds promising! Some people will kill over their pets."

"My thought exactly! The problem there is that Mrs. Fortenberry said the neighbor has been in the hospital for the past five days with COVID. He will probably survive, but he didn't kill Diamond. And coming all the way here to kill the man when he could do it in without leaving his neighborhood doesn't seem too likely, when you think about it."

"Did Diamond have a day job?"

"He claimed to be a lawyer when he had that YouTube channel dealing with legal questions, but he wasn't a member of the Indianapolis bar. Mrs. Fortenberry said he kept coming and going in his car—a silver gray Honda Civic, several years old—so often that she thought maybe he was a ride share driver. I doubt that, though. It doesn't seem to fit."

"I wouldn't want to be a stockholder in Uber, Lyft, or Ryde right now," I mused, "or depend on a side gig as a driver. There are fewer and fewer places to drive to that are still open! People like us, who can work remotely from home, are lucky these days."

"Some TV anchors are starting to do that."

She watches more than I do.

"What, broadcasting from home?"

"Yeah."

"I wonder if Conrad Starshak could do that with his radio show."

"Why not?"

Chapter Eleven
Murders Old and New

Johanna Rawls' banner story in Thursday's *Observer & News-Ledger*, **SBU COP CATCHES TP ROBBER**, contained no surprises and no significant errors. A mug shot of Glen Monroe, the petty villain of the piece, looked out at me from page one. The photo with the jump on page 5A showed him in his tell-tale cow print mask as Gibbons and Banfield escorted him into the city jail. The murder had moved inside the paper, with a page 2B profile of Stuart Diamond's life in Indiana based Johanna's follow-up to Lynda's digging.

I skimmed all that and moved on. For the first several hours of the day—the first day of spring—I was immersed in the fallout of our employee's criminous behavior and routine work with Popcorn (news releases, speeches, social media, a brief virtual meeting of the coronavirus task force) all from my home office on the porch.

When I came up for air in the afternoon, I called Mac. He didn't have to work on *his* porch, if you call what he does work. With campus closed, he was teaching and whatnot from the comfort of his man cave.

"What did you think of Lynda's background report on the dead man?" I asked him.

"Most impressive, old boy!"

"And what did you think of Starshak as a suspect?"

"I salute Lynda for calling him to my attention. However, if everyone who posted critical and even scurrilous comments about another on social media were to subsequently murder that person, the COVID-19 death rate would pale by comparison." This comment was ill-timed, I thought, that being the day Ohio reported its first death from the virus-born illness. (Later testing determined the date to be earlier, however.) "In addition, Jefferson, Lynda admirably established Mr. Starshak's alibi in her report."

I'd been waiting for this, and I pounced:

"Only if he was broadcasting from his radio station's studio there in Iowa. Suppose he was broadcasting remotely, say from a hotel room in Erin, where he registered under a different name."

"Bravo, Jefferson! How very astute of you to see that possibility." Mac took a pause. I'm almost sure he was puffing on a cigar. I deduced that Kate was gone, possibly delivering some of those masks she had sewn, and that he was on their patio (where smoking is grudgingly permitted). "The happy thought occurred to me as well, prompting me to call Mr. Starshak's employers—if that is the correct relationship—at radio station KSFW earlier today. The station manager informed me that Conrad Starshak was in fact broadcasting his program, *Beyond Reality*, remotely on the night of Monday, March 16."

"Ah ha!"

"However, the remote location was his home. Mr. Starshak has a home studio from which he always broadcasts. The station manager was quite proud to assure me that KSFW has high quality standards which are strictly monitored and enforced. He assures me there is no chance that Mr. Starshak literally was 'phoning it in,' in the words of a rather moribund cliché."

Oh.

"That sounds awfully pat," I pointed out.

"Also, there is a call screener who has to be patched through to the landline where the home studio is located."

Okay, okay, I give up.

"How did you even get this guy, the station manager, to talk to you?"

"I have a friend who—"

"Never mind." I shifted gears. "Thanks to Lynda, we know a lot more about this fake Diamond"—*hey, that's not bad!*—"but we still don't know who he really was. Any thoughts on that?"

"More than thoughts. I know who he was."

"What!"

"I was just about to call you before you called me. Oscar informed me within the last half-hour that the Bureau of Criminal Investigation has established that Stuart Diamond was, in reality, one J. Calvin Davis."

This was where I was supposed to express my astonishment, but I wasn't up to the task.

"Why does that name ring a faint bell?" is the best I could do.

"Davis was an Erin lawyer who stole money from several of his clients before he apparently committed suicide nine years ago."

"Oh, yeah. I remember now. That was a huge brouhaha—front page stuff in the *Observer* for days."

"Even so, I paid scant attention at the time. It was a few months before the murder attendant to the 'Investigating Arthur Conan Doyle and Sherlock Holmes' colloquium thrust us into the world of real-life criminal investigation for the first time. Now, however, it is a matter of intense interest to me as our current case becomes the murder of a man already thought to be dead. Very intriguing, that. You realize the fact that the victim was a former Erin resident changes everything, Jefferson?"

"Of course! It means the killer could be somebody who knew who Diamond really was and had a reason to kill him—a reason that had nothing to do with the TV show or The Speakeasy."

"Precisely! That should be of some comfort to Chef Lipinski and Ms. Carson, while somewhat complicating our own task.

"Meanwhile, old boy, I am pleased to inform you that last evening, employing a search engine and a network of friends that you must concede is extensive, I almost certainly solved the century-old murder of Jackie O'Brien. Perhaps it would not be too vain of me to say that some detection enthusiasts might consider my performance to be armchair sleuthing at its best. Perhaps that will in some small measure mitigate that Lawrence IGA fiasco."

Sometimes the man leaves me speechless. It took a while to work myself up to sputtering:

"How in the name of Nero Wolfe could you do that? And why were you futzing with a century-old murder instead of the one at hand?"

"To answer your last question first, it was part of the process of elimination. We now know that access to the long-rumored Jackie O'Brien cash hoard could not have been the motive for the murder of J. Calvin Davis for the very good reason that the ill-gotten fortune no longer exists."

"You mean O'Brien spent it all before he took the bullets?"

"By no means! Be patient as I explain. The key to the solution of Jackie O'Brien's murder, and the destiny of his presumed fortune, lies in the actions of two key individuals after his death. If you knew nothing other than the fact that a man was shot dead, who would you say was the most likely killer?"

"The wife, hands down. The spouse is always the first suspect."

"Bravo! Not ignoring the obvious, my thoughts turned first to O'Brien's widow, Marilyn. I was able to establish that she left Erin about six months after his death. Up to that time she lived quietly and modestly, with no indications of great wealth to give the lie to her protestations that she knew not what happened to her husband's illicit lucre. Four months after her departure, Erin Police Chief Melvin Quade retired at the age of forty-three and also sought greener pastures."

"I'm picking up a pattern here."

"Indeed. I must grudgingly give them credit for their prudence and planning, as well as their patience in waiting so long. Two years later, after living in what used to be called sin, the two married at their sumptuous six-bedroom home in Fort Meyers, Florida, a residence that in 2017 sold for $4.6 million. While it is quite possible that Chief Quade had enjoyed a comfortable second income protecting Mr. O'Brien's illegal ventures, I believe that O'Brien was more valuable to the happy couple dead than alive.

"You will recall that the Smith & Wesson .38 with which he was most likely killed was popular with both police and gangsters of that era. If Melvin Quade did not pull the trigger, as seems likely, he was behind the person who did. As police chief, he would have both access to and leverage over any number of individuals willing to perform that task. And, of course, Chief Quade was in command of the investigation that almost inconceivably found no witnesses to a murder carried out in a speakeasy full of patrons."

"That's a pretty good circumstantial case," I conceded.

"I find it so. Especially since no one else has suggested an alternative. One of the problems that historians have faced in speculating about the case is that no one obviously benefited from Jackie O'Brien's death. He was popular and had no Chicago-style rivals. Upon his death, his network simply disintegrated. Franklin W. Galton did not appear on the scene to create a similarly well-organized enterprise until three years later.

"Although the moralist in me wishes it were otherwise, the Quades apparently lived happily together into the 1960s. Melvin died in 1967 at the age of 89. Marilyn was twelve years younger and died two years later. She left their money to the Fort Meyers Zoo."

So, Sebastian McCabe had solved the century-old murder of Jackie O'Brien—he thought. And who could prove otherwise? The facts all fit.

"All right," I said, after due consideration. "I buy it. Diamond—or, rather, J. Calvin Davis—wasn't killed because he found the O'Brien fortune. But I don't see how eliminating one motive—and one that was always a long shot, at that—gets us very far in solving the murder."

"It does to this extent: Eliminating the treasure hunt theory increases the chance that the motive was purely personal against Davis."

"So, we go back to basics," I said. "Did Davis have a wife in Erin who's still around?"

I could almost hear Mac nod. "He did indeed, old boy: Your friend Mary Landfair, before her second marriage, was Mrs. Mary Davis."

Chapter Twelve
Doubly Dead

When I recovered from the shock, I said: "We're casual friends, not friend friends. I only know her from the Convention & Visitors Bureau. I never even thought about her marital status."

"She is now married to a man named Rowan Landfair," Mac said. "He was mentioned in Johanna's story about the night Chef Lipinski was at The Speakeasy."

Oh, right.

"Isn't that bigamy?"

"Fortunately for her, no. I explored the law on that. J. Calvin Davis was declared legally dead by the proper authorities, which made her second marriage equally legal in the state of Ohio although her first husband was still alive."

"*Was* being the operative word there. Now he's doubly dead. How did Davis make people think he was no longer among the living? I'm fuzzy on the details."

"As was I, so I asked Oscar that very question. Mr. Davis left a suicide note indicating that he would drown himself. His credit card showed that he bought weights and a ticket for the Erin Ferry. That is rather subtle, for which I give the now-deceased credit for cleverness. No body was found, of course, but that is not unusual in the Ohio River. After five years, his wife had him declared dead and remarried shortly thereafter."

"How shortly?"

"Less than a year after the official declaration, Oscar said. That timeline struck me as possibly indicative of a certain haste, but I looked into the law on that as well. I found out that under Section 2121.01 of the Ohio Revised Code a missing person can be declared legally dead even earlier than five years if the individual in question "was at the beginning of the person's absence exposed to a specific peril of death." That would certainly apply in this case. Therefore, Mrs. Landfair did not act with such dispatch as to indicate a desire to be free of her first husband as quickly as possible."

"Maybe she didn't know she could move faster on getting him declared dead." Not that I had anything against Mary Landfair, other than being worn out by her caffeine-fueled energy.

"Surely her attorney would know, if he or she is at all competent. No, Jefferson, we have no reason to believe the new widow was in any great hurry to get out of her marriage to J. Calvin Davis. Now, however, the situation is much different. She has been Mrs. Landfair for three years and presumably well settled into a new life. Her first husband's resurrection from the dead cannot have been welcome."

I processed that out loud.

"In order for Mary Landfair to have killed Davis, she first would have had to realize who he was. On the one hand, how could she not know her own husband? They were in the same room at The Speakeasy, even though I don't recall them getting up close and personal. But, on the other hand, she did tell me Stuart Diamond seemed somehow familiar. Why do that if she knew or suspected who he was, with all the trouble his being alive would cause her? Why call attention to it?"

Mac ignored the rhetorical questions, probably because he had no answer beyond the obvious "she wouldn't." Especially not if she were the killer. Because as long as Davis's true identity was hidden, so was her motive. *Unless that's just what she wanted us to think!* But I wasn't going down that rabbit hole. That would only give me a headache.

"Although we never knew J. Calvin Davis," Mac said, "we should have suspected that Stuart Diamond had a previous connection to Erin when he lied about how he knew of the legendary speakeasy ghost. We both realized at the time he could not have read of it in one of your books. Let that be a lesson to us to let no anomaly go unchallenged, no matter how apparently unimportant."

Let it be a lesson to you: You're supposed to be the sleuth.

"Well, anyway, now that we know who Diamond was, what else are you thinking?"

"I have been reflecting on the remarkably high number of false deaths in the Sherlock Holmes Canon. Most notably, *The Valley of Fear* and 'The Adventure of the Norwood Builder' feature essentially the same plot trope in which an individual stages his own death and hides in a secret room. Of course, Sherlock Holmes himself appears to be dead in 'The Final Problem' but stages a resurrection of sorts in 'The Adventure of the Empty House.' And several other Canonical characters are also either believed or feared dead. 'The Noble Bachelor,' 'The Crooked Man,' 'The Man with the Twisted Lip,' and 'The Disappearance of Lady Frances Carfax' spring readily to mind."

"They do? And how, pray tell, does this meditation on Sherlockian scenarios help solve the murder of Mary Landfair's first husband?"

Mac paused. "Admittedly, I can conceive of no way in which it does."

"I didn't think so." I shifted gears. "I wonder how the widow's taking it?"

"She fainted when she got the news from Chief Hummel," Ralph Pendergast informed me in a phone call an hour or so later. "I was there when it happened. It wasn't pretty, Cody. I sent her home and told her not to come back. She can work from there, and she should. Mary has some underlying health issues that could be a serious concern if she came into contact with somebody who had that new virus.

"I suppose I should transition to my home office as well. We won't be doing any real business for a while anyway. The governor of California issued a shelter-in-place order today, and I expect that action to spread to other states. It's already clear we'll have to cancel the jazz festival this summer. Our work at the CVB is going to be planning for a future that may look very different. But at this moment, I am most concerned about Mary."

Ralph, a prissy type with rimless glasses and slicked-back dark hair rapidly receding into history, was the bane of my existence when he was SBU's provost and academic vice president—Saylor-Mackie's predecessor, with a slightly different title and less authority. But after leaving the university to run the Convention & Visitors Bureau, Ralph somehow became a human being instead of a computer in a three-piece suit. I realized that a homo sapiens lurked in there somewhere when I once caught him listening to jazz after hours, but the change of jobs really liberated him.

"It's a strange new world," I commiserated. "J. Calvin Davis won't even be able to get a normal funeral open to all comers. But I suppose that would be a bit touchy anyway, what with the way he stole from his clients and made them and his wife think he was dead."

"That whole sorry episode was before I came to Erin, Cody, but I can imagine the turmoil it caused in such a close-knit community. Yes, I suppose a social-distanced funeral is a blessing of sorts for Mary."

Then Ralph finally got around to why he called me:

"I'm sure this murder has ripped open a lot of old wounds for her. Since it's better to run over hot coals than to walk slowly"—*nice image!*—"the sooner the killer is caught and this matter put to rest, the better. The better for everybody, Cody, but especially for Mary. I'm so sure that McCabe is on the case that I won't even ask. But I'd like some assurance that he's making it a priority. We've had our differences in the past, but I can't deny his track record in solving murders."

To say that Mac and Ralph had their differences during the latter's tenure at SBU is like that old euphemism of calling the American Civil War "the recent unpleasantness." If Ralph and I were oil and water in those days, Ralph and Mac were more like oil and fire. Which doubtless is why Ralph called me instead of Mac.

"Don't worry," I said, "the Davis murder is at the top of his agenda." *Now that he's finished with that toilet paper robbery and a century-old shooting.* "Of course, he didn't know until today that the victim was Mary Landfair's first husband. That makes it a whole different investigation. I don't suppose you have any fear that she killed him?"

"What? Mary, a killer? Don't be absurd, Cody." *The old Ralph is back for a special appearance!* "If I thought so, I wouldn't be making this call. No, my only fear with regard to her as a suspect is that Chief Hummel and the prosecutor may fix on the easy but wrong scenario of the murderous spouse."

"We're on the same page, then: Mac and I don't think Mary's a good suspect, either. But I'm sure Mac will want to talk to her as somebody who was once close to the victim."

"Not in person, he won't, not even with protective masks," Ralph said. I could almost hear him shake his head. "There's no need to take the risk."

"Could we do a video conference? Mac likes to look at a person's face during an interview."

"I don't see why not. We occasionally use Zoom at the office. I'm sure Mary can set it up on her home computer as well, if she hasn't already, and answer your questions that way. She has nothing to hide."

"I hope not."

Chapter Thirteen
Background to Murder

Mac and I talked to Mary Landfair from our respective offices that evening, as we had earlier with Oscar. I Zoomed in early, glad we didn't have to use Skype, What'sApp, Google Hangouts, Houseparty, Webex, or some other technology that I would have to get Popcorn to explain.

So, my laptop and I were huddled on my screened-in porch, and there was Mac ensconced in the world's greatest man cave. But who said life is fair? I saw a stack of books on his desk: Camus's *The Plague*, Defoe's *Journal of the Plague Year*, García Márquez's *Love in the Time of Cholera*, Jack London's *The Red Plague*, and Stephen King's *The Stand*. I discerned a certain uniting theme there.

"So, what are you reading these days?" I asked.

He pretended to think that was a real question.

"I just finished Poe's 'Masque of the Red Death.' The ending haunts one, Jefferson." He picked up a book and read: "And now was acknowledged the presence of the Red Death. He had come like a thief in the night. And one by one dropped the revellers in the blood-bedewed hall of their revel, and died each in the despairing posture of his fall. And the life of the ebony clock went out with that of the last of the gay. And the flames of the tripods expired. And the Darkness and Decay and the Red Death held illimitable dominion over all."

"Cheery."

"Camus gives more hope."

"That wouldn't be hard. Hey, speaking of masks, I need to get one from Kate." I knew the difference between a masque and a mask, thanks to the opera murders,[10] but one sparks thoughts of the other. "I figure it could do no harm. Besides, I might want to steal some toilet paper."

"You wound me with your allusion to a matter in which I failed so ignominiously."

"Don't say 'failed.' Think of it as an incomplete success!"

And so forth.

Mary Landfair joined us at the appointed time, 7 P.M., looking haggard and sapped of the energy for which she was notable. Her fair hair looked like a bird's nest. Even through the screen of the laptop it was clear she wore no makeup. For a change she looked her age, mid-forties, and then some. She had a large Sussex County travel mug in her hand, no doubt filled with caffeine-laced coffee. A watercolor of a Venice canal scene decorated the wall behind her.

"Thanks for speaking with us at this difficult time," Mac said. "You must be quite upset."

"Upset? More like stupefied. It's all too much at once. I just told everything I know about Cal to Assistant Chief Gibbons. He doesn't have much personality, does he? I still can't believe Cal's alive—*was* alive. Oh, hell. Hit me again; I won't feel it."

She chugged java.

"You have my deepest sympathy," Mac intoned, and I quickly echoed the sentiment.

"You're a little late, guys. I needed it while the bastard was alive, pardon my French. I can't believe he did this to me. What am I saying? Yes, I can. That man never had any consideration for me or our kids whatsoever."

I couldn't tell whether Landfair thought Davis's offense was being alive until Monday or getting murdered,

---

[10] See *Death Masque*, MX Publishing, 2017.

but I didn't ask. Besides, I'm not sure she knew. She didn't give the impression of a woman who was thinking clearly.

"How long were you married to him?" Mac asked.

"Too long. Fourteen years. I helped put him through law school by working at a series of admin jobs before I landed at the Convention & Visitors Bureau." Not bitterness, just a factual statement.

"You knew him well, then. If you could be so kind as to tell us about him, as you did for Colonel Gibbons, it might help with our inquiries."

"He was a skunk."

Tell us something we don't know.

"And yet you married him," Mac stated.

"It wasn't obvious he was a skunk at the time!" She sighed. "I was so foolish. Rowan—my current husband—and I dated in high school and college. He was—is—really the love of my life. But somehow, I got the idea that he wasn't romantic enough. I broke it off when we were seniors in college. Even though it was my idea, I felt miserable about it even then, like I'd stabbed myself in the heart. I was so screwed up. I met Cal on the rebound. He was everything that I thought a lover should be—good-looking and charming and always knew the right thing to say. Only later did I figure out what a great actor he was. Or bullshit artist; take your pick. In a bigger town, he could have had a great career using his dramatic skills as a trial attorney.

"But this is Erin. He didn't have a great career, but he made a decent living for a one-man shop. At least, that's what I thought. He kept track of the money, so I assumed everything was fine. Cal and I had a nice house, two kids in private schools—both living out of state, now. We ate out a lot at nice restaurants, took cruises and European vacations. But everything wasn't fine. He borrowed against our home and racked up almost a hundred thousand dollars in credit card debt. Some of that was losses at the Forty Thieves.

How's that for a financial plan—gambling at a casino? I was stunned when I found out."

There's a term for Davis's treatment of his wife: financial infidelity. Unfortunately, it's not rare.

"Then Cal did the worst thing of all: He stole money from his clients. The whole thing came a cropper when one of them—I forget which—figured out what was going on and went both to the prosecutor's office and to another attorney, Willie Bloomer. Willie didn't wait for the prosecutor to take action. He filed suit against Cal for theft and damages, which got a lot of media coverage, causing several of Cal's other clients to get suspicious and contact Willie. The whole thing snowballed. You probably know what happened after that: Cal was indicted, and the lawsuits piled up."

"Until then you had no suspicions of your husband?"

"Hell, no! I was just bowled over when the first lawsuit hit. Looking back, I guess I should have suspected that *something* was wrong. Cal drank too much and ate too much by about sixty pounds. But I completely missed all the signs. Maybe I wanted to. I had a pretty comfortable life, you know. Why rock the boat just because my husband liked to gamble a little? Nobody's perfect, right? And if I thought of Rowan now and then, well, that was the road not taken."

"You were still married to Mr. Davis at the time of his supposed suicide?"

She nodded. "Right. I wasn't kidding when I made my marriage vows. I was going to suck it up and stick with him even if it meant visits to prison. Maybe I'm a chump, but that's what I intended." *You're not a chump.* "Then the son of a bitch took the coward's way out and killed himself. Only he didn't, which was even more cowardly."

"You believed he did, however."

"Of course! I never would have married Rowan otherwise. I swear I had no clue Cal was still alive. I'm sure Ida didn't either—his sister, Ida Garrison, that is. Their parents are both dead, lucky for them."

"Davis kind of left you holding the bag, didn't he?" I said.

"I'll say!" Landfair's energy was back. "I had to declare bankruptcy because there wasn't enough money in the estate to pay all the claims against it. I felt really sorry for Cal's cheated clients, but there was nothing I could do to help them. The money just wasn't there. I've tried really hard for years to bury the memory of that whole mess, because I get so angry when I think about it. I guess you can tell I'm angry now. If Cal wasn't dead, I'd kill him!"

"You might want to keep that thought to yourself," I advised.

Mac jumped back in:

"Believing Mr. Davis to be dead, you married Mr. Landfair."

"Better late than never. That's what I told myself, and it was true. Rowan reconnected with me shortly after Cal disappeared. I was a little reluctant to get involved with him again, afraid to make another mistake, but I finally had to admit to myself that I still loved him. And he loved me enough to wait until Cal was declared dead, and then some. We wanted to be sure he was really gone. But are Rowan and I even legally married?" She sounded frantic, as if the thought had just hit her like a hammer blow.

"You can rest easy on that one," I reassured her, as Mac had done for me earlier. "Davis was legally dead, so you're legally married to Rowan." *And now Davis is really dead anyway.*

"However," inserted Mac, "you might have to return any life insurance settlement that came to you."

She gave a hollow laugh. "There was none. Like I said, no consideration for me."

Mac cleared his throat with a Wagnerian rumble. "I am sure you realize that an objective observer might conclude that you had every reason to hate your former husband—both emotional and financial. The same person might reasonably infer that the six bullets pumped into his body indicate hatred rather than, say, financial gain, as the motive."

"But I didn't even know that was him!"

Mac didn't correct the bad grammar, a sure sign that his mind was fully engaged in sleuthing.

"And that brings us, Ms. Landfair, to the unavoidable question of how you failed to recognize a man to whom you had been married for fourteen years."

"How could I!" She spoke rapidly in a rising voice, more exclamation than question. "Look, his hair color was different, he had a beard, he wore glasses, he'd lost weight, and he even cultivated a speaking voice like some overly dramatic actor. Plus, I never had more than a few words with him in person last week. I'm sure he managed it that way. I saw him mostly on YouTube. He did seem vaguely familiar to me in those shows, but I couldn't put my finger on it. I thought maybe I'd seen him on some other show first."

"You were a devotee of his program?"

A vigorous headshake. "No, I thought it was hokey as heck. But what reality show isn't? I only checked it out in the first place because I learned that 'Stuart Diamond'"—air quotes—"was coming to Erin."

"Although you failed to realize that Stuart Diamond and J. Calvin Davis were one in the same, someone else may have made the connection and acted decisively," Mac informed Landfair. "I mean, of course, someone who was victimized by Mr. Davis's predation. Do you remember any of them as being particularly distraught or greatly harmed?"

She took another long pull on her big mug of coffee while she gave that a think. "To tell you the truth, I've managed to block out the names. It was the only way I could survive in a small town, knowing that I could run into one of them at any time and they might blame me for what Cal did. That was a nightmare, and this is another nightmare. Rowan is just devastated by all this."

"Understandably," Mac said. "It cannot have been easy for him to learn that your first husband was alive all these years. Please have him give us a call when he has a spare moment."

"Rowan doesn't have a lot of those these days. He's a nurse at St. Hildegard Health and they're starting to see COVID cases. Besides, what could he tell you? He didn't even know Cal under either name."

"Merely routine, I assure you. Clearing the forest so we can see the trees, as it were."

Landfair shrugged. "Sure. What's your cell number?"

Mac gave it to her, adding casually, "What were you doing on Monday evening?"

"You won't believe this." She gave a little giggle. "Rowan was at the hospital and I was home reading one of your mystery novels, *Out of Thin Air*. That was a good one. I didn't guess the ending."

She was putting the mug back up to her smiling mouth as she left the meeting.

"What do you make of all that, Jefferson?" Mac inquired.

"I think she has terrible taste in literature. And I also think Rowan Landfair makes a jim-dandy suspect. What happily married man wants husband number one to suddenly show up back from the dead?"

"Granted. He would, of course, have to know that the individual *was* husband number one, a fact of which even Ms. Landfair was unaware. I am willing to grant her veracity on that point, by the way. And according to her, Rowan Landfair had never even met J. Calvin Davis."

"Right—'according to her.' I find Mary credible, but sooner or later Oscar and Gibbons are going to come up with the idea that she and Rowan could be in this together. They both had good reason for wanting Davis out of the way. And even if Rowan never met the guy, Mary lived with him for years. It's going to be hard for our friends with the badges to believe that Davis only seemed 'vaguely familiar' to Mary through his new beard and glasses, despite what I said earlier about her calling attention to it."

"Well, there is ample fictional precedent. In the Sherlock Holmes story called 'A Case of Identity,' Miss Mary Sutherland fails to recognize her fiancé as her stepfather. And in 'The Man with the Twisted Lip,' Mrs. Neville St. Clair doesn't see her husband behind the makeup—although she only saw him from a distance. A closer parallel is the Agatha Christie novel in which a woman marries a man not realizing that he is actually her first husband, who was believed dead. It was one of Mrs. Christie's less credible constructions."

"I hate to bring this up, Mac, but we're not fictional characters."

"Are you quite sure, old boy?"

"Sometimes you go too far."

Mac was spared from responding by an incoming phone call.

"Sebastian McCabe here. Oh, hello, Chef. Yes, it is quite true. That is also true. Did you ever have any suspicion that your new collaborator was not who he said he was? I see. In the light of his true identity, does anything that he did or said strike you as important? Well, if either of you think of anything, please let me know. And Chief Hummel, of course, if appropriate. I understand. Thank you. Good evening."

Mac looked bemused as he disconnected. "You heard my part, Jefferson, and can probably guess most of his. Chef Lipinski learned from Johanna Rawls that Stuart Diamond was in reality an Erin local, and he believes that should take the focus off the television crew who barely knew the man. No, Chef Lipinski had no suspicion that he was anything but a serial YouTuber with a fascination for the occult. No, he cannot think of anything the man may have said or done that would shed light on the reason for his murder. Nor can Ms. Carson, who spent much more time with the deceased. Chef

Lipinski will call Oscar in the morning and renew their plea to be able to return to Santa Fe."

"Persistent cuss, isn't he?"

"That is in the nature of entrepreneurs."

Before I could volley back on that one, Lynda sashayed into my office-away-from-office, carrying a reporter's notebook and looking pleased with herself. With the kids down for the night, she also looked quite delectable in a red kimono and matching nails.

"Would you boys be interested to know the names of the clients Davis ripped off, since they all had good reason to use him for target practice?" she asked.

"Most definitely," Mac averred. "The question virtually answers itself."

Before the Cody brain could go too far down the path of wondering how "virtually" came to mean "not really," as in not-in-person, Lynda explained:

"While you two were gabbing, I was researching. I picked up the names of all the victims—at least, the ones who filed suit. The suits are online. So are a boatload of stories about the case by Fred Gaffe, some of his last news stories before he retired to write the 'Old Gaffer' column. And did you know that Davis shared office space with Irene Cassorla Kessler?"

Mac arched an eyebrow. "Judge Kessler?"

"The very same. She wasn't a judge then, of course."

"Mary Landfair said he was a one-man shop," I interjected.

"The judge isn't a man, although that's actually off-point. What I got out of a passing reference in one story is that they weren't partners, just shared office space and expenses. I've already texted both of you with links to the suits and the stories."

"Brava!" Mac said. "Thank you, Lynda. Who were the victims?"

Lynda consulted her notebook. "For starters, Harvey Gold—that's 'Long John' Gold, of Long John Gold's Treasure Chest on Court Street."

"The pawnshop?" I said.

"That's it. I've never been in there, but from the outside it looks like an antique store or a thrift shop to me."

"The difference," I explained, "is that Long John probably doesn't sell *Star Wars* action figures and other toys I played with as a kid. And he charges six percent on loans, plus six dollars a month storage fee on pawned items."

Back to the notebook. "Then there's Lucius Burdette, operator of the Orpheum movie house—he's Holly's uncle, you know. And, um, Myrtle White."

"Your hairstylist!" I exclaimed.

I knew Ms. White slightly, a friendly, upbeat black woman who walks with a limp. I've admired her grit ever since Lynda told me she wears a back brace. That's got to be misery when your life's work involves standing all day.

"I'm sure she had nothing to do with the murder," Lynda said airily, "but I'll talk to her for you on Zoom and give you a full report. I promise to ask tough questions, never mind that she's a genius with my hair."

"That is a most generous offer, and we gratefully accept it," Mac said, as if we had a choice.

"I was going to get in touch with Myrtle anyway. Since she had to close her shop, she's been trying to stay afloat by offering consultations for only fifty dollars. Maybe she can squeeze me in tonight."

"Fifty!" I repeated weakly.

"The beauty box with shampoo and moisture packs is a hundred and fifty."

"Go for the consultation."

"I don't want you to listen in when I talk to her."

"Wouldn't think of it!"

"You go call your parents, darling, and I'll give you boys a full report later."

Chapter Fourteen
Digital Salon, Virtual Suspect

To: Mac
Cc: Jeff
From: Lynda
Subject: Myrtle White interview

I recorded my Zoom interview (and hair consultation) with Myrtle, so you and Jeff can see the whole thing for yourselves if you want. But this report covers everything both of us said, plus my impressions based on my knowledge of Myrtle. She's been working her magic with my hair for almost eight years. Remember how I looked on our wedding day?[11]

Myrtle has a computer set up in her salon, Glam Gurlz, with chairs and mirrors showing in the background to establish the right mood. Two other stylists were renting space from her before the lockdown, and there's room for a third. Their chairs are all empty now, of course.

She greeted me with a friendly, "Hi, Lynda! How's it going?" You know how she is, that big smile across the broad face. Long eyelashes. Her own hair is dyed blond and in cornrows this week, a look that wouldn't work for me at all. I loved the black and yellow dashiki she was wearing.

"Fine, thanks," I said. "I don't really have a double chin. It just looks like that on camera."

---

[11] Fabulous! Although why that's in this report I have no idea. – *T.J.C.*

"Try pulling back your skin with tape. That'll help. How are the kids?"

"A handful. How are you doing, Myrtle?"

"The name of the game is survival, both health-wise and business-wise, and I'm surviving." She pointed to a mannequin head to her right. "I'm shooting a video tutorial on how to wash and maintain curly hair, which I'll put up on YouTube to remind my customers I'm here selling product and doing these video consultations. I had you down for an appointment next week, but I can see that this week would have been better."

"My hair *is* getting a little long."

"I'll say! But cut as little as possible. It looks like you need about an inch off, so take half an inch. You can always cut more. If you overcut, you have to wait for it to grow out. That can feel like a long wait."

"Well, I was thinking of wearing it longer anyway, like I used to. I always liked a French braid, you know."

"Okay, but while you're doing your own hair you might want to consider a top knot, a bun, or a ponytail. Those are simple styles."

We discussed some options, along with the appropriate use of texturizing spray, hair spray, and pomade or gel, but you probably aren't interested. You can skip through that discussion on the video if you look at it.

"So," I said when the consultation (well worth the $50) wound down, "I guess you heard that Stuart Diamond, that guy who was murdered at The Speakeasy, was really J. Calvin Davis, who was supposed to be long dead already."

Her eyes got big. She has beautiful chocolate brown eyes. "I did! Isn't that outrageous? Well, I shall shed no crocodile tears for Cal Davis."

"How so?" I tried to sound innocent, channeling my performance as Marian the Librarian in my high school's production of *The Music Man* in 1999. I love that play. The old movie, too.

"That low-life crook stole thousands of dollars from me."

"No!"

"Yes! You know I had an accident that put me in this brace, right? Nine-ten years ago, right before I opened the salon. I slipped on the threadbare carpet at my apartment house and took a tumble down two flights of stairs. I was lucky I didn't get killed. It was the landlord's fault for not maintaining the property."

"I never heard those details. How awful for you!"

She nodded. "Yeah, well, the next part was even more awful. I hired Cal Davis to file suit. He told me the case was thrown out by the judge in something called a summary judgement. Only it wasn't. Davis reached a settlement for fifty thousand dollars and had the landlord's insurance company make out the check to him on behalf of me. Apparently, that can be a legit thing if the lawyer is honest, which Davis wasn't."

"So, you never got anything?"

"Not a penny, because Davis wasn't around to collect from. I was just lucky most of my medical bills were covered by my parents' medical insurance. But if I'd had the money Davis stole from me, the pain and suffering damages, I wouldn't have had to borrow so much when I started this salon. Do you know whether it's true what I heard, that Mary Landfair was his wife?"

"It's true."

"Oh, wow. Sorry to hear that. Poor lady. I know her a little, nodding acquaintances, and she seems nice. This whole he-wasn't-really-dead thing has got to be messing with her head. But as for Davis, dying twice is no worse than he deserved."

I made sympathetic noises.

"You didn't recognize him when he came back to town under the Diamond name, I suppose?"

"I never even saw him."

"Wasn't there a picture of him in the paper?"

Myrtle shrugged. "I don't remember. But if there was, he must not have looked the same."

I couldn't dispute that, with the whole dyed-hair-and-beard thing Davis had going.

"Hmm. Well, it sure seems like *somebody* knew who he was and hated him enough to put six bullets in him." I gave a little chuckle to show that I was about to make a joke. "I hope you have an alibi for the night he was killed."

Myrtle smiled. "Just my roommate." That would be her five-year-old son, Antoine. "We were home watching TV all evening."

If you want my vote, I believe every word she said. I'm going to try a top knot.

Chapter Fifteen
Requiem for a Fraud

When I went out to pick up *The Erin Observer & News-Ledger* in our driveway the next day, I saw Ginger Ronson-Patch doing likewise next door. She was dressed for her morning run in shorts and a tank top. We quickly fell to exchanging war stories from a safe distance. I told her I was working from home.

"Lucky you," she said. "If Ohio goes into a shelter-at-home mode because of COVID, I'm screwed and my patients are screwed. The personal touch is everything in my profession."

My trim but muscular neighbor is a physiotherapist. Her husband, Aaron, works at his father's Patch Auto Body. ("Car Crunched? We can Patch It Up!"). Andy Patch, age 4, is Donata's best friend, although play dates were off for now.

"On the other hand," Ginger added, "the ergonomics of working from home are going to cause my clients some new physical problems that are going to keep me busy later. People crane their necks in Zoom conferences or strain their arms and backs from hunching over the laptop."

"I'll watch out for that."

"Do you have any eggs?"

"Eggs?"

"You know, those white oval things. Some people eat them. In fact, so many people eat them that I couldn't find any at the store. Maybe there's panic buying because of the pandemic. If you have any, I was wondering if I could borrow some."

Opportunity was knocking so loud I could barely hear myself think. "I'm pretty sure we can spare a few. Do you have any paper towels?"

We quickly struck a trade deal, which Lynda later judged to be a good one.

Even before I had the newspaper fully open at the breakfast table, I could see the headline for what's known in the newspaper trade as the "second-day story"—the logical follow-up reporting—on the Davis murder: **VICTIM WAS ERIN NATIVE**. The subhead spelled it out in three lines: *Disgraced attorney/ J. Calvin Davis/ Was thought dead.* Side-by-side photos of Davis as he was around the time of his disappearance and in his Stuart Diamond disguise (taken that Friday the 13th at The Speakeasy) made it easier to understand how he fooled even his wife. You could see a resemblance if you looked for it, I guess—but then, some people see Elvis at Walmart.

Johanna Rawls and Bernard J. Silverstein, to give them their full monikers, again shared the byline on a story that began:

> YouTube star Stuart Diamond, shot to death Monday night at The Speakeasy gastropub, was in reality Erin attorney J. Calvin Davis, who was believed to have killed himself in 2012 in the midst of accusations that he stole money from clients.
>
> "I'm shocked," said Lisa Carson, director of the *Dining (Way) Out* reality TV program that Davis was in Erin to co-host. "We worked closely together for a short period, but I never really knew him. I certainly never guessed that he was anything other than a successful YouTuber named Stuart Diamond."

Davis's former wife, Mary Landfair, declined to comment beyond saying, "I had no idea. I still can't believe Cal was still alive." She requested privacy.

The story went on to provide seven paragraphs of background, including the names of three victims of Davis's sticky fingers.

"A lot of this sounds familiar," I told Lynda, "like maybe from what you told us you learned in your internet research of the lawsuits and what I told you we learned from Mary Landfair. A coincidence? I think not!"

"Well, you can take the girl out of journalism, but you can't take the journalism out of the girl," Lynda said. "I saw no reason not to share all that with Johanna, like I did with what I learned about Davis's post-Erin life. It's all public info anyway."

Unable to argue with that, I kept reading. The only Davis victim willing to comment for the story was pawnbroker Long John Gold, who proclaimed the deceased "even slimier than the average lawyer, not to speak ill of the dead."

Oscar, quoted in the twelfth paragraph, managed to give the impression that the same diligent policework which identified the victim would soon uncover his murderer. "Knowing his true identity has opened up many more avenues of investigation," he declared, blandly but accurately.

The story ended with Lisa Carson saying that all the major recording was already done on the program, "but I'm uncertain whether it will ever air. In the light of the tragedy, that might not be in good taste."

When has that ever been a problem for reality TV?

"Have you noticed how thin the *Observer* is these days?" Lynda asked, multi-tasking as she fed the boys and kept an eagle eye on their big sister. "The size of a newspaper is advertiser-driven, and there's not much point in advertising a restaurant or a gym that's closed. Another nail in the coffin of local journalism! I'm afraid there will be even more staff cutbacks at the paper." Grier Newspaper Group, the parent company, had already done a lot of that since piling up debt to fend off a corporate raider a few years back.

"Want another cup of coffee?"

"Please!"

I poured; she drank, holding on to the mug as if it were a life preserver.

"So, what's on your agenda today, darling?" she asked.

"Before I go on the SBU clock, as if I'm not *always* on the SBU clock, Mac and I have a video conference with Oscar in—" I looked at the time on my smartphone. 7:30. "Right now. Bye!" I kissed my comely spouse, not giving the job as much time as it really deserved, then rushed off to my office on the porch.

Mac and Oscar were already both on-screen when Mac accepted me into the meeting.

"Nice of you to join us," Oscar said.

"I'm only two minutes late," I said. "I lost track of time."

"Spare me the marital details."

How did you know?

"Oscar was just telling me about a certain political pressure being exerted on him to solve the Davis case with dispatch," Mac said.

"As if I was dogging it!" Oscar threw in. *Weren't you? Even Lynda has done more on this case!* "It's Leonidis Garrison, the councilmember. He's on my tail."

The owner of Garrison's Antiques & Collectibles on Main Street had been appointed to city council as a placeholder when Reverend Sutterlee moved up to acting mayor. Deciding he liked it, he ran for and won a seat in the following election.

"Is Ida Garrison his wife?" I asked.

"Bingo!" Oscar confirmed. "His wife and Cal Davis's big sister."

"I gather that Mrs. Garrison is counting on her husband to use his position to light fires under you, and that if he does not do so, domestic tranquility will not ensue," Mac summarized.

"Yeah. What you said."

"What is your current thinking about the case?"

"It's a quagmire."

I love that word.

"Elucidate, please," Mac said.

"This double identity thing opens up a whole new can of worms. Was the victim killed because of who he was, Davis, or because of who the killer thought he was, Diamond? We've been down that road before,[12] only this one is a little different because there really is no YouTuber named Stuart Diamond apart from the one created by J. Calvin Davis.

"Anyhow, what I've been thinking is this: Let's say the murderer was somebody who recognized Davis and thought he should stay dead—somebody who hated him enough to pour six bullets into him when one or two well aimed would have done the job. That person could have lured him to his death at The Speakeasy by threatening to reveal who he really was, or maybe saying they needed to hash things out or some such."

"You think Davis knew there wasn't going to be shooting—video shooting—that night at the gastropub?" I said. "That he lied to Charles Bexley to get the key?" We'd thought of that, of course, in conjunction with Mac's ill-fated treasure hunt theory.

"I'm saying that's a possibility. Otherwise, Carson and Lipinski are lying about there being no video—in which case they are the killers, not a bad idea—or the killer

---

[12] See *Holmes Sweet Holmes*, MX Publishing, 2012.

somehow fooled Davis with a message that appeared to be from Carson or Lipinski, probably Carson. What do you geniuses think?"

"Your logic appears sound," Mac said. "It would be reasonable, then, to turn our attention to whomever had reason to kill Davis. Who is on your suspect list, Oscar?"

"That's a no-brainer. The wife must have been nursing a nine-year grudge for the mess he left her, not to mention the ticklish situation of her now being married to somebody else."

"Not that ticklish," I said, once again saving Mac the trouble. "Mary's legally married to Landfair, and J. Calvin's untimely resurrection does nothing to change that."

Oscar didn't give an inch. "Maybe killing wasn't what she had in mind when she lured him there, but it escalated to that. Maybe she only planned to tell him off and strongly suggest that he leave town."

Mac waxed skeptical. "And she brought a gun?"

"Maybe for her own protection."

"Do you know whether she owns a gun?"

"She doesn't. At least, not legally. Gibbons checked."

"If payback is the motive, and it is certainly a plausible one, have you considered the victim's former clients whose funds he misappropriated?"

Oscar gave himself a caffeine fix while he tried to put the best possible face on his answer. But all he could come up with was, "We haven't focused on them yet. The body's barely cold, you know."

"Lynda talked to one of Davis's cheated clients last night—Myrtle White," I informed Oscar. "She owns the Glam Gurlz hair and nail salon on College Street." I summarized Lynda's report, ending with: "It's not easy to put one over on my wife. Believe me, I know! If she thinks Myrtle was telling the truth, she probably was."

He grunted noncommittally to that.

"One of the other victims of Davis's larcenous activities was Lucius Burdette," Mac observed.

"Uncle Lucius?" Holly Burdette's face suddenly appeared next to Oscar's. "Get out!"

Mac cocked an eyebrow. "That surprises you?"

"He never mentioned it to me. But then, why would he?"

"Well, for one thing, you were with Stuart Diamond at The Speakeasy on Friday," I said, remembering her quote in the *Observer* calling the ghost of the gastropub "cool." "If he knew Diamond was Davis, that would be a reason to mention it."

"I wasn't 'with' the man. We were in the same big room. Somebody may have pointed him out to me from a distance, I think. I'm not even sure. And how would Uncle Lucius even know that Diamond was Davis?"

A good question, to which I had no good answer.

"You are close to your uncle?" Oscar asked Holly.

"Yeah, he's like my surrogate father here in Erin. I don't see my dad much. Well, I do now with Zoom, but you know what I mean." Said dad is a police officer in Paducah, Kentucky. Maybe that's why she's working for Oscar and finishing up a master's degree in criminal justice. Or maybe not. I haven't heard her talk about her family much.

A phone rang and Holly scampered to her desk to answer it. "Chief Hummel's office," I heard her say.

Oscar looked her way, off camera, then turned back to Mac and me.

"Seems like I have a little conflict of interests here," he drawled in a low voice. "On the one hand, all of Cal Davis's victims should be interviewed. On the other, one of them is a close relative of a key member of my crack staff. And on top of that, there's a mini-crime wave going on in our fair town now that animal spirits can't find their natural outlet in bars. See my problem?"

This was painful, watching Oscar asking for Mac's help without, you know, asking for his help. Mac bailed him out, and none too soon.

"Jefferson and I would be happy to speak to Lucius Burdette, and to other victims of the duplicitous Mr. Davis. Unofficially, of course. May we mention your name, Oscar?"

"Yeah, but not too loud, if you know what I mean. And keep me informed. I think you're drilling a dry hole there with Davis's cheated clients, but maybe—"

"It's Mr. Lipinski on the line, Chief," Holly called. "He really, really wants to talk to you."

"Okay, thanks. I'll take it."

This is going to be good—the Chef vs. the Chief!

Oscar picked up the call from the phone on his desk and put it on speakerphone, an invitation to eavesdrop.

"Hummel here!"

"This is Stephen Lipinski, Chief. I'm surprised I haven't had a call from you telling us we're free to leave town and be about our business."

"Oh? How do you figure that, Mr. Lipinski?"

"We were informed by a local newspaper reporter late yesterday that the man we knew as Stuart Diamond was really a local crook who faked his own death to avoid prison and lawsuits." *Nice summary of the situation!*

"Yeah, so?" Oscar said.

Lipinski's voice jumped through the phone. "Oh, come on! Isn't it obvious the killer was somebody who knew the victim and was out for revenge?" Apparently, he was no longer flirting with the supernatural theory. "Get your head out of your butt!"

Wrong move, Chef. That sound you hear is Oscar's feet being set in stone.

"The only thing obvious, Mr. Lipinski, is that the list of people with a reason to want the victim dead isn't a short one," he said in a calm, chill, dangerous voice. "That's not particularly unusual. And we don't exactly have a smoking gun here. In fact, the gun that killed Davis is probably at the bottom of the Ohio River so it can't be traced back to the killer. If it's not, we'll find it and that may lead us to the killer. I've got three officers working on it. Please be patient."

"Patient? You mean you expect us to stay in this one-horse town indefinitely?" *To be strictly accurate, there are quite a few horses in Erin pulling Amish buggies.* "Do you even have the right to do that?"

Oscar rolled his eyes in a manner reminiscent of my beloved spouse.

"Well, now, Mr. Lipinski, it's only a request, legally speaking. But if you don't honor that request, I'm going to be very unhappy. And if I'm unhappy, you're going to be unhappy."

"We'll see about that!"

Lipinski hung up.

"That, Oscar, was perhaps your finest hour," Mac said.

I seconded the motion.

"It was fun," Oscar said. "I love bullying bullies, especially when they're high on my suspect list and they know it. I'm betting Lipinski and Carson won't leave the Harridan Hotel, much less Erin. It would be nice if my troops turned up the murder weapon with one of their fingerprints on it, but I'm not betting the rent money on that one. Let me know what you get out of Uncle Lucius."

Chapter Sixteen
Ghost Town

I pedaled into town on my Schwinn while Mac piloted his big red machine. With Nouveau Shape closed, I needed the exercise. Plus, I wanted to see what the central business district looked like under near-lockdown.

Speaking of ghosts (please see all previous chapters), downtown Erin was on its way to becoming a ghost town. Beans & Books and Bobbie McGee's Sports Bar were shuttered. Daniel's Apothecary dispensed pharmaceuticals but not sandwiches and milk shakes, except for carry-out. Myrtle White's salon sat sadly empty. Artistic Ink Tattoo Studio was closed, with its neon signed turned off. The Looney Ladies Gallery on Mulberry Street, which last week hosted a show of female fabric artists, today bore a sign on the front door, black letters on bright yellow:

**GALLERY CLOSED
DUE TO COVID-19.**

Then in smaller print, two more lines:

*Stay safe and we'll see you soon.
Wash your hands for at least 20 seconds!!!*

But Witches Brew, the occult store next door, still sold crystals and tarot decks. Maybe the owners considered their products essential in light of the health crisis.

Based on the light street traffic, I wondered if any of the small businesses still open were doing much trade. From Bruce Gordon's floral shop to Mo's Mysteries & Marvels, many of them would be hurt by the closing of SBU even if Ohio didn't follow the trend to shelter-in-place orders. College towns thrived on students and their parents, both of which were now in absentia. GK was right to fret about that.

I rendezvoused with Mac at *The Erin Observer & News-Ledger*'s free parking lot on Main Street, not far from Lucius Burdette's Orpheum Theater. There was plenty of room in the lot. Journalism is an ideal profession for working outside the four walls of an office. In fact, Lynda always says that reporters should be away from the office most of the time, digging up news.

"This is surreal," I told Mac as we donned our Kate-sewn protective masks with appropriate designs—red Cody plaid for me, deerstalkers and magnifying glasses for Mac.

He nodded his hairy head. "Surreal is *le mot juste* for the situation in which we find ourselves marooned," he agreed. "I am reminded of Eliot's 'The Waste Land,' Part I, 'The Burial of the Dead.'" *Who wouldn't be?* "No doubt you recall that the fourth stanza begins with the currently apt words 'Unreal City.'"

Oddly enough, I did, being an old English major myself. And I always thought that line sounded more like something from beat generation icon Allen Ginsberg than T.S. Eliot, but Mac changed the topic before I could say so.

"How providential," he rumbled. "There is the late Mr. Davis's brother-in-law."

Whether it was the work of heaven I had my doubts, but Leonidis Garrison was exiting the front door of the newspaper's offices. The owner of Garrison's Antiques and Collectibles is a bit of an antique himself, stout with a walrus mustache, longish hair, and wire-rimmed glasses. It was no novelty to see him dressed in a short-sleeved white shirt and a Lone Ranger tie, but I was surprised that a guy who wore both suspenders and a belt didn't sport a protective mask. We kept our distance as we caught up to him on the sidewalk.

"Good day, Councilmember!" Mac hailed.

Garrison shook his head. "Not so good, I'm afraid. I've just been in to see Frank and give him a piece of my mind." Frank Woodford is the long-time editor and general manager (de facto publisher) of the *Observer*. He does most of his work on the golf links, schmoozing Erin's movers and shakers, while Ben Silverstein runs the news operation. I've always figured that Frank mostly reads the sports pages, although I'm told he's written the occasional editorial.

"That story on the front page today was a knife in Ida's heart," Garrison went on. "Can you imagine what she's been through over the past decade? She finds out that her little brother's a crook, then he kills himself, then she finds out nine years later that he didn't kill himself—that he's been alive all this time and didn't contact her, but now he's dead at the hands of a murderer who filled him with more holes than a sieve. And all of this is on page one!"

"Are you sure about that?" I asked.

"Hell, yes, I'm sure! The headline was like three inches tall."

"I mean, are you sure Ida didn't know that Davis was still alive until he wasn't?"

Garrison just stared me down, though from a safe distance. I tried not to blink.

"I believe that what Jefferson has in mind is that if perchance Mrs. Garrison knew that J. Calvin Davis yet lived, someone else also may have known," Mac said. "There is a bit of a conundrum, you see, as to whether the deceased was killed for being who he really was or for being a YouTube personality named Stuart Diamond. For the former to be true, the killer had to have seen through his change in appearance or learned of his true identity in some other way."

"Hmmph," Garrison grunted. "I get what you're saying. I also get that if Ida knew Cal was still kicking, she might be an accomplice to something or other. Which she wasn't, because she didn't—didn't know that he was alive, didn't know that he was in town, didn't know that he was this Stuart Diamond guy."

"Perhaps we could talk to her."

"What for?"

"We are trying to find out as much about the deceased as possible."

"Sleuthing again, eh? You should leave that to the cops. That's what we pay them for. Oscar Hummel is getting a two-point-three percent raise in the next fiscal year under the budget we just passed, which is substantially higher than the rate of inflation in 2019. Anyway, Ida's in no shape to talk to you or anybody else about her piece-of-crap brother. She's too upset. So, that's not gonna happen."

"Who do you think might have wanted to kill your late unlamented brother-in-law?"

"Try whitepages.com."

"Sure, I wanted to kill Davis," said Lucius Burdette. "Why deny it? But I didn't have time to stand in line that long."

The three of us each sat in one of the 48 seats of the weirdly empty Orpheum Theater, at least 10 feet apart even though we were all wearing masks. Burdette's was of the blue paper variety. His strawberry blonde hair was unkempt in the front and non-existent at the back where he had a bald patch. The buttons of his plaid shirt fought a losing battle with his expanding waistline.

"Seriously, though," he added, "I thought the bastard was already long dead. Haven't thought about him in years. But now that I know he was out there, living his life and not paying the penalty for what he did to me and the others, it does bother the hell out of me, you know? The last few days, I've been thinking about it a lot more than is good for me."

"We understand that J. Calvin Davis stole money from your father's estate," Mac said.

That was in Lynda's written report.

Burdette nodded. "Right. And there was a pile of it— more than a million to be divided between my brother Cornelius and me until Davis got his hands on it. Dad sold some family land to a developer back in the seventies and invested the money in mutual funds." *That was a great time to get into the market!*

"Cornelius is Holly's dad?" I said.

"Right. I don't know what he intended to do with his share of our inheritance, but I went into the movie business on the expectation of it. I signed a long-term lease for this place with the Masons. You may remember it used to be their Masonic Hall before they moved to the new building."

They must have seen you coming.

"Why a movie theater? I mean, why did you do it? The competition from the multiplexes with the recliner seats must be murderous."

"Tell me about it! But it's not about money. I've always loved movies. Before this, I managed a DVD store. I thought it would be cool to have an old-fashioned movie house in downtown Erin, serving real butter on the popcorn. I figured there was a niche for it. So here we are. Now I'm forty-six years old and without Dad's money I'm still paying off the projectors."

"Business debt aside, is it a profitable enterprise?" Mac asked.

Burdette gave that a hollow laugh. "Not so's you'd notice. I grossed about six hundred thousand last year and netted less than forty thousand, with most of the profits coming from drinks and candy. My biggest seller is frozen Junior Mints. I have three employees, all of them teenagers, and four or five volunteers who help out when they can. Some months I don't pay myself. Of course, my gross take right now and for the foreseeable future is zero. Normally this is a good time of the year, too. In early summer, on nice days, business tanks. But spring is good. So that's a missed opportunity. Fortunately, I have a very understanding wife with a good job in marketing at Altiora."

"In short, your life would have been very different had J. Calvin Davis not pillaged from your inheritance."

Burdette shrugged. "Until the murder brought it all back, I'd put it behind me. I'm pretty lucky, really. I'm living the dream I had since I took film classes in college, thanks to Tory's indulgence. Tory's my wife. Hell, just to be alive is a plus. I heard that one of Davis's victims killed himself way back when."

Mac's right eyebrow almost reached his forehead. "Indeed! That would certainly give the suicide's loved ones a strong revenge motive. Do you recall the name of the unfortunate soul?"

"I'm not even sure I ever heard it, or who told me. Maybe it was just a rumor. I don't know."

"Just for the record," I said, "where were you on the night of March 16, when Davis was killed?"

"I was right here, showing movies for the last time. The state's shutdown order for theaters took effect at the close of business that day. The film was *Emma*. Not a bad way to go out, I guess."

We were barely out of the theater when my phone erupted with a call from Lesley Saylor-Mackie.

"Something tells me this is bad news," I said by way of salutation.

"The worst, Jeff. Father Joe has COVID, and not a mild case. From what I understand, his high blood pressure adds a risk factor on top of his age. He's on a ventilator. He really needs our prayers right now." It took a few seconds for that to register, as if my brain didn't want to accept that Father Joseph Pirelli, the heart and soul of St. Benignus University for almost as long as I'd been alive, had a potentially fatal illness. I guess I'd always assumed he would live forever, unlike ordinary mortals.

"This is just for your information, Jeff," the Provost continued. "We can't make an announcement or even comment on his health because of HIPPA regulations."[13]

"I understand."

"Knowing Father Joe, he would want complete transparency, but he's in no condition to authorize that."

After I hung up in a daze, I explained to Mac.

"That is sad news indeed, Jefferson." He reflected silently for a solemn moment before adding: "The great Hasidic master Rabbi Nachman of Breslov once said, 'All the world is a narrow bridge and the most important thing is to not be afraid.' That bridge seems narrow indeed of late, old boy, and getting narrower all the time."

---

[13] The federal Health Insurance Portability and Accountability Act of 1996 includes privacy protections that prohibit an employer or health facility from disclosing an individual's health information.

Chapter Seventeen
Social Distancing

Long John Gold justified his nickname by standing half a foot taller than me at about six-seven, weighing in at maybe three hundred pounds. His crew-cut hair might have been gray, but it was cut too short for me to be sure. His mouth was framed by a mustache and goatee, which were certainly dishwater gray. I put his age at mid-sixties. With tattoos of mermaids on his arms and a gold earring in one ear, I expected him to greet us with a hearty "argh!" when we walked into his pawn shop on Court Street.

But instead, he said:

"Hello, gentlemen! Welcome to Long John Gold's Treasure Chest, where somebody else's misfortune is your good fortune."

This greeting was delivered with an asthmatic wheeze punctuated by a smoker's cough. At least, I hoped that's what kind of cough it was.

"You sure have a lot of guns," I couldn't help commenting. Dozens of them, maybe hundreds, were on display in a series of locked glass cabinets behind the counter where Long John Gold presided. Most were handguns. The rest of the place was stuffed with guitars, jewelry, watches, cameras, and such like.

"Yep," Long John conceded. "I sell a lot of guns in normal times, and these are not normal times, with this virus scare and people having fewer and fewer places to go to get out of the house. People get edgy when they're cooped up too long. What are you looking for?"

How about a Sig Sauer .45—the one that killed J. Calvin Davis? It could be hiding there in plain sight!

"Information," Mac said. "This is Thomas Jefferson Cody and my name is—"

"Sebastian McCabe. You don't exactly keep a low profile in this town, McCabe. Let's skip the foreplay. If you're not shopping, you must be doing your amateur sleuth thing about the murder of Cal Davis. Am I right or am I right?"

That's quite a choice.

Mac nodded. "Admirably succinct, sir."

"I don't know anything about who offed him, but I hated the son of a bitch. And do you know why? No, it wasn't the money he screwed me out of in my divorce. It turns out that a lot of divorce attorneys steal from their clients. Did you know that? I didn't either until I Googled it. Unfortunately, I didn't do that until it was too late. Cal padded his bills and charged me thousands of dollars in fraudulent expenses. What should have been a simple divorce became a nightmare. I would have rather given the money to Mitzi—that's my ex-wife—than to that shyster. She was just as honked about the whole thing as I was, believe me."

"And yet, that was not the reason you hated him," Mac prodded.

That earned a head shake from Long John. "No, I hated him because he acted like he was my friend before he ripped me off. That stung. We didn't visit each other's house, mind you, but we used to golf together now and then. That started because he was in here so often. Whenever he needed some quick cash, he would pawn his Rolex for a few thousand dollars."

I think my Timex cost $37.99 years ago at JCPenney. But I haven't worn it since Mac did that stupid magic trick where he removed it from my wrist without me noticing.

"You felt betrayed by Davis," Mac translated, "which gave you ample reason to want him dead."

"I thought he *was* dead!"

That sounded convincing enough. But how much credence should we give a guy who's just a peg leg short of being a character in *Treasure Island?*

"You did not recognize him in his guise as Stuart Diamond?" Mac asked.

"Never saw the man."

"Not on YouTube?"

"No."

"Not in *The Erin Observer & News-Ledger?*"

"That rag?"

"Not in The Speakeasy?"

"I've avoided bars since I got sober eight years ago, so again, no."

Time for a new approach.

"Where were you on Monday night?" I said.

Gold chortled. "Somebody had to ask, I guess. I was at home with She Who Must Be Obeyed. She'll tell you."

He whipped out his smartphone, made some jabs with a thick finger, and the next thing I knew we were on a video call looking at a woman with short, spikey silver hair and a round face. Despite the hair color, I figured she was a decade or so younger than Gold.

"Hi, Mitzi," he said. "I'm here at the store with Sebastian McCabe and Jeff Cody, the unlicensed PIs. They're investigating the murder of that slimebag Cal Davis. Say hi."

"Hello, gentlemen. Pleased to meet you."

We made appropriate noises in return, and then Mac confessed himself to be confused. "I understood that Mitzi was your first wife," he told Gold.

Gold shrugged. "What can I say? Our divorce was even less successful than our marriage. She never got around to moving out. Or I didn't get around to moving out. I'm not sure how that was supposed to work, but it didn't work. At least this way I get my therapy free."

Even through the phone Mitzi Gold must have been able to see the question marks on our faces, because she explained:

"I'm a relationship counselor in independent practice, a Clinical Fellow of the American Association of Marriage and Family Therapists. My ex was joking about his therapy, but the effect of these lockdowns is going to be no joke. I expect to be taking on quite a few new clients—virtually, of course—as more and more couples are forced to spend time alone together all day. The lack of personal contact with most of the world, combined with increased contact with their housemates, will stress both introverts and extroverts. And it will have a profound impact on romantic relationships—some will fracture, while some will grow even stronger."

"That makes sense," I opined. *But so far, so good at the Cody domicile!*

Mitzi Gold, apparently an extrovert, amplified her point. "Take, for example, a couple I've been counseling where the wife is very jealous. She calls her husband all the time when he's not around, and she checks his phone when she thinks he's not looking to see who he's in contact with. There's a fundamental lack of trust there that indicates a relationship in trouble. Being forced to spend more time alone together as other options are closed off by businesses being shut down may bring the marriage to a crisis and resolve the tension one way or the other."

I'm not sure I'd trust a divorced woman who still lives with her ex-husband to be my relationship counselor. But then, I didn't need a relationship counselor. So far as I knew.

"I trust that your own rather unconventional marital arrangement will survive the test," Mac told Mrs. Gold dryly. Or is that wryly? "I understand that you two were together at home on the night J. Calvin Davis was murdered."

"That's right. We were bingeing on *Antiques Road Show*. We heard about the murder the next day. I still can't believe that Davis was alive and here in Erin for several days."

"Your former husband has rather strong feelings about the deceased."

Gold snorted.

"That's his nature," Mrs. Gold said. "It's not mine. Negative energy is toxic."

"Do you have any thoughts about who might have committed the murder?"

"Just one, but I don't think I should say."

"Oh, come on!" I said. "You can't hang that out and just leave it there."

"I assure you that anything you say to us will be held in the strictest confidence," Mac said.

We were all playing roles here—Mitzi Gold's fig leaf of reluctance, my encouragement, Mac's promise of confidentiality. She was going to tell us all along. She just wanted to be coaxed into it so she could feel good about herself. That was as obvious as the beard on Mac's face when it's not covered by a mask.

"Well," she said, "this is just an idea. I have no proof. But if Irene Kessler—Judge Kessler—was more involved in Davis's shenanigans back then than anybody knew, wouldn't that give her a reason to make sure he could never tell anybody?"

Chapter Eighteen
Justice Denied

"Talking to you about Cal, even off the record, is at least slightly irregular," said Irene Cassorla Kessler, presiding and administrative judge of the Sussex County Court of Common Pleas. "But then what isn't these days? I just authorized the sheriff to release low-risk, non-violent inmates who aren't charged with sex crimes. He was none too happy about it. Neither am I, frankly, but the county Justice Center at capacity could be one big petri dish for the coronavirus."

Kessler was an attractive, shapely woman in her mid-fifties, with auburn hair worn shoulder length and then some. I wondered whether the closing of hair salons presaged the arrival of gray roots for her within a few weeks, then immediately chided myself for the unworthy thought.

"I'm surprised the courts are still open," I said.

"That wasn't my call. The chief justice of the Ohio Supreme Court sent an email a week ago asking that we stay open for business. She called it a 'request.'" I could hear the air quotes around the last word.

I'd encountered Judge Kessler in social situations from time to time, almost always wearing eye-catching jewelry and fashionable dresses not bought at Walmart. Today she wore basic black—her judicial robes—as we met between court sessions in her chambers at the courthouse, just a block down from Long John's and a few doors away from the police station. An equally black protective mask dangled from one ear.

I had a nagging feeling in the back of my mind that we should have called Oscar, or stopped in, with a progress report before making this stop. But one thing led to another too fast as Mac immediately saw merit in Mitzi's Gold's speculative scenario about the judge.

"You don't mind if I eat, do you?" Kessler said.

That tuna salad sandwich is halfway to your mouth.

"Not at all," Mac assured her. "I understand that you and Mr. Davis were associated, but not partners."

"That's right," she said between bites. "We shared office space, a paralegal, and an admin. Other than that, our practices were separate. In theory, one of his clients could have sued one of mine, or vice versa, although that never happened. As you correctly noted, we weren't partners. We didn't split fees or even see each other's financials."

You seem eager to make that clear.

"How did that arrangement come about?" Mac asked, eyeing Kessler's rapidly disappearing sandwich covetously. We hadn't stopped to eat.

"Like a lot of bad choices, it seemed a good idea at the time. You have to understand the background: I came to the bar rather late in life, in my early forties, after a career as a social worker. You have no idea what it's like for social workers in the legal system. Most lawyers treat them like trash that somebody forgot to haul out of the kitchen three weeks ago. I was never going to change that, so I decided to change myself by going to night law school at Chase College of Law.

"I passed the bar about the same time my first husband told me he never really wanted to be married. Which was strange, because I found out later he was already engaged to the second of his three wives. He was a social worker, too, so the financial settlement wasn't great. As a freshly minted lawyer, I had substantial law school debt with no great prospects for getting hired by any of the Erin firms. And I didn't want to leave Erin because I thought it was a good place to raise my daughter. Which it has been."

Kessler wiped her mouth with a napkin and sucked the last remnant of cola through a straw. Coke or Pepsi? Even today there is no more divisive topic in America.

"Anyway, there I was, trying to figure out what to do next. Enter Cal Davis, one lawyer who always treated me and my clients with respect when I was a social worker. He asked me my plans. And when he found out I didn't have any, he offered to let me set up in his office with access to his two employees in return for paying half the monthly expenses. I assumed this meant he wasn't doing so well and needed to cut his overhead. But as time went on, I wondered how that could be. He had a lot more clients trooping through the building than I did. It turned out that he spent money faster than he made it. He apparently had no financial discipline."

I guess you could say that. His major creditor was a casino.

"But you were completely in the dark about that at the time," Mac stated, not making it sound like a question. But it was a question.

"If I hadn't been in the dark about Cal, I wouldn't have stumbled. That debacle was a blot on my name for years. Can you imagine how much egg I had on my face when it came out that he cheated his clients? I was mentioned in almost every *Observer* story about Cal's fall from grace. I'm sure it escaped most readers that I couldn't possibly have profited in any way from his crimes.

"But the worst part was the sympathetic clucks from other attorneys. 'Tough break, Irene. We know you had nothing to do with it.' Phoney-baloneys! At best, they must have thought me naïve or inattentive. And I was the head of the ethics committee for the bar association at the time! I strongly suspect that more than a few of my fellow attorneys found that highly amusing."

"The voters do not seem to have held it against you," Mac observed, "nor have your fellow judges who chose you as presiding and administrative judge for the court."

Kessler smiled, taking about a decade off her age. "Well, I've worked hard to prove myself. And people have short memories. At least, they used to. Now I live in fear that something I tweeted nine years ago will come back to haunt me some day. You may have noticed that we live in a very harsh world where nothing is forgotten or forgiven, especially when it comes to public figures."

"You don't sound very forgiving yourself when it comes to J. Calvin Davis, Judge," I pointed out. "If you will forgive me for saying so."

I'm prouder of that last sentence than I should be, but Kessler was quick to respond:

"Maybe I'm making up for lost time. Forgiving Cal wasn't an issue for years, as a practical matter. I thought he was dead. Of course, by the time I found out he wasn't, he'd been murdered."

"You had no inkling, then, that Stuart Diamond and J. Calvin Davis were one and the same?"

She shook her head. "None at all. And, I must say, I feel a little foolish about that. I followed the saga of *Dining (Way) Out* coming to Erin with great interest. I'm a big fan of the show—great bubble gum for the mind. So I saw the photo of Diamond in the *Observer* months ago, but I never suspected that he could be Cal. Who would ever dream it? Cal Davis was supposed to be dead."

"You never saw his YouTube program?"

"I've never seen *any* YouTube program, per se. Just film and TV clips here and there. I spend too much on my monthly cable bill to watch anything else. I'm thinking of switching to a streaming service or two and cutting the cable."

Good move. Streaming will save you a bundle, as long as you don't pile on services the way Lynda did.

"You were not present at The Speakeasy last Friday?" Mac asked.

"No. My husband and I don't go out a lot." I seemed to recall that he was a dentist.

"Were you home together last Monday night?"

Wasn't everybody?

Her smile seemed genuine. "Nicely put, McCabe! Very smooth. As it happens, I do have an alibi. Dennis and I were at a small fund-raiser for Marvin Slade's re-election campaign as county prosecutor. It went on far too long, and seemed even longer, from six o'clock until after midnight."

Mac moved quickly on.

"Who do you think might have killed J. Calvin Davis?"

"If I had an opinion about that, I wouldn't tell you even off the record. But I will say this: Cal should have been tried for his crimes and, if found guilty, sentenced to an appropriate punishment. That would have been justice. Everybody would have been better off, including the killer—assuming the murderer was a former client. Every murder is an offense against not only the dead person, but against the whole community and the very idea of an ordered society. That's why society needs to address the wrong through the legal system. And, by and large, we do a decent job of it."

It was a good speech, but not good enough for me.

"What about the old *cherchez la femme?*" I pressed. Maybe it was the good-looking *femme* in front of me that sparked this notion. "As you said, 'We live in a very unforgiving world.' Could Davis have been carrying on with someone not his wife whose reputation today couldn't stand the exposure that Davis's return to Erin might bring? Or whose husband is good at holding a grudge?"

"Strictly speaking, I don't know. Cal and I didn't banter with each other about our private lives. Our professional relationship was quite satisfactory, but also quite professional. He could have been having an affair with every woman on city council for all I know."

Kessler pointedly looked at the clock above my head, then gathered the detritus of her lunch and deposited it in the wastebasket next to her desk. "But my guess is not. Cal didn't seem the type to me, and I think I know the type. I'm sure a lot of wagging tongues in town thought he was parking his boots under my bed, but he wasn't. Nor did he ever try. Now you'll have to excuse me, gentlemen. I need to get to court."

Mac stood. "Thank you, Judge. I appreciate your candor in sharing your thoughts."

"And I appreciate your promised discretion in keeping those thoughts to yourselves, whether they are worth anything or not."

Chapter Nineteen
Crime on the Rocks

"I guess you shouldn't tell Oscar what she said. That wouldn't be discretion."

"Indeed," Mac agreed. "And what did you get out of all that?"

"Hungry. I could use a tuna salad sandwich about now."

By this time, we'd reached the *Observer* parking lot. I was eager to get on my bike and head home for a late lunch. But Mac rambled on.

"Anything else?"

"I think Her Honor is a straight shooter, but I've been fooled before. She did go out of her way to distance herself from the guy who threw her a lifeline when she needed it, but I don't blame her for that."

"Nor do I, Jefferson. That lifeline for her, the sharing of expenses for their respective law practices, was also a lifeline for him. Maintaining that arrangement after she became head of the bar association's ethics committee, and while he was looting his clients, was either hubris or a particularly cynical attempt to shield himself. Davis was not an admirable person, which is why we have no lack of suspects in his murder."

"Most of those suspects are people who haven't seen the man in nine years and should have moved on," I pointed out.

"'Should have,' I agree. However, it is said that 'revenge is a dish best served cold.'"

"*Star Trek II: The Wrath of Khan.* Khan said it."

"I believe the expression goes back a little further than that, to the French diplomat Talleyrand. At any rate, I find it quite plausible that the years have only added to the sense of grievance felt by Davis's cheated clients. At various difficult points in their lives, they must have looked back and imagined that things would have worked out very differently if they had only had the money that was stolen from them. Although money is not the answer to every problem, it often seems to be when one lacks it.

"The great difficulty, old boy, is that no one—*no one*—admits to having recognized Stuart Diamond as J. Calvin Davis under another name. Is it credible that they are all lying?"

"They don't have to all be lying—just one."

"Only one person recognized him while the others did not?" Mac removed his protective mask and fired up a cigar, a sure sign that the McCabe brain was in overdrive. "That is scarcely more credible than the notion that all or most did and are lying about it!"

"It would make plenty of sense if the only one who recognized him was the person closest to him when he was Davis, and that person is someone who we know also saw him in person close up as Diamond."

"Do you really think that Ms. Landfair is the culprit?"

He had me there. "No. Not really. I was just being logical. I promise that won't happen again. You'd better come up with something else."

"Davis's disgruntled clients not only pursued criminal charges, Jefferson; they also sought satisfaction through lawsuits. Perhaps we should talk to their attorney, Willie Bloomer. My preliminary inquiries in that direction have established that he resides in a nursing home. Access to him may be limited because of the restrictions imposed by the state during this dratted pandemic. Nevertheless, I will formulate a plan."

With no tuna salad in the house, my lunch was a peanut butter and banana sandwich—known as "The Elvis" at Daniel's Apothecary.

"What have you been up to?" I asked Lynda. She was appropriately dressed for the second day of spring in a sleeveless floral-patterned dress in a riot of yellow, orange, and green. I felt underdressed in my khakis and SBU polo shirt, but Popcorn called my ensemble "business casual."

"The kids took such a long nap I was able to crank out three pages on the new book and walk three miles on the treadmill." A home treadmill is no replacement for the fancy workout equipment at Nouveau Shape, but we couldn't always get to the gym even before it was locked down. And though I prefer my bike for exercise, the weather doesn't always allow it. "How's your day been?"

"Very informative. Did you know that Khan wasn't the first person to say that 'revenge is a dish best served cold'? I didn't either. Beyond that, I'm not so sure I learned much of any value." I detailed our encounters with Lucius Burdette, Long John Gold, his in-house relationship counselor Mitzi Gold, and (strictly off-the-record) Judge Kessler.

"We didn't exactly strike gold," I summarized. Lynda rolled her eyes at the play on words, which I thought was uncalled-for. "But there's always Mary Landfair, who may have been Davis's biggest victim."

"I can't believe that nice woman would shoot her ex six times," Lynda said.

"How many times would you believe? Never mind. I can't either, for whatever that's worth. Rowan Landfair might do just as well, though—either on Mary's behalf without her knowing it, or protecting his own position as her spouse. But we haven't talked to him."

"Why not?"

"We asked Mary yesterday to have him call us, but he hasn't yet."

"Sounds suspicious. Anything new on Father Joe?"

I'd texted her with the gloomy health news as soon as I got the word.

"Not yet. I think it's going to be a while before we find out which way that goes. His age and chronic illnesses are against him, so keep praying."

"I'm on it."

I spent the rest of the afternoon with my nose firmly pushed to the grindstone, dealing with texts, emails, and phone calls from Saylor-Mackie, Hadley Reams, Popcorn, and a host of disgruntled students and alumni whose complaints wound up in my lap (or, rather, on my laptop) because my job title is "communications director," and they were communicating.

Saylor-Mackie wanted my take on her nascent plans for some sort of virtual commencement ceremony in May before she took the idea to the full task force. Reams wanted to know whether SBU planned any layoffs. ("Not at this point. We hope to be able to keep all our wonderful employees on the payroll. But we are closely monitoring the situation, just as every responsible non-profit is.") Popcorn reported that her grandchildren weren't allowed to get close enough to hug her, which hurt. She blamed her physician daughter.

I had three virtual meetings to take care of issues that might have been handled by hallway conversations if the hallways of participants weren't miles apart. For the record, GK's home office looks like something out of the "Mansions" section in the Friday *Wall Street Journal*. He told us that Father Joe had been moved to ICU.

By five o'clock, I thought I was all Zoomed out. But Lynda forgot to tell me that she and Kate decided we should all get together for a virtual cocktail hour. So, I gamely fixed Lynda a Manhattan and poured a light beer for myself. I was living it up. We sat together in front of my laptop, holding the hands that weren't otherwise occupied.

"Oh, what a gorgeous dress!" Kate exclaimed. My sister was turned out in a "Hound of the Baskervilles" sweatshirt over shorts, her pile of red hair flowing all over the place instead of atop her head. Her right hand held a cocktail glass full of martini, shaken not stirred, and three large olives. She was standing at the island in her kitchen, within easy reach of bar supplies.

"Thanks," Lynda said. "I just couldn't pass it up. It was on sale online."

Uh-oh. I'd had a passing thought that closing retail stores to hamper the spread of the coronavirus would also save a lot of wear and tear on Lynda's credit cards. Silly me.

This was not the usual cocktail hour at Casa Cody. Donata soon held up her latest drawing for Aunt Kate to fawn over, the twins crawled on Lynda, the McCabe daughters popped by for cameo appearances, and I fetched another beer. I'll spare you the periodic interventions from my nephew Brian and his ventriloquist figure, an Irish setter named Murphy.

"So, how's the sleuthing going?" Kate asked after a half-hour or so of family togetherness.

"Progress has been slow," Mac reported accurately. How had he and Kate not talked about this already? Maybe she'd been saving up. Mac was way ahead of me on beer, by the way, but he has his own tap there in the man cave and lots of practice. "We now know what we *know*, but we do not yet know what we do *not* know." *That's easy for you to say.*

"Leonidis Garrison doesn't want us to talk to his wife, Davis's sister, and Rowan Landfair hasn't called us back," I supplied.

"Maybe I can help get Ida Garrison for you," Lynda said. "I happen to know that she's a good pal of Polly's friend Louise LaRosa."

"We would be grateful," Mac said. "In the absence of a phone call to set up an interview with the husband of the deceased's former wife"—*got that?*—"our next step is to interview one Willie Bloomer."

"Night club comic?" Lynda guessed.

"*Au contraire!* He was a quite serious fellow in his day—the attorney who represented Mr. Davis's clients in a series of lawsuits. My research indicates that Willie, not William, is his given name. He now resides at the Elysian Gardens nursing home and is currently permitted only one visitor at a time because of the pandemic. However—"

"Oh, good Lord!" Kate exclaimed. She was staring down at her phone. "This is a text from Helen Archer. She has a fever and cough, and no sense of taste or smell. That doesn't sound good at all. She says, 'Between you and I, I think I have that virus.'"

"Isn't she, like, a hundred years old?" Lynda asked.

"Not quite. Eighty-four, I think. Well past the age for being at special risk for COVID-19, though. And that loss of taste and smell is a real tell-tale sign."

"She's that retired high school English teacher friend of yours, right?" I said.

Kate nodded. "That's Helen. I met her at that painting class I teach at the senior center. Her fiancé died in an auto accident in 1958 and she never married."

I remembered the rest of that story: Miss Archer stayed close to her late beau's parents, who left her a sizeable inheritance.

"She devoted her whole life after that to her students," Kate amplified. "They all love her. And she won tons of awards for teaching, but she never told me that. One of her former students did—the principal at Archbishop Bernardin High."

Kate's thumbs flew over the keys of her phone, responding to the text as she talked.

Mac frowned. "Surely no competent English teacher, much less a highly honored one, would say 'between you and I'! The rules of grammar dictate that a preposition, such as 'between,' must be followed by an objective pronoun, in this case 'me.' 'Between you and me' is always correct, although perhaps seldom heard."

"I told her to go to the doctor without delay," Kate reported, for some strange reason more concerned about Miss Archer's heath than her grammar. "She said she will. Helen doesn't have any living relatives except for a wastrel nephew, Ted Archer." *I love that word "wastrel."* "He hardly ever even calls her, much less stops by. So, I've been visiting when I have a chance and texting in between. I just took her banana bread a week ago." A lot of banana bread was baked all over America in the first months of the pandemic. I like mine with walnuts.

Mac's eyebrows knotted in concern. "If she has been infected, you could be COVID-positive as well."

"I only saw her for a few minutes, Sebastian. And we both wore masks, even though we stayed several feet apart. At my age and with no other health issues, my risk of serious consequences isn't nearly as great as hers. I'm very worried about her."

And with that, Kate finished off her martini in a gulp.

"The scariest part of the pandemic," said Lynda, "is that we're just at the beginning of this thing. Another Manhattan, please?"

Chapter Twenty
Unrest Home

Mac woke me up on Saturday with a call at 7 A.M.

"Good morning, Jefferson!"

"It was," I mumbled.

"I apologize for the early hour, by your standards, but I just spoke with Rowan Landfair." I sat up, suddenly awake. "He professed himself puzzled as to how to help, but willing to do so. You will recall that he is a nurse. His schedule at St. Hildegarde is such that he has no opportunity to meet with us in person, but he has agreed to a virtual meeting later today."

How quickly videoconferencing has become easy, free or inexpensive, and unremarkable. I'm old enough to remember when Skype was a fairly big deal.

"First, however," Mac rolled on, "I intend to see Willie Bloomer at the Elysian Gardens. He is allowed one guest at a time." Later, the state would drop even this concession, permitting no visitors to nursing homes or assisted living facilities for several months. The policy made sense, given the relatively high rate of COVID-19 deaths at such places, but it brought a lot of pain to the families who couldn't call on their loved ones in person, and perhaps even more pain to the isolated elderly. But you know all that.

"Well, thanks for keeping me in the loop. But since I won't be there—"

"Oh, but you will, old boy! Virtually, of course, by way of a Facebook Messenger call on our phones. You will be able to see everything that I can see at Elysian Gardens in real time, so that you can record it later in your chronicle of this adventure."

"Do I really want to? Some of those nursing homes can be pretty grim."

Grim? *Au contraire*, as Mac would say. From the outside, Elysian Gardens looked like some Roman emperor's palace from the glory days. They didn't skimp on the columns or the fountains. I know that because Mac called me on Facebook early so that I could get the lay of the land. He swept his phone around, giving me a full view of Willie Bloomer's residence in all its splendor.

"Not too shabby," I commented.

"I had expected—Oscar!"

"Why would you expect Oscar?"

"That was an exclamation of surprise, old boy." Mac turned the phone so that I could see Oscar Hummel coming out the front door of the building and moving our way. He was togged out in his blue Erin police uniform, all the way up to the official service cap.

"Good morning, Oscar!" Mac boomed. "Have you anticipated us?"

Puzzlement was writ large on the Chief's broad face. "Huh? I'm just visiting Mom." That explained the full uniform on a Saturday, which is normally Oscar's off day. Alma Hummel loved that uniform. "And what do you mean by *us*?"

"Jefferson is watching on the phone."

"Oh. Hi, Jeff." He waved. "So, what's up?" He glowered at Mac. "And why haven't you reported back to me, as per our deal?"

"Why have you not reported to us?" Mac parried.

If looks could kill . . .

"I've got Mentzel and Lehmann looking for the gun and Gibbons poking around to see what he can find out about the TV people before they get away from us." *In other words, nada.* "Your turn."

"We also have little to report, Oscar, and certainly nothing of any urgency." Mac quickly summarized our talks with Lucius Burdette and the Golds, skipping any reference to Judge Kessler. "Now we hope to speak with Willie Bloomer, who was the attorney for Davis's victims."

"Good luck with that. I seem to recall that he was a piss-and-vinegar type when he was in practice, although I never had much to do with him professionally. He didn't handle criminal defense cases."

"When did your mother move to Elysian Gardens?" Mac asked.

"Oh, she couldn't afford to stay here. And I couldn't get her to move out of her apartment anyway. She's just in the rehab unit for a few weeks—recovering from a hip replacement. Too much yoga, maybe." I knew this from Popcorn, though I hadn't thought to pass the intelligence on to Mac. "But I'm really scared she's going to get stuck in this place because of COVID. Or even worse, that she'll catch it while she's here.

"That damned virus is messing up everything, you know? The Erin Eagles season has been canceled! And who knows when the pro season will start? The Reds' Opening Day next week was scratched, parade and all, first time in forever. That's almost un-American!"

"You have my deepest sympathy," Mac said, as if he were greeting the bereaved at a funeral.

"Yeah, well." Oscar looked away for a minute, then looked back. "That's not so important, really. I'm worried about Mom. I just want her to be safe."

Mac and I gave the requisite banal assurances. But I wondered whether anybody could be safe, given the rate at which reported cases and deaths around the world were accelerating.

"I hope you're socially distancing from Popcorn," I joshed.

"That's none of your beeswax."

Safe sex was taking on a whole new meaning during the pandemic, not that Oscar and Popcorn . . . Never mind.

Oscar suddenly decided he needed to get going to "spend a few hours in the office."

Mac must have looked rather awkward as he held out the phone so that I could see everything as he entered Elysian Gardens. The inside was just as nice as the exterior, with high ceilings and a lot of marble. Mac checked in at the front desk and truthfully assured the friendly young woman there that Mr. Bloomer was expecting him. She told him the room number and gave him a visitor's pass to hang on a lanyard around his big neck.

Willie Bloomer sat in a wingback chair watching one of the *Jaws* movies. (This reminded me of an old joke: *"What do you call it when a shark refuses to eat a lawyer?" "Professional courtesy."*) He looked like a once-big man who had deflated, with mottled skin and very thin gray hair. Based on his apparent age, he must have been near the end of his career as a lawyer when he sued Davis nine years earlier.

"Mr. Bloomer? I am Sebastian McCabe."

"Who else would you be?" He picked a remote off a small table to the right of him and turned off the TV. To the left of him was a metal cane, the kind that has feet so that it stands up by itself. "It's not like my daughter ever visits me. I haven't seen her in months."

"I understand that she is at high risk for infection by the novel coronavirus because she is over sixty years old and has a complicating health condition," Mac said. "She visited you every day until earlier this week."

This isn't information a place like Elysian Gardens would share with a non-relative, but Mac has his ways.

Bloomer waved that aside with an airy hand motion. "Whatever. Judy doesn't visit me anymore. What did you want to see me about?"

Mac changed the subject. "Do you remember J. Calvin Davis?"

"Davis? Hell, yes, I remember that rat. He took the easy way out—killed himself. Left my clients high and dry. No money in the estate. At least, none that anybody could find." I had a flashback to Jackie O'Brien and his missing cash. Which was silly. "I always thought maybe he slipped some of it to the wife before he offed himself. Couldn't prove it, though. Not that I tried that hard. Those were contingency cases. I could have done a lot of work for no return."

Can't have that!

"Do you read the newspaper, Mr. Bloomer?"

"The *Observer*? I've been a subscriber for almost sixty-five years."

"Then surely you must know that J. Calvin Davis did not, in fact, kill himself and that he was alive until Monday of this week."

"What? No! That's not possible." He became agitated. "Davis killed himself in 2011. He took the easy way out. There was no money in the estate. At least, not that anybody could find. I always thought—"

"Mr. Bloomer," Mac said gently. "J. Calvin Davis was shot to death on Monday night. It was on the front page of Wednesday's *Observer*."

"Are you sure? Oh, well, maybe I did read something like that." He shook his head. "Davis was still a rat."

"What about his officemate—Irene Kessler?" I asserted.

Bloomer squinted at me through the phone. "Who the hell are you?"

Mac introduced us. Bloomer grunted.

"About Irene Kessler?" I prodded.

Bloomer smiled lasciviously. "Easy on the eyes, that one! I tried to date her up once before she was a judge, when she was between husbands. Not only didn't I get to first base, I didn't even get to the ballfield. That's because she's a smart gal. You'd be surprised how many judges have the IQ of a rock, but not Irene. I think Cal snookered her, though, just like he did everybody else."

"Then I guess you don't think there's much chance the judge killed J. Calvin to keep him from telling some inconvenient truth about her?" I guess I was leading the witness, but he didn't object.

"What? Davis killed himself. Everybody knows that."

Find wall, hit head.

"He's as dead as Clark Woodsfield," Bloomer added. "I call that irony."

I couldn't see Mac, since he was holding the phone, but I bet he raised an eyebrow to that.

"That is a new name added to the dramatis personae of this case," Mac said. "Who was Clark Woodsfield?"

"He was another poor bastard that Davis cheated. Took it so hard that he swallowed a massive overdose of sleeping pills. At least, that's what those in the know figured. I couldn't exactly ask him why he did it." Bloomer gave a harsh laugh. "Woodsfield and I had some preliminary discussions about me representing him in a suit against Davis. Davis stole a decent chunk of money he held in escrow for Woodsfield from a real estate deal, a couple of hundred thousand. I only met with Woodsfield one or twice, but I could see he was deeply depressed and not thinking very clearly.

"After he killed himself, I talked to his lover about suing on behalf of the estate, but Bexley wasn't interested. He said he felt bad enough taking the money Woodsfield left him, and he wasn't going to go after more."

"Bexley!"

Bloomer took Mac's exclamation as a question.

"That's what I said, isn't it? Woodsfield's partner was a guy named Charles Bexley, an engineer at the Altiora Corp. Or at least, he was. I don't know whether he's still around town or not."

Chapter Twenty-One
Contact Tracing

"Maybe the old guy was faking the memory loss," I told Mac as he settled into his boat-sized Chevy.

He just stared at me through the phone.

"Okay," I tried again, "maybe he killed Davis, but he forgot."

Mac was unpersuaded.

"Even assuming that (a) Mr. Bloomer was the only person who recognized his old antagonist in the guise of 'Stuart Diamond,' and (b) was so outraged at justice denied that he decided to impose capital punishment on Davis, and (c) could walk more than a few feet on that cane, and (d) could secure a mode of transportation to The Speakeasy— assuming all that—one does not simply walk away from an assisted living facility of an evening with no one knowing. In addition, I have already ascertained that Willie Bloomer was playing bingo with other residents on Monday evening."

"Oh."

"I am sure you realize, however, that this visit was far from unproductive."

"Yeah. We know the name of the Davis client who killed himself, the one that Lucius Burdette heard rumors about. And we know that he was romantically involved with Charles Bexley, so why didn't Bexley mention that to us?"

"Precisely, old boy! That certainly bears investigation. If Mr. Bexley blamed Davis for Clark Woodsfield's death, that would be an even stronger motivation for revenge than the mere financial loss suffered by the other Davis clients. And, of course, the murder took place in a gastropub of which Charles Bexley is the co-owner. However, our revisit with him will have to wait. We have a Zoom appointment with Rowan Landfair in half an hour. Did you receive his invitation? Good."

Lynda wandered into my office a few minutes later. It was a sunny spring morning with a nice breeze coming through the screens of the porch.

"How's it going?" she asked.

"So-so. I'm grateful for the technology that lets me do my job from home, but I feel like I'm in a science fiction novel I read once—maybe by Isaac Asimov—where the only contact people have with each other is over a screen."

"This isn't science fiction, *tesoro mio*, it's a horror story, and it's real."

The fact that she was rubbing my shoulders as she said this somewhat undercut the fatalistic words and the notion that physical contact no longer a thing. One thing led to another (but not *that* other) and I was rather relaxed by the time I joined Mac and Rowan Landfair in Zoomland.

Actually, Landfair was at the hospital, St. Hildegarde Health, wearing green medical scrubs and matching paper mask. Probably in his early forties, like his wife, he looked tired and his dark hair was a little shaggy.

"Thank you for agreeing to talk to us," Mac began. "You must be quite occupied."

"Hey, I'm sorry it took a while to get back to you. I'm on a break right now. Yeah, we're all busy here, even with the ban on elective surgeries. This is a small hospital, not like the big regional ones. And we've had a number of COVID patients sent from nursing homes. We also have, uh, a rather prominent individual from the academic world on a ventilator." *Why don't you just say Father Pirelli? Oh, yeah— HIPPA.* "Anyway, I don't know anything about what happened to Davis, so I have to admit lacking a sense of urgency in calling you. But Mary's been nagging me to do it. She's losing sleep over this. I've never seen her so unraveled."

"And you've known her since high school," I threw in.

He nodded. "I would have married her then if I could have. But you know what they say happens."

Excrement, or a word to that effect. Actually, people don't say that so much anymore. I always get a little thrill when I realize that a cliché has worn out its welcome and passed out of common use.

"You will forgive me for pointing out that both you and Mrs. Landfair have what an objective observer would consider to be solid motives for wishing to return J. Calvin Davis to the grave," said Mac. "She would want to protect her current life and marriage to you, as well as her reputation in the community. You would have special animus toward the dead man because, by your own admission, he came between you and the woman you have loved since high school."

That woke Landfair up. "Are you nuts?" he sputtered. "How the hell would I even know that the YouTube guy was Davis? I never knew the man years ago—never wanted to. You'd be surprised how easy it is to avoid somebody, even in Erin, if you work at it. It's not like we moved in the same circles. He was a lawyer and I was a nurse. And I never saw him in person when he came back to Erin. Mary said he looked different anyway, and even if he didn't look so much different why would I think he was a guy who was dead?"

The words came spilling out at the end like coins from a slot machine at a big payoff.

"All good points," Mac conceded.

"Oops, sorry!" A young black woman in scrubs and mask appeared behind Landfair, then disappeared again. Apparently, he had his laptop set up in the nurse's break room.

"And most important of all"—Landfair seemed to arch his back as though he were standing straighter, even though he was sitting down—"Mary loves me, and nothing matters next to that. Nothing! I wouldn't give Cal Davis the satisfaction of thinking he was important enough to kill. If I could kill anybody, which I couldn't. My skill set goes in the opposite direction."

I would have bet real money that Landfair meant every word of that little speech. After more than 25 years of hanging around Sebastian McCabe, I know baloney when I hear it, and that wasn't it. But Mac saw the other edge of the sword:

"Your wife's love of you would be a strong motivation for her to protect you, of course," he observed nonchalantly. "She said you were working on the evening of her first husband's death."

"You're checking my alibi? Oh, give me a break! Yeah, I was working. Ask around here if you want. We're short staffed. If I wasn't here, somebody would notice. It's not like you need one of those contact tracing apps they're working on to know where I was."

Chapter Twenty-Two
Dead on the Water

"Even if Rowan Landfair had such an app, it would only tell us with certainty where his phone was," Mac pointed out later. "The man could have been somewhere else entirely. We only have his word that anybody would notice if he slipped out of the hospital for an hour or so. Was there ever such a collection of weak alibis?"

"Not in fiction, anyway," I quipped. "In one of your books, a tight alibi is usually a dead giveaway to the killer."

Mac couldn't fire back right away because his mouth was full. We were grabbing a quick bite at Tony Ranieri's Cal-Zone food truck parked outside of The Speakeasy before dropping in on Charles Bexley for a bit of a chat about the late Clark Woodsfield. Bexley told Mac that he and Haldane would be there all day, supervising a thorough sanitizing of the place and some minor refurbishing that could be done during the gastropub's down time. While Mac indulged in the eponymous pseudo-Italian calzone stuffed with cholesterol-laden salami cooked up by the former Speakeasy bartender, I finally had a much-desired tuna salad sandwich on a hoagie bun. The consistency was just right—not too wet.

"In fiction—" Mac finally began, only to be interrupted by his cell phone.

"Yes, Oscar?"

He didn't need to put it on speakerphone for me to hear the Chief.

"Another murder. The Old Gaffer."

"Hell and damnation! Where? When? How?"

"At the Erin Ferry. That's where I am now. The coroner's here, too. Gaffe was strangled with some kind of cord while he sat in his car about an hour ago."

"Garroted, in fact!" Mac's dark eyebrows furrowed. "How unusual. And does it not strike you as odd that Fred Gaffe would be crossing the river to Kentucky at a time when increasing numbers of businesses are being closed in both states? Where did he have to go?"

I knew what he was thinking: A common destination via the ferry is the Greater Cincinnati International Airport, located in Boone County, Kentucky, but—as Lipinski had pointed out during his rant to Mac a few days earlier—planes were flying mostly empty these days.

"His car trunk was pretty well filled with toilet paper, Clorox, hand sanitizer, and groceries. I figure maybe he was visiting somebody who couldn't get out or couldn't find some necessities because of all the panic buying. That's the kind of thing he would do. Do you want to get over here or do you want to keep yapping?"

"The former. Jefferson and I will see you in a few minutes."

"At least one suspect has an alibi for this one," I pointed out as we climbed into Mac's car, with me in the back again for social distance. "Landfair must have been talking to us from the nurse's break room at St. Hildegarde right at the time it happened."

"That is cold comfort, Jefferson—especially to Fred Gaffe!"

Fair point.

"I hate to make things even worse," I said, "but the Old Gaffer's murder might have nothing to do with the Davis case. I've said for years that I wouldn't want to be his life insurance company, what with all that he knows about people in this town. He knows—*knew*—where all the bodies are buried, and who buried them." I missed him already.

"That is a possibility not to be dismissed, old boy. However, bear in mind that he also wrote the *Observer*'s news stories about J. Calvin Davis's larceny and supposed suicide. Although that is by no means beyond the bounds of coincidence given his large journalistic output over many decades, it is worth keeping in mind."

The Ferry Landing is in downtown Erin at the point where Market Street and Vine Street come together at the Ohio River's edge, just beyond Front Street[14]. The Treadwell family has been operating the unimaginatively named Erin Ferry for 167 years. Captain Elijah Treadwell used to smuggle slaves to freedom on an earlier version of the ferry as one of the conductors of the Underground Railroad. He lived and later died at what is now the much-remodeled McCabe house at 23 Half Moon Street.

The parking lot, intended for those who leave their cars behind and ride the ferry on foot, was full of official cars and an EMS vehicle when we arrived. As we approached the landing after parking Mac's Chevy, two EMTs and a covered body passed us going in the other direction.

The sun in the cloudless sky shone on the sparkling water of the mighty Ohio, a light breeze blew our way, and I found myself thinking: *What a great day to be alive.*

But the ferry was festooned with yellow crime scene tape. We could see Oscar there in conversation with the much shorter Dr. Arlene Eppensteiner, who punches well above her weight. She's a hard-working, hard-driving professional about my age with frizzy dark hair spilling over her white lab coat. Ohio law doesn't require her to visit the scene of a suspicious death, but she does whenever she can. If she smiled in recognition when she caught sight of us, I couldn't tell because she was wearing a white protective mask. Oscar was also masked up, in light blue.

---

[14] See map on p. 9.

Also on the ferry were various other medical and police officials, a doleful-looking young woman with a shocking pink pony tail, and a dark blue Buick that must have driven off the new-car lot sometime during the Clinton Administration.

"Hail, hail, the gang's all here," Eppensteiner said as we walked onto the ferry. Or at least, I think so. Her voice was a little muffled.

"Hello, Arly," Mac and I chorused as Officer Mentzel logged us into the crime scene. She's asked us to call her that, maybe because we've stood over a few bodies together or maybe as a political reflex. County coroner is an elected position in Ohio.

"I understand that Fred was strangled," Mac said. "Rope, perhaps?"

Ropes hung here and there all over the ferry.

Eppensteiner shook her head. "We don't know what it was because the murderer didn't leave it behind. But it wasn't thick enough to be rope. It was something thin and tough that left no fibers in the wound."

"Fishing line?" I speculated.

"Not that thin."

"Maybe it's still here somewhere," Oscar said. "We'll keep looking." The "we" included Gibbons, Mentzel, and two or three other officers.

"Time of death?" Mac asked.

"You don't need me for that. It's obvious when he died. In fact, I'm finished here. I'll let you know if the autopsy turns up anything interesting, Chief."

She nodded at everybody and left.

"Time of death?" I asked Oscar.

"Gaffe drove onto the ferry at about one-fifteen and paid Daphne Saunders, who takes the cash or tickets," Oscar said.

He nodded toward the young woman. Her pink ponytail stuck out of an SBU Lady Dragons baseball cap. She wore a red sleeveless T-shirt, showing off a colorful tattoo of a butterfly on her right arm, over a pair of impossibly short cut-offs. If they were any more cut off, they wouldn't be there at all. Although the day was warm for March, she stood hugging herself, head down, as if she were freezing.

"It's possible to buy tickets in advance, like Davis did when he faked his suicide," Oscar said, "but Gaffe paid her with a five-dollar bill. Then about ten minutes later, when the only other car on the ferry drove off, she realized that the Buick was staying put. She went over to the car and looked inside. His head was down. She thought he was sleeping. He wasn't."

"May I ask her a few questions?" Mac said.

"I dunno. She's pretty shook up. We talked to the pilot, by the way, and he was too busy steering the ferry to see anything. He's her uncle."

Being a selective hearing specialist, Mac ignored Oscar's dubious response and walked over to the young woman. Oscar followed, but didn't say a word over the next ten minutes.

"Daphne?" Mac said quietly.

Her head jerked up. She had blue eyes and freckles. I saw the freckles because her pretty face wasn't covered by a mask. Well, she worked outside. I wondered, though, whether she sanitized the money she touched all day.

"Professor McCabe!"

"I am sorry to see you again in such difficult circumstances, Daphne. Your hair was aqua when you were a student in my film noir class last fall, was it not? I thought so. You earned a very solid B-plus that term. As I recall, your mother is a member of the Treadwell family."

Daphne nodded. "Right. I get paid, though. I've been working on weekends since I was fifteen. It's not all that much fun in rain or cold, but this is awful. I bet nothing like this ever happened on the ferry in its whole history."

Safe bet!

"And what did happen, from your point of view?"

"When we got to the Kentucky side, I leaned my head through the open driver's side window and told the guy at the wheel it was time to get off the ferry. I have to do that once in a while. They get busy with their phones or whatever. Anyway, his head was down, so I thought he was asleep. I yelled, 'Sir! Sir!' You know, to wake him up. I can yell pretty loud because I have brothers. When he didn't move, I'm like, 'Oh, shit, maybe he had a heart attack.' So, I opened the door and shook his arm. He slumped over in the passenger seat and I saw his neck. It was all purplish and I knew that something really bad had gone down."

She shivered and bit back tears.

"Chief Hummel said there was one other car on the ferry," Mac noted.

"Right. A red Toyota Camry. I see a lot of those. It was long gone by the time I realized Mr. Gaffe was dead."

"You knew Mr. Gaffe?"

"Not really. I knew who he was."

"Did he take the ferry a lot?"

"I don't think so. Not while I was working."

"What can you tell us about the Toyota's driver?"

"Not much. I didn't pay attention."

"Male or female?"

"I don't know. They were shaped kind of blocky. I didn't notice whether they had boobs, but even guys like that kind of have boobs, you know? And they wore a red mask, a big one that covered their nose and most of their face. All these masks kind of freak me out. I mean, I know it's good to wear one now for health safety, but it's still creepy."

"Clothes?"

"They had on a big floppy hat, with a white shirt and black pants."

"Did Mr. Gaffe talk to this other driver?"

"Not that I saw. The other driver got out and walked over to the railing, but Mr. Gaffe stayed in his car."

Mac raised an eyebrow. "You observed this and yet you did not see the other driver strangle Mr. Gaffe?"

And that's when the tears finally let loose. "I guess I wasn't paying any attention at the time. I must have been texting Phil when it happened—Phil Canning, my boyfriend. He just lost a good summer internship in Louisville because of the pandemic. That's a bad thing, and he's upset, but I'm honestly kind of glad because it means he won't be going away for the summer."

Oh, to be young again!

Mac put on the metaphorical kid gloves as he continued asking questions. Daphne couldn't say whether the "blocky" driver of the Toyota was tall or short or medium, but she was pretty sure "they" didn't wear glasses.

Mac thanked her for her help and suggested that she shouldn't try to drive herself home.

"I already called my dad," she said. "He's waiting for me in the parking lot. I can see him pacing."

"Go ahead," Oscar said. "You've had enough for today. You can come to the station and make a formal statement on Monday."

Her blue eyes widened. "But I already told Professor McCabe everything I know! You just heard me!"

"That didn't count."

She started to say something, thought better of it, and huffed off.

"That went well, Chief," I opined.

He glowered. "I thought I was being pretty damned sensitive."

We let that pass.

"It strikes me, Oscar, that the biggest anomaly in this murder is also the biggest clue, if only we can interpret it," Mac said.

"Well, sure, that was obvious to me, too." *I doubt it.*

"I mean, of course, the location. Jefferson has observed that Fred Gaffe, amiable fellow though he was, had a knack for accumulating information that could be embarrassing or worse to the parties involved. Turning that habit of his into a murder motive does not require much imagination. However, of all the places one might have chosen to dispose of him, why do so where the murder might be so easily observed? And why choose such an unusual method?"

Chapter Twenty-Three
Murder with a Past

"Strangulation is silent, that's why that method," Oscar offered. He must have had that answer ready, judging by how quickly he tossed it out.

"Quite so," Mac acknowledged. "And yet, that advantage is hardly enough to justify the risk of murder in the proverbial broad daylight." He stroked his facial forest for a while before coming up with: "The killer must have faced an immediate threat, and hence a need to act with great dispatch despite the risk. That suggests a weapon that was conveniently at hand."

"Such as what?" I asked.

"When we know the answer to that, old boy, this murder may be solved."

"Well, while you're thinking great thoughts along those lines," Oscar said, "I'm going to put out an APB for a red Camry driven by somebody matching the description our pink-haired witness gave us."

"That somebody could be in Louisville by now!" I said.

"Hi, guys!" came the familiar voice of Tall Rawls. The press was on the scene.

Back in Mac's car, after about twenty minutes of Mac deferring to Oscar as the one who should answer Johanna's questions, and Oscar feeding her bromides, I checked in with

Lynda by phone. She was still processing the Old Gaffer's death, and it was a wet job.

"He had newspaper ink in his veins," she said with a sniffle. For Lynda, that was her finest tribute to a veteran reporter whose post-retirement column she had edited for years. It also gave her an idea: "We should check with Ben to see what he was working on. He wouldn't be the first journalist killed during pursuit of a story."

"What an excellent idea!" Mac said when I told him. "Never underestimate the lovely Lynda, Jefferson." *Fat chance of that!* "While you were talking, it occurred to me that the last time I saw Fred Gaffe was eleven days ago when we were both among those interviewed by J. Calvin Davis, alias Stuart Diamond, at The Speakeasy. The two men were also together at the gastropub on Friday the thirteenth, as recorded in the *Observer* the next morning. That co-presence adds impetus to our planned meeting with Charles Bexley and Nicholas Haldane. It may be instructive to get their reaction to the news of today's murder, as well as quizzing Charles about the late Clark Woodsfield."

"You mean the Old Gaffer?" Even Bexley's walrus mustache looked surprised. If he wasn't shocked to learn of the columnist's murder, he was a good actor. But, come to think of it, he was a good actor! He played Bob Cratchit in the Lyceum Theater's production of *A Christmas Carol* a couple of years before. "I can't believe it!"

Believe it.

"As a newcomer to Erin, I found his column quite informative, if somewhat overwritten," Nicholas Haldane put in. The four of us sat at opposite ends of a long table in the middle of the deserted gastropub, all wearing masks.

"You don't think this had anything to do with the Stuart Diamond murder, do you?" Bexley said.

You must have never read a mystery novel.

"Whether the two murders are connected is the very crux of the matter," Mac informed him. "However, surely you know that Stuart Diamond was in fact a criminous former Erin resident named J. Calvin Davis? The headline screamed from the front page of the *Observer*."

"I saw that, but Diamond is how I knew him. Anyway, he's dead. What did he have in common with Fred Gaffe?"

"One connection is that they were both here one week ago yesterday."

Bexley shrugged that off. "So were a lot of people."

I couldn't see the frown on Haldane's slight face behind his rainbow protective mask, but I could tell from his eyes that he didn't like the way this conversation was trending.

"A tenuous connection, I grant you," Mac said, "but a connection, nonetheless. Did either of you happen to observe the two of them in conversation that night?"

Haldane didn't have to think about it. "A TV show was being filmed here. I was too nervous and too busy to observe anything else."

"Same here," Bexley said. "I had a million things on my mind that night."

"That is understandable. Nevertheless, both murdered men were here then. The conventional scenario, one might almost say the cliché, would be that Fred Gaffe was a Man Who Knew Too Much—that he somehow had knowledge that threatened to expose the killer of J. Calvin Davis. If that is the case, perhaps Fred gained that knowledge here. It could have been something Davis told him, or something he heard or saw."

"That's not very likely, is it?" Haldane pushed back. "The murder wasn't until three days later."

"It is entirely possible," Mac countered. "Perhaps whatever knowledge Fred acquired was damning to the killer only after Davis was murdered—or the killer thought it might be. This is all highly speculative, of course, and idle speculation at this point."

Speculative? I'd call it getting deep into the weeds without a weedwhacker.

"It would be equally idle," Mac rolled on, "to speculate whether seeing you, Mr. Bexley, might have reminded Fred that Clark Woodsfield killed himself because of the money he lost to the late Mr. Davis's larceny. Although he never wrote about that in the *Observer*, he might well have known it. And you and Mr. Woodsfield were quite close, I understand."

"Hell, yes, we were close!" Bexley exploded. Haldane put a supportive hand on his shoulder as if to calm him down. "He wanted me to marry him—we'd have had to go to another state in those days—but I'm not the marrying kind. We were close enough that I can tell you he didn't kill himself over Davis."

"You mean he was not one of Davis's victims?"

"Oh, Davis screwed him over, all right. That shyster stole a little over half a million dollars that was part of an escrow account from an apartment building Clark sold— something called an Interest on Lawyer Account. A half a million isn't pocket change, but Clark's holdings were worth many times that. I know that because he left a big chunk of it to me." Bexley's voice got thick with emotion. "That's where my share of the money to start this place came from."

"Then why did he kill himself?" I had to ask.

"Clark was dying very painfully of pancreatic cancer. I kept telling him to keep up the fight. But instead, he decided to end the pain permanently with a handful of prescription painkillers. He left me a note asking me to forgive him. J. Calvin Davis was a scumbag, but he wasn't responsible for Clark's death. If I'd known Davis was here at the pub, I would have thrown him out—not killed him. But how would I even know? I don't think I ever met the man back when he was Clark's attorney. If I did, I've forgotten."

"I suppose the HIPPA privacy law would make it difficult or impossible to verify Mr. Woodsfield's in extremis cancer," Mac mused.

"You suppose wrong, McCabe. Dr. Sharfman knows that I held Clark's medical power of attorney. I'm sure that if I asked him to, he would confirm for you that Clark was his patient and that Clark had very little time left when he chose to end his life." He rattled off the oncologist's phone number. "Give me a day to prepare him for your call."

"Thank you," Mac said. "I am sorry for what Mr. Woodsfield had to suffer, and also for what you had to suffer."

By this time, I was feeling sorry for what *Mac* had to suffer. Every door in this case opened into a blind alley.

"If you think the murder is related to Davis's thievery, maybe you should be talking to the victims that are still alive," Haldane said.

Been there, done that.

"Or maybe Davis and the Old Gaffer were both killed for reasons that have nothing to do with ancient history," his partner said. "And maybe the two murders are unrelated. Whatever the case, I hope Chief Hummel and his crew are doing better than you at pegging the killer."

Ouch! And don't count on it.

Mac, being a sleuth, picked up on Bexley' testiness.

"I apologize for my intrusion, which I appreciate comes at a very difficult time for you and your business."

"You have a way with understatement," Bexley shot back. "Right now, we don't have a business. Restaurants are allowed to offer carryout, but that doesn't help a gastropub much. Food isn't how we pay the rent. There's some talk of extending carryout to alcoholic drinks, which might be a lifeline. But for now, we're dying on the vine while one of our former bartenders—and not a very good one—is peddling low-rent Italian from a food truck right outside our building."

Tony Ranieri, he meant. *Tony Ranieri!* I had a flashback to Tony telling TV4 Action News that he'd been "let go," which immediately touched off a storm in my brain.

"You fired him, didn't you?"

I asked both of them, but it was Haldane who said:

"Charles delivered the bad news, but it was a joint decision as part of a reduction in force. We were overstaffed earlier this year. But, frankly, I wanted to get rid of Ranieri anyway. He sent off signals, perhaps unconsciously, of unwelcomeness to some of our diverse patrons."

"Now we don't have any patrons," Bexley said. He seemed kind of stuck on that. "And the publicity that I'd been counting on from the *Dining (Way) Out* program probably won't happen. They aren't likely to broadcast the episode in the wake of the murder. That would be too tacky even for reality TV."

Is there such a thing?

"Can you give me Father Ortega's phone number?" Haldane asked. "I want to ask him to exorcise that ghost."

His partner shot him daggers with his eyes. "Give me a break, Nicholas!"

"I've got his cell," I said, "but what you need is a series of prayers called Office for the Dead." If Haldane had been paying attention during the good father's interview with Diamond/Davis, he would have known that.

"It's the old *cui bono*—who benefits?" I told Mac a few minutes later, standing outside The Speakeasy and looking across the street where there was no longer a line of customers outside Tony Ranieri's food truck. "And psychological satisfaction is a great benefit."

He cocked an eyebrow. I had his attention.

"Here's what happened." I was channeling Adrian Monk, even though I'm not like Monk. I don't care what Lynda says, I'm not like Monk. "Tony nursed a grudge against Bexley that only grew worse when he learned about WSTV coming to The Speakeasy. He probably figured that Bexley, or both partners, would be in the gastropub that Monday night. Maybe that's how they usually spent their off-day evening, getting ready for Tuesday; I don't know. Anyway, Tony got a gun and went in there prepared to use it. He shot fast so he wouldn't lose his nerve—so fast that he didn't realize the man who happened to be standing at the bar when he entered was Davis, AKA Diamond. The two men have similar builds. Maybe the light was dim. *Bang!* Tony plugs Davis six times, thinking he's Bexley. The fact that Davis died in roughly the same place and manner as Jackie O'Brien was sheer coincidence. Coincidences do happen in real life, even if they are *verboten* in popular fiction."

The only thing that kept me from patting myself on the back was the logistics of it.

"Ingenious, Jefferson! And Fred Gaffe?"

"You said it yourself earlier with all that speculation: The Man Who Knew Too Much! I always thought the Old Gaffer knew too much."

"Shall we see what Mr. Ranieri has to say about that?"

"Let's!"

What Ranieri said first was, "Back for more?"

"Not food, just conversation," I said. "You must really hate Charles Bexley for firing you."

I thought I'd hit him fast and hit him hard. But I could have sworn the laugh behind his mask was the real deal. "Hate? You've got to be kidding! I owe Bexley big time. Or I should say, Haldane. He's the one who had it in for me, I'm pretty sure. I could tell by the way he looked at me. Anyway, if they hadn't pushed me out the door, I'd have never started my own business. And look at me now. The hours are long here in the Cal-Zone, but I'm killing it!"

"Funny you should use that word," I said heavily. "It occurred to me that maybe the murderer had it in for the owners of The Speakeasy."

He wrinkled his eyebrows. "How do you figure that? The killing didn't hurt them. The state shut down the place, not the murder."

Ranieri had a point, but I was undaunted.

"Well, if that hadn't happened, I don't think the murder would exactly make it the hot place to be. A killing in real time isn't quite the same as a century-old homicide attached to a good ghost story. Meanwhile, you can't dish up calzones and panini for crime-scene gawkers fast enough. But The Speakeasy's loss and your gain was just an unintended side benefit of your attempt to kill Bexley, who fired you."

"What!"

"You mistook Davis-slash-Diamond for him."

"That's crazy! They don't look remotely alike! Bexley has a mustache like Teddy Roosevelt"—*or Leonidis Garrison!*—"and that other guy had a beard. I've seen pictures of him. Never mind that I don't own a gun and I've never even shot one. Those things scare me."

My fantasy of a quick confession was collapsing like an umbrella.

"Did J. Calvin Davis rip you off as your attorney?" I pressed.

"He wasn't my attorney. Where'd you get that idea?"

That only stalled me for a few moments. As I stared at the food truck, the name spelled out in large letters on the side suddenly struck me as possibly significant. What if the play on words was actually a triple play? "Was he your secret partner, the *Cal* in Cal-Zone?"

I'm on a roll here!

"What? That's crazy, man! I never even heard of the guy until this week. I read about him in the paper. I was in high school when all that stuff happened nine years ago." He addressed Mac. "Is he always like this?"

"Fortunately, no."

"Where were you on the night of the murder?" I asked Ranieri. I was prepared for something like, "At home with my wife/girlfriend/boyfriend/all of the above." Instead, he said:

"At my other job."

"Job?" I repeated weakly.

"A lot of micro-business owners have other jobs. I'm a part-time bartender at the country club. They have a golf night on Mondays. At least for now. I'm hoping it doesn't get shut down."

"You knew that was going to happen," I said bitterly.

"I suspected it," Mac acknowledged.

"And you let me make a fool of myself!"

"By no means, old boy! That your solution was wrong in no way detracts from the fact that it was, as I said, ingenious. I thought it best to let the theory play out."

"Played out is the word for it! Ranieri didn't do it, Bexley didn't do it, Haldane didn't do it—"

Mac's eyebrow calisthenics stopped me. "What?"

"Just a notion. Suppose that Nicholas Haldane killed Clark Woodsfield to remove a romantic rival and J. Calvin Davis somehow knew it."

It didn't take me long to see the holes in that one.

"But Woodsfield was dying anyway. Bexley said Dr. Sharfman will verify that. Plus, Bexley is Haldane's alibi. He certainly wouldn't lie for the man if he knew that he killed Davis for the reason you theorize."

"Exactly! That is what makes the idea challenging and intriguing. If we can overcome those objections, Jefferson, we either have the solution to the Davis murder or the beginnings of an excellent mystery novel."

I wanted to strangle him.

Chapter Twenty-Four
A Sister's Story

If you think all of that was enough sleuthing for one day, I'm right there with you. After Lynda and I celebrated the sacred ritual of cocktail hour, I expected nothing more exciting than a raucous dinner for five followed by playtime, a little TV, and a lot of reading. (I was halfway through *Hound Dog Homicide*, one of Dunbar Yates's early Hector Gumm & Beauregard mysteries set in Louisiana; Lynda was reading ghost stories by Roger Johnson.) But Ida Garrison, the councilman's wife and Cal Davis's sister, had a different take on the way I should spend my evening.

"She would like us to meet her at the City Hall parking lot because, quote, 'that's the last place you'll find Leonidis on a Saturday,'" Mac informed me when he called. "Mrs. Garrison is taking this precaution despite the fact that her husband is attending an Ancient Order of Hibernians meeting this evening. She appears quite determined that he be unaware of this conference with us. You will recall that when I asked Mr. Garrison if she would talk to us, he took it upon himself to answer for her in the strongly negative."

His exact words were, "So, that's not gonna happen."

But I mentioned Garrison's intransigence at the time to Lynda, who called Triple M, who called Louise LaRosa, who called Ida Garrison, who called Mac. Why didn't she call me? Anyway, it was Lynda's fault that our Saturday evening was upended, but I could hardly complain.

Mac drove us to the City Hall parking lot, where we found Ida Davis Garrison leaning possessively against a red Yamaha motorbike with her arms folded. An equally red helmet dangled from one of the handlebars. I've known married couples who were a matched set physically, such as the diminutive Margaret and Gordon Cole of Happy Homes Realty, but the Garrisons personified the old adage that opposites attract. Ida was at least a head shorter than her somewhat older husband, trim yet solid and busty, with shaggy dark hair and gray roots. She wore jeans, boots, a checked shirt, and an impatient look, but no makeup.

"Let's get this over with quickly," she said. *My sentiments exactly!* "Thanks for meeting me here, by the way. Leonidis would have a conniption fit if he knew I was talking to you, and the poor man's blood pressure is high enough as it is. He thinks he's trying to protect me, but he doesn't even know the worst of it. I just pray that he never does."

Ida Garrison didn't look especially in need of protection to me. I'd hire her as a bodyguard in a New York minute just based on her aggressive body language.

"And what is this information that you do not wish him to know?" Mac asked.

She lit a cigarette, her hands shaking ever so slightly. That gave Mac tacit permission to fire up a pricey cigar.

"This is just between us chickens, right?" she asked.

"You can count on our discretion," I assured her, stealing Judge Kessler's word. Mac seconded the promise.

"I guess I'll trust you. Louise said you're okay. The thing is"—she sucked on the cig—"I knew Cal was alive, and I knew he was coming back to Erin for a few days. Leonidis had no idea. It would crush him that I didn't tell him the truth about Cal, and it might hurt him in the next election because people would think that he knew, which I swear he didn't."

Mac raised both eyebrows. "This is a revelation of some consequence. When did you learn that your brother's presumed suicide was a hoax?"

"He called me maybe a month after he disappeared to let me know that he was alive and okay. I'll never forget it. He was crying and said he let me down. I was the big sister who took care of him when we were kids, you see. I told him he didn't owe me anything—he owed those clients that he cheated. But the truth is, he did let me down. That whole mess was a body blow to me when it unraveled. I was glad our parents weren't alive to see it. Anyway, I begged Cal to come back to face the music, but he said he was too ashamed. I think he just didn't want to pay the price. He was my brother and I loved him, but he was so used to lying by then that he even lied to himself. And I guess I lied, too, by not telling anybody, not even Leonidis, that he was still alive.

"Cal called me now and then over the years, always from a different cell phone number each time. He never told me where he was or what name he was using. Then a couple of months ago he called and said he was coming home, but only if I promised not to tell people who he was. Well, what could I do? He was my brother. I promised. That's when he explained the whole thing about the TV show and his life as Stuart Diamond."

"Why do you think he informed you he was returning to Erin?"

"I'm sure he was afraid that I would recognize him on the street and blurt out his name, so he wanted to loop me in and make sure I kept his secret." She shook her head. "But he needn't have worried. He was older, thinner, and with a beard, glasses, and darker hair. I wouldn't have known it was Cal. I'm sure nobody did, not even his wife."

"You are certain of that? About Mrs. Landfair, in particular?"

"That's what I said, isn't it?" Ida Garrison blew a prodigious cloud of smoke. "I'm a hundred percent sure! I watched Mary that night at The Speakeasy when she was in the room with him. She was interested in what was going on—that's part of her job, I guess, for the Visitors' Bureau—

but no more than that. She didn't pay any special attention to Cal."

"If she was fooled, then it hardly seems possible that anyone knew his true identity."

The dead man's sister shook her head in a way that seemed rueful, but not about Mac's comment. In fact, she agreed. Her mind was elsewhere, though.

"I'm sure no one did. But Poor Mary! I've always felt sorry for the way Cal left her holding the bag. And guilty, too, for not letting her know that he was alive. I was happy for her when she remarried and moved on with her life. Now comes this nightmare to upend things! I know she's probably the chief suspect, being the wife, but I also know she didn't kill Cal. I don't know who did—I have no clue—but it wasn't Mary. I'd bet on that."

You might want to rethink that, Ida. Your family doesn't have a good history with gambling.

"Did your brother in his most recent phone call indicate a special reason for coming to Erin, other than the television program?"

She thought about it. "He just said he had a good gig going on YouTube—I called it a scam in my own mind, but he called it a gig—and that he lucked into something even better with that TV show. They wanted a ghost in an eatery and Erin had one. Like I said, that was the first time he ever told me what he was doing and what he called himself. He may have used other names, I guess."

"Why did you decide to tell us all this?" I asked.

She rubbed her shoulders, as if hugging herself. "It's bothered me for years. I had to tell somebody. And since I'm not religious, I couldn't tell God. Just keep it to yourselves. You promised."

Chapter Twenty-Five
The Last Gaffe

Usually the way I know I'm awake in the morning is that it dawns on me I'm thinking about something and it's not a dream. On Sunday morning, I woke up thinking about Daphne Saunders.

"Could she really be so oblivious she didn't know whether the driver of the other car was male or female?" I asked Lynda.

"First of all, darling, she's a college student. If that's not explanation enough for obliviousness, she said she was texting her boyfriend."

"Point taken."

With public Masses suspended because of the pandemic, it felt strange not to go to church on Sunday. But we did watch the 11 A.M. service livestreamed from our parish, St. Edward the Confessor. Generally speaking, it went okay—except for the gaffe when someone accidentally activated a filter that made the pastor, Father Peter Nguyen, look like a potato while delivering his homily.

After Mass, I called to check on my parents in Virginia.

"Still kicking, but not so high," Mom reported. Being in a wheelchair, she doesn't get out much anyway. But Dad admitted to being a little restless and bored, having sold his real estate brokerage last year. "Play chess or cards with Mom, but not Scrabble," I advised. Words are her business, for Cornelia Randolph Cody is a poet of no small distinction.

Later, while Lynda baked banana bread for the older neighbors, I joined Mac in his man cave to talk about the case. He sat at his sizeable desk while I occupied a chair in a corner of the room, to one side of the bar with the TV mounted over it. We were at least twice the recommended six feet apart.

"Has it occurred to you, Jefferson, that the term 'social distancing' is singularly inappropriate?" I was not so foolish as to think he would give me a chance to answer the question, nor did he. "What is really meant by the term is physical distancing. One can be social at any distance, especially with the video technology at our disposal."

"Just be sure to flatten the curve," I said. "It's the new normal. After all, we're all in this together."

Bandying about these newly popular and already annoying clichés wasn't doing much to buoy my spirits, depressed in almost equal measure by two murders and a world-wide pandemic. But it was no doubt providing plenty of grist for "The Write Stuff," Mac's blog about bad grammar and hackneyed language.

"And thanks to the World Wide Web," he sailed on, "physical distance is even more irrelevant when it comes to gathering information. For example, I have been able to learn from a simple internet search that almost ten years ago, which is when Clark Woodsfield died, Nicholas Haldane was happily operating his restaurant in Savannah and would not meet Charles Bexley for another three years."

Which was further confirmation that Haldane had no reason to do away with Woodsfield. This was like putting a nail in the lid of a coffin that was already buried.

"Good to know," I tossed off. "In other words, he's as innocent as Daphne Saunders."

A McCabe eyebrow lifted. "Daphne?"

"Never mind. Let's call Ben."

That was the first item on our afternoon agenda—following up on Lynda's suggestion that the *Observer*'s news editor, Ben Silverstein, might know what the Old Gaffer had in the works for his column at the time he died. Ben didn't assign topics to the freelancer, but occasionally suggested ideas. "Plan to write about something dangerous to a killer but be sure to let him know in advance so that he can strangle you" was probably not one such idea, but you never know.

Mac made the call using his cell phone, with the speaker on.

"This must be about Fred's murder," Ben said. "Such a tragedy. What's up?"

Nobody ever said Bernard J. Silverstein was slow on the uptake, even though his affection for three-piece suits and a gnarled wooden pipe gave him something of a 1940s air to my mind.

Mac outlined the straw at which we were grasping – the possibility that Fred Gaffe was done away with to prevent him writing the next Old Gaffer column.

"Do you know whether the projected subject matter of his next effort had anything to do with J. Calvin Davis or Jackie O'Brien, for example?" Mac asked. *O'Brien again?* "Both men were subjects of Fred Gaffe's writing in the past, in different ways."

Fred had covered Davis's supposed death as a reporter near the end of his career as a daily journalist, and he had written about O'Brien—the man and the ghost— more than once in his columnist days.

"That's a good theory," Ben said, "but it won't fly. I kind of assumed Fred would write a retrospective about Davis's supposed suicide and all that, but he told me that Johanna did such a complete job in her background story on Davis that she didn't leave anything for him. I think he was a little disappointed about that because, after all, she basically just recycled Fred's reporting from the time.

"Anyway, his next column is about a U.S. Senator from Erin, Joseph P. Marx, who almost became a vice presidential candidate in 1936 but didn't make it because of a whispering campaign that he was a secret communist. I guess his last name didn't help any. Fred submitted the column on Friday. We'll make a big deal out of it being his last. 'The Last Gaffe,' you might say. I doubt if he was working on the column after that one yet."

Another dead end. Mac took it well. "Do you have any thoughts on Fred's death?"

"Beyond being sad and angry, you mean? No, I don't. He was a great guy and a great reporter. Even retired, he was a great reporter."

"Do you have any idea why he was going to Kentucky at the time he was killed? His trunk was loaded with materials that have been in short supply these days."

"I couldn't even guess. You might call his niece. Fred and his late wife never had any children, but Betty was close to both of them. She must be devastated."

Betty Malvers was an administrative assistant on the executive floor at Samson Microcircuits. The Erin-based company ran into more than a little legal trouble a few years ago,[15] but managed to claw its way back after a cash infusion from an outside investor.

"I'm still numb," the bereaved niece told Mac when he called her. "I can't believe this happened. Uncle Fred was the nicest person I know. It's horrible that only ten people are allowed to attend the funeral because of this stupid virus. The church should be packed. Everybody loved Uncle Fred."

Somebody didn't.

"At least his family is small enough to fit. He just had my mom and dad and us kids. Aunt June died years ago, and Uncle Fred always said he was a one-woman man. That's why he kept working for so long—he had nobody to go home to."

"Perhaps this is irrelevant," Mac said, "but I am curious as to where he was going at the time he was killed. Do you happen to know?"

---

[15] See *Erin Go Bloody*, MX Publishing, 2016.

"That just shows you how nice he was! He told me Friday he was taking toilet paper, food, and I don't know what all to a former colleague, another retired reporter who lived over the river. Sally Hendricks is her name. She's a little older than Uncle Fred and in much worse physical condition, from what he told me, so either she couldn't get out or she was afraid to because of the virus—I'm not sure which. I don't think she has any near relations, so Uncle Fred stepped up. He didn't have a ton of money, working for the *Observer* his whole life and not being from a rich family. But he shared what he had."

She started crying. Mac gave her space for that.

"Why would anybody hurt a sweet old man?" she asked when she could speak again. It sounded like a plea to the unfeeling universe, but Mac answered:

"We know from your uncle's editor that the subject of his next column was not one likely to inspire homicidal intent. However, perhaps he nonetheless had information damaging to the killer, some knowledge that—though he did not plan to write about—nevertheless resided in his brain as a threat."

Betty Malvers laughed through her tears.

"Did you ever talk to Uncle Fred? Or should I say, did you ever listen to Uncle Fred? He never had an unspoken thought."

That's true, come to think of it. I've heard him called "The Old Gasser."

"If he knew something really juicy," she added, "I don't think anybody could kill him fast enough to keep him from spilling it."

Chapter Twenty-Six
Homicide Deterred

"There are those who tell even more than they know, and those who know more than they tell," Mac rumbled after Betty signed off. "I prefer to be the latter."

"So, what are you not telling me?"

"The killer of Stuart Diamond. Please do not look at me that murderous way, Jefferson. It is not that I know who the killer is, but that I have some confidence I know who the killer is not. Nor do I know the motive. I prefer to say no more at this point lest I prove wrong. No, I am unmovable on that point. My hasty and false conclusion in that toilet paper affair still rankles. I am a chastened man.

"Besides, the murder of Fred Gaffe still puzzles me. Upon sober reflection, it does indeed seem unlikely that he was knowingly keeping a secret for which he was silenced. The concept of keeping a story to himself was foreign to him. He was a gregarious soul who did not save all his stories for print. And yet, the traditional motives of love and money seem barred by Miss Malvers's testimony that he was 'a one-woman man' and had no great financial resources."

I was unwilling to give up the Man Who Knew Too Much theory.

"Maybe Fred didn't think whatever he knew was interesting or important enough to share," I posited, "but the killer saw it as a threat and wanted to get to him before he spilled whatever it was as a throw-away line in a casual conversation someday."

Mac nodded. "That is indeed within the realm of possibility, which is why I specified he would not *knowingly* keep a secret. However, that possibility does not help us. If Fred Gaffe did not grasp the importance of some knowledge he had, certainly there is no way for us to conjecture the nature of it."

He stroked his beard. I considered reminding him that the CDC's pandemic guidelines said not to touch your face, but I didn't want to interrupt the genius at work. "There is something that *would* help us," he said at last, "and it is not beyond hope. Perhaps, unbeknownst to the killer, Fred Gaffe already shared the information and neither he nor anyone else understood its import."

That did not compute. "You mean in his Old Gaffer column about the 1936 election?"

"No, I mean in his interview with the man he knew as Stuart Diamond."

"But we were there during that interview. It was innocuous!"

"So it seemed at the time, I grant you. However, perhaps if we saw the recording of the interview, something would strike us when viewed in the context of Fred Gaffe's subsequent murder. Perhaps the killer was not present for the interview and did not realize that Fred had already shared the harmful information, and it was even recorded. Or perhaps the killer was present and is confident that the interview, and the entire program, will not be aired because of the 'Stuart Diamond' murder."

"Which the killer was also responsible for! Maybe."

While I pondered the ins and outs and the ups and downs of all that, to the rhythm of my head pounding as it always does when pondering stuff like that, Mac picked up the phone and called Lisa Carson at her hotel room.

"Yes, we're still here," she said acidly. "It's not like we have a viable option."

Mac asked if she would be willing to let him see the video of Fred Gaffe's interview.

"Will it help us get out of this burg any faster?"

"That is my profound hope, Ms. Carson!"

"Then I'm in! I can get the recording and send it to you via Zoom tomorrow, if that's soon enough."

"That will be fine."

She agreed to send him a Zoom invitation for 10 AM.

"And might I ask," Mac added, "will The Speakeasy episode of your program be broadcast despite the tragic circumstances attendant to it?"

The question earned a heavy sigh. "That's above my pay grade, a WSTV decision, but I doubt it. Management is pretty squeamish."

"I think I know why you wanted to know that," I told Mac after he disconnected. "One of the questions you always like to ask is what changed after a murder. In this case, one of the things that changed is that the show may not go on. Maybe the killer—"

Kate entered the room, looking so grim I shut up.

"What's wrong?" I said, beating Mac to it.

"These texts from Helen Archer really worry me. I've been calling her since Friday and getting no answer. I'd call her nephew but he's basically AWOL from her life, which is why I got involved."

"What does her most recent text say?" Mac asked.

Kate consulted her phone. "She wrote this morning and said, 'I can't stop coughing and I have a fever.' I told her, 'You need to go to a doctor immediately.' She said, 'I don't want to be a burden to nobody.' I said, 'I'm coming right over.' She said, 'I won't come to the door.' What do you think, Sebastian?"

He stood up. "I think it is inconceivable that a much-honored English teacher, however ill, would write, 'I don't want to be a burden to nobody' rather than 'anybody.' That is even worse than the earlier 'between you and I,' which has troubled me for days. Now I know why. We are staring in the face of a terrible evil unleashed by this virus." *I know you take grammar seriously, Mac, but—* "Or perhaps I should blame Original Sin, which is itself a kind of virus."

"What are you babbling about?" Kate asked before I could.

"Miss Archer surely did not write that, which makes me confident that her life is in grave danger."

Helen Archer came to the door before I had a chance to jab the bell a second time.

"Kate!" she exclaimed. "What a surprise! Is that your husband?"

The retired teacher stood about five-foot-three, solidly built, and had her hair dyed a convincing shade of light brown. She wasn't lacking in wrinkles, but her dress didn't have any and her lipstick was carefully applied. I put her age north of eighty.

"This one is my husband and that one is my brother," Kate informed her. *An embarrassment of riches, I'd call that!* "I've been calling you, but you didn't answer."

"Oh, dear. I misplaced my phone a few days ago. I'm sure it will turn up eventually."

"It was after your nephew visited that your phone disappeared, was it not?" Mac asked.

"Why, yes, I suppose it was." She looked fondly at Kate. "We had a very nice visit and I told him all about you, dear."

I was getting the picture now, and it was a particularly ugly one.

"Come on in and have a drink," Miss Archer said. "I was just having a little bourbon, neat, while I watched the governor."

We said yes to the "come on in" and no to the drink. Inside the house, small but tidy and filled with high-quality furniture, we sat down in the room with the TV. Miss Archer turned off the governor in mid-sentence. That was the day he made the unsurprising announcement that a stay-at-home order, Ohio's version of shelter-in-place, would take effect at midnight the next day, Monday.

"This pandemic stuff reminds me of my grandfather talking about the 1918 flu," Miss Archer said. "He swore that he got through it by nipping whiskey out of a flask all day long." She sipped from her small glass of bourbon. "I figure it couldn't hurt!"

Lynda would love this woman.

"But you're not ill?" Kate said.

"Never better! Well, that's a lie. I'm an old woman and time's winged chariot is carrying me away. But I'm in excellent shape for my age, except that my memory is a little sketchy. I don't know where I put that phone, for instance."

"I believe that I can find it for you," Mac said.

She looked at him shrewdly. "Well, that would be very nice, but how in the world could you do that?"

"He's smarter than he looks," I said, earning scowls from both McCabes. "And he's a detective."

She nodded absently. "Of course. I remember, now. You're a regular Miss Marple, aren't you, Mr. McCabe? I hope you catch whoever killed Fred Gaffe. Such a nice man. I used to teach with his late wife at Malcolm C. Cotton High."

"What an asshole!" Kate exploded as she shut Helen Archer's front door behind us. She meant Ted Archer. "He stole her phone, knowing from Helen that she was in regular communication with me. Then he sent me texts, pretending to be his aunt—"

"But lacking credibility because of the poor grammar," Mac inserted.

"—describing symptoms to create the idea that she had COVID-19. But why?"

"There can be only one reason," Mac said. "He planned to kill her with the expectation that she would leave him her money."

"Kill her!"

Mac nodded. "If he smothered her with a pillow, 'discovered' the body, and told the hospital that she had COVID symptoms but refused to go to a doctor, who would question it—especially in light of the texts to you?"

As if to punctuate that rhetorical question, my phone erupted. Seeing that Hadley Reams from the *Observer* was calling, making it business and not social, I began walking away from Mac and Kate as I answered. And I thought: *Now what has some SBU student, faculty member, administrator, or maintenance worker done wrong?*

"Hi, Hadley. What's news?"

"Hi, Jeff. Sorry to bother you on a Sunday. I'm just wondering if you can confirm for me that Father Joe Pirelli is in the hospital with COVID."

Oh, crap!

"Where did you hear that?"

"I have my sources."

"Don't you date a nurse at St. Hildegarde?"

"Let's leave my love life out of this, okay? I know Father Pirelli has the virus; I just need you to confirm it for me on the record."

"I can neither confirm nor deny"—*what a cliché!*—"medical information about any St. Benignus employee. HIPPA prohibits it."

"What's HIPPA?"

I explained.

"Can't you just tell me off the record?" Hadley said. "Then I would have two sources and my editor would let me go with it."

"Good try, Hadley." He was coming along nicely as a reporter. "You know I'm normally agreeable to going off the record with you, but in this case I think that would still be a violation of federal law."

We jousted for another five minutes or so. I didn't crack, even though he told me he was going to write the story anyway if he could get a second source.

"Do what you have to do," I said in what I hoped was a professional tone. I hated that it would look like SBU was trying to hide something, but HIPPA is a real thing.

"But if it wasn't true, you'd find a way to warn me off the story, wouldn't you?"

"I'll let you draw your own conclusions on that." *Meaning yes.*

I rejoined Mac and Kate and learned that a decision had been made.

"You and I are going to pay Ted Archer a visit," Mac told me. "Kate, however, is going home."

She didn't look happy about it. "Mac's afraid I'd do something violent to the bastard. And he's right!"

Maybe it's a case of confirmation bias, but when Ted Archer opened the door of his apartment, he looked like a weasel to me. He had fair hair, a wispy mustache, weak chin, low forehead, with a slim build on a none-too-tall frame. Where had I seen him before?

"Yeah?"

Maybe he was conserving his energy. He certainly hadn't invested any in throwing on the white T-shirt and jeans.

"My name is Sebastian McCabe and this is Thomas Jefferson Cody."

He straightened up. "Oh, hi. Your wife is Aunt Helen's friend, right?"

"Quite so. A very good friend indeed."

Ricoletti's Ristorante! That's where I'd seen Ted Archer. He was a waiter at Erin's finest restaurant, where

Lynda and I dine when I'm feeling flush. We celebrated our engagement there, the week she asked me to marry her.

"What can I do for you?" Archer didn't invite us in or move from the doorway.

"You have something that belongs to your aunt—her cell phone," Mac said. "We are here to retrieve it."

Archer managed a nervous laugh. "I don't know what you're talking about."

Approximately 99.5 percent of the time, somebody who says "I don't know what you're talking about" knows precisely what the other person is talking about.

"You know precisely what I am talking about." *See.* "In a rare visit to your aunt, you purloined her phone. Perhaps the initial intention was just to isolate her, or perhaps your entire plot was fully hatched in advance. In any case, you knew either from Miss Archer or from the text messages on her phone that Kate was watching out for her. Is that what gave you the idea to send a series of messages to Kate under her name that would later support your story that she was suffering from COVID and died of it?"

Archer preferred to remain silent. He also looked like a cornered rat.

"You either knew or assumed that the coroner does not perform an autopsy on every elderly person who dies," Mac went on. "Your testimony that Helen refused your entreaties to go to the doctor, backed up by the symptoms reported to Kate and the burgeoning number of COVID cases, would probably suffice to have her death ascribed to the virus. In reality, you intended to murder her with the expectation that you would inherit the results of her lifetime of fruitful work and frugal spending, plus what she was left by her fiancé's parents. Was it a pillow over her face that you planned?"

"You're crazy! You're a freaking lunatic!"

"I want that cell phone, Mr. Archer. I will not leave without it."

"Maybe I do have it," Archer mumbled.

"Maybe?"

"All right, I have it! I picked it up by mistake. It looks just like mine. I'll get it."

He retreated a couple of feet back into his apartment. But when he tried to close the door, Mac prevented him with a well-placed foot.

"Do not take too long looking for it," Mac instructed. "Every second I wait makes me more inclined to discuss this matter with Chief Hummel. Your criminal intent would be hard to prove, I grant you, but I doubt that you want to attract his attention."

Archer was back in about half a minute and plunked the phone into Mac's waiting hand. Mac didn't thank him. Instead, he said:

"Helen Archer had better continue to live her long and happy life. And when she does shed her mortal coil, I shall see to it that there is an autopsy. I also have high hopes that she will change her will if you in any way profit from the current version. There is no lack of charities that share her interest in children."

Archer's eyes were blue, but they almost blazed red with hatred for Mac. "Get the hell out of here!"

"It is my pleasure to do so, I assure you!"

"It's almost like there are two pandemics—one of virus, and one of crime," I said back in Mac's car. "Glen Monroe stole toilet paper, of all things! I read in *The Wall Street Journal* the other day that there's practically a cottage industry in COVID-related scams. And now a would-be murderer tried to piggy-back on the virus like a parasite."

If Mac admired the colorful simile, he didn't say so. What he did say was:

"It is indeed likely that reports of a high death rate from the virus among the elderly set Ted Archer to thinking there was a way he could kill his aunt and get away with it.

Before there was a method, however, there was a motive: Helen Archer stood between her nephew and the object of his desire—the wealth he coveted and assumed would be his upon her death. The thought must have consumed him. Money is a jealous lover, Jefferson."

Chapter Twenty-Seven
A Dead Man Speaks

"Just a trim," I told Lynda the next morning, one week after Davis's murder. I wanted to look good for virtual meetings before going to my office on the porch.

"Who's the barber around here, darling?"

"Hmph," I responded. Never argue with a woman who has scissors in her hand. Besides, I knew how lucky I was that she was willing to do this and had attained some proficiency at it. Half the TV anchors broadcasting from their basements these days looked like they cut their own hair.

"I've been thinking about the case," she said. "Maybe it's not a case. Maybe it's *two* cases, with two killers. It wouldn't be the first time in our experience."

"True enough, my sweet. Whatever got Fred Gaffe killed might have had nothing to do with the murder at The Speakeasy. Mac hasn't ruled that out. Of course, the Old Gaffer *did* have a connection to Davis—he wrote about his sticky fingers when it all came unraveled nine years ago. But, you're right, that could be a coincidence. Anyway, Mac says we'll know who the Gaffer's murderer is when we find out what he knew that the killer had to hide."

Lynda bit her lip in thought. "But how are you even sure Fred was killed because of something he knew?"

"Well, for one thing, he tended to know a lot, and some of it not so nice. And for another, we can't think of a better motive! He didn't have a romantic attachment or a fortune, so love and money are ruled out."

My in-house barber stepped back with a critical look on her face, but it wasn't directed at my comments. "I hope I didn't cut too much. Take a look in the mirror."

I did so.

"It's fine," I assured her. *It'll grow back. It always does.*

Hadley Reams's "sources say" story, **SBU LEGEND IN HOSPITAL WITH COVID**, made the bottom of the front page, illustrated by a head shot of Father Joe.

"Unfortunately, it's all true," I commented sadly.

Thinking about Father Joe's age, and the toll of the virus on older people, reminded me of Alma Hummel. I gave Oscar a call.

"She's okay health-wise, thanks for asking," he said. "But she's going to get pretty lonely with this stay-at-home order. Hell, I'm going to get lonely. I've been playing poker on Wednesday night for years. How are we going to do that virtually?"

"There must be a way. People are already talking about Zoom seders for Passover. Hey, are you having virtual dates with Popcorn?"

"None of your business."

"I said 'virtual,' not 'virtuous.' How goes the murder investigations?"

"We're plowing through. We stopped about a half-dozen red Camrys, but none of the drivers matched the witness's description of Fred's killer; all the alibis of likely suspects for Davis's murder check out, although in some cases the two suspects alibi each other; and we haven't found either murder weapon."

"Oh."

At 10 A.M., I was on Zoom myself with Mac and Lisa Carson to look at Stuart Diamond's interview of Fred Gaffe. Stephen Lipinski joined us at the beginning to make his feelings known, which he did with some force.

"This is such bullshit!" he exploded. "It should be obvious that—what was his name?—Davis was killed by somebody he ripped off years ago. There's no justification for forcing us to stay here while my restaurant in Santa Fe tanks."

Lipinski looked every inch the New Mexican in his bolo tie with the silver and turquoise slide. He probably had a silver belt buckle, too. Carson was dressed in a simple white blouse, nicely setting off her black hair, and black and white plaid slacks. I wondered if their suitcases were packed and if they'd be going off in separate directions, she to WSTV headquarters in pandemic-slammed New York. For now, though, he had his arm around her.

"I assure you that I am doing all that is in my power to clear up this matter with dispatch," Mac said. "Thank you for your cooperation, Ms. Carson."

She didn't say he was welcome. "Let's just do it, please. "I gave you permission to record this Zoom session, but I want you to agree that you won't use the Fred Gaffe interview for any commercial purposes."

"Of course."

The video began with the preliminaries, the white-haired and hefty Fred Gaffe putting on the mic while the bearded fraud Davis, AKA Diamond, chattered meaninglessly to put him at his ease. Seeing the two of them, knowing that they had no idea they would both be dead in a little over a week, hit me harder than I expected. How could they be so alive when they were six feet under? That's a kind of miracle we never even think about when we watch TV shows or movies with deceased performers.

Spoiler alert: The interview unfolded pretty much as I remembered it, no big surprises.

"I hear you're quite familiar with the Speakeasy ghost," Davis said.

The Old Gaffer nodded. "Jackie O'Brien's been haunting this building as long as I can remember."

"And how long is that?"

"Oh, going back to the forties, I guess."

He launched into his memoir of going to the Cricket Café as a young boy and seeing the beer taps turn on by themselves. Nothing significant there that I could see, except Gaffe's reference to Jackie O'Brien being killed right in front of the bar—exactly where his interviewer would be shot to death within days.

"Who do you think fired the shots that killed Jackie a hundred years ago this Halloween?"

"No real idea. Lots of folks assume it was another bootlegger. But it could have been a jealous husband, for all I know. Still a mystery, isn't it?"

I wanted to reach across the boundary between life and death to tell the Old Gaffer that the murder of Jackie O'Brien was no longer a mystery. But I guess he knew that now, wherever his spirit was.

"Did you attend to the body language, Jefferson?" Mac asked me after the video was over and Carson and Lipinski had signed off.

"You mean the way Davis and Fred looked at each other?"

"Precisely."

"Yeah. I didn't see anything between them—no spark of recognition by Fred. And I didn't hear anything in what Fred said. The whole exercise was a bust."

"*Au contraire*, old boy!" He looked so excited I wanted to reach across the computer screen and hit him. In a brotherly way, of course. The McCabe brain apparently had been in overdrive while I'd been processing the miracle of video. "We have learned something of crucial significance. To wit: There was no indication in that interview that Fred Gaffe knew the true identity of Stuart Diamond sitting across from him. Therefore, there is no reason to believe that he did know. Nor did anything that Fred said hint at some important knowledge that would warrant his elimination.

"Undoubtedly, Betty Malvers was right: Whenever her uncle knew anything interesting, he shared it. There remains the possibility that the killer wrongly *thought* he knew something damaging to the killer, but that is highly conjectural."

"See previous comment. How is the Davis-Gaffe interview not a bust for us?"

"Because it has cleared away the forest and allowed me to see a tree that should have been obvious all along. Fred Gaffe did not tell anyone what he knew because he never had a chance. Therefore, the secret that got him killed was knowledge he acquired immediately before his death—that is to say, on the ferry. Since Daphne Saunders testified that Fred never left his car—she was sufficiently attuned to her surroundings to notice that, despite her preoccupation with her boyfriend's summer internship woes—that knowledge must have been something that he *saw* from the car, for which bad luck he was immediately killed."

Mac may have cleared out his metaphorical forest, but I was still lost in the woods.

"What could he possibly have seen on the ferry that was worth killing for?" I asked.

"The gun that killed J. Calvin Davis! Think back to Oscar's telephone call with Chef Lipinski on Friday morning. He rightly said, 'The gun that killed Davis is probably at the bottom of the Ohio River.' I submit that Oscar was premature. That gun was not in the river then but is most likely in the river now, and Fred Gaffe had the misfortune to see the killer throw it there on Saturday morning."

I don't know what I'd been expecting, but nothing like that. This was just about the biggest rabbit that Sebastian McCabe had ever pulled out of his hat.

"The killer must have turned around from tossing the weapon and seen that Fred was looking in his direction," he expounded. "Perhaps he walked over to the car and Fred—who, as Ms. Malvers colorfully put it, 'never had an unspoken thought'—imprudently made it clear what he had seen. This time the murder weapon was something at hand, an impromptu garrote. If we knew what it was, that might point definitively to the killer. After all, who is normally equipped with something that could be turned to that purpose?"

Maybe a woman in a string bikini.

"Since we don't know the murder weapon, what else have we got?" I said.

"Fred never saw the killer's face, which was concealed by a protective mask. Therefore, he or she must have been someone that Fred could identify either by body type or by a distinctive mask, as Aurelia Banfield identified the toilet paper thief."

"You mean somebody he knew? That doesn't narrow it down at all. The Old Gaffer knew everybody!"

Chapter Twenty-Eight
Square One

"Seems to me that we're back to square one," I said back in Mac's man cave. "But what does that even mean, anyway? What's square one?"

"Etymologists disagree," Mac said in a distracted way. "I lean toward the theory that the expression comes from the board game Chutes and Ladders, known as Snakes and Ladders in the UK, in which an unlucky spin can send an unfortunate player back to the beginning of the game— square one."

"Sorry I asked."

As Mac spoke, he absent-mindedly performed an old magic trick to liberate his unconscious mind to work on the mystery. He took four playing cards, the kings, and squared them with their faces up. Then he showed the cards one by one. But instead of the fourth king, the King of Clubs, the back of the card showed. He started over. This time Clubs was displayed but instead of the King of Hearts, the back showed. A third time Hearts returned but instead of the King of Diamonds, the back showed. I was picking up a pattern here. But I was fooled! The fourth time, all the faces showed. But when Mac turned the cards over, the back of all four cards were mirrors. He turned them over again, and the other sides were mirrors as well.

"It's done with mirrors, old boy," he non-explained.

"Well, anyway," I said, dragging the conversation back to the task at hand, "why don't we just skip the board game imagery and go back to the drawing board?"

"It was your imagery, was it not?"

"Never mind that. I think it's time to take a fresh look at everybody we've talked to in this case, including whoever you've ruled out and those who make no sense to me as suspects. That's what I mean by going back to the drawing board." I was energized now, with the synapses in my brain firing like bottle rockets on the Fourth of July. People who chug caffeine must feel like this all the time.

"If you're right about the reason the Old Gaffer was garroted, Mac, we only need to solve Davis's murder since the same person killed both. Motive is problematical for Davis, and the means—in the form of the murder weapon— is presumably at the bottom of the beautiful Ohio, so let's focus on opportunity. Make a chart of where everybody claimed to be on Monday night when Cal Davis met his Maker. Once we see all those alibis in black and white, maybe something will stand out that we've missed up to now. Oscar said his troops have been working over the alibis, but they might have missed something."

"By thunder, Jefferson, the idea has merit," Mac conceded, and went to work on the computer in front of him. After about fifteen minutes, occasionally checking his memory against mine, this is what he came up with:

SUBJECT	ALIBI
Charles Bexley	*With Nicholas Haldane*
Willie Bloomer	*At Elysian Gardens*
Lucius Burdette	*At Orpheum Theater (alone)*
Lisa Carson	*With Stephen Lipinski*
"Long John" Gold	*With Mitzi Gold*
Mitzi Gold	*With "Long John"*
Nicholas Haldane	*With Charles Bexley*
Irene Cassorla Kessler	*At Marvin Slade fundraiser*
Mary Landfair	*At home (alone)*
Rowan Landfair	*At St. Hildegarde Health*
Stephen Lipinski	*With Lisa Carson*
Kerri Raines	*With Nuno Robles (playing miniature golf at Putters)*
Tony Ranieri	*At Country Club job*
Nuno Robles	*With K. Raines (Putters)*
Conrad Starshak	*On the air*
Myrtle White	*With son*

"Subject?" I said, referring to the heading on the first column. "Why do you call them subjects?"

"For most of them, 'suspects' greatly overstates the situation."

"Well, that's true," I agreed glumly. "But I did say not to leave anybody out, and I don't think you did. I forgot there were so many couples that alibi each other, though."

"Regrettably so. The testimony of one's inamorata can hardly be considered objective. The assistant producer, Nuno Robles, and the videographer, Kerri Raines, do not appear to have that sort of relationship, however, and the receipt from their round of miniature golf verifies their story."

"Yeah, that's one alibi that's pretty solid," I agreed. "There are a few others. Willie Bloomer didn't go anywhere on the murder night, that's for sure. Lynda confirmed Conrad Starshak was broadcasting. Judge Kessler, Rowan Landfair, and Tony Ranieri all have good alibis if they check out—and Oscar said they did. You could argue that Landfair could have slipped out of a busy hospital, but I don't buy it."

"Jefferson!" Mac sat up. "I believe I see—"

"Wait a minute! You *did* forget somebody, Mac—two somebodies, in fact!"

He cocked an eyebrow. "And that would be?"

"Leonidis Garrison and his wife, Davis's sister Ida. We never even considered them as suspects. But why not? Fratricide is not unheard of and killing a brother-in-law might be even more common." *I know how often I've been tempted.* "There could be all kinds of family dynamics there that they didn't tell us about. And how do we know that they didn't recognize Davis beneath the beard and the dye job? We only have Ida's word for that."

Sebastian McCabe just stared for what seemed to me a long time as he processed that. Then he became animated, his right hand closing into a fist. "Hell and damnation! 'Oh, Watson, what a fool I have been,' as the Master said in 'The Adventure of the Creeping Man.' Worse than a fool, Jefferson—I have performed more like a caricature Watson in a bad Sherlock Holmes film."

"I entirely agree, I'm sure." *But what the hell are you talking about?*

"You are right about the Garrisons, of course—we committed the unforgivable lapse of not considering them as suspects. Therefore, I assumed that Ida was telling the truth when she said she would not have recognized her brother in his current incarnation if she did not already know who he was. You will recall that I therefore assigned a high degree of credibility to the statements by others, those we *did* consider suspects, that they, too, did not pierce J. Calvin Davis's disguise. And if they did not know who he was, they had no reason to kill him because of Davis's predation. That is what

I meant when I said I knew who did not kill him. I reasoned that the killer must have been someone from Stuart Diamond's present, not J. Calvin Davis's past. However, once we grant the possibility that Ida did not tell the truth, my reasoning is a house of cards that collapses quickly."

"Don't look so down," I advised. "If Ida lied about that, it was to make it appear that she and/or her husband had no reason to kill Davis-cum-Diamond. Therefore, one of them did it. Case closed!"

"It is not quite that simple, old boy. One could imagine other reasons for Mrs. Garrison to lie. Perhaps, for example, she wanted to protect someone else who has an obvious grievance against Davis but professed not to know that Diamond was he. Ida could have suspected or been certain that this person was not fooled by the masquerade. That would explain why she admitted to knowing Diamond's true identity, which she would have every reason *not* to do if she were herself the murderer. There is no way to know whether she was prevaricating, short of a competently administered lie detector test. However, we cannot assume that she, or anyone else, was telling the truth about not knowing that Stuart Diamond was the much-loathed Davis."

My head hurt.

"So," I said, "square one?"

"Rather worse, I think, given that I have lost my confidence that I know who did not commit the murder of the wayward attorney. At any rate, whichever cliché we prefer, square one or drawing board, your prescription to re-examine every testimony from the beginning remains valid."

When he walked across the room and drew a fortifying beer from the tap, I knew we were in for a long haul. And it was. We took turns reciting everything we could remember each one of the "subjects" saying, with the other filling in the blanks. Mac played back the interviews with Charles Bexley and Nicholas Haldane from his memory banks, for example, and I made a few minor corrections since exact words were important. Then I recalled Lucius Burdette's answers to our questions, and Mac tweaked it a bit. We made a bit of a game of it without keeping score.

The last two names on the alphabetical list, Starshak and White, were people we had not talked with personally about the case, but Lynda had.

"We could give our memories a rest by watching the video she made of her Zoom call with Myrtle White," I suggested.

"Excellent notion! Although she gave us a rather extensive report, the video will give us the opportunity to observe Ms. White's body language."

In a few minutes, we were looking at a split screen of two pretty women. Myrtle's dyed blond hair, in cornrows, contrasted sharply but attractively with the black of her smiling face.

"Hi, Lynda! How's it going?"

"Fine, thanks. I don't really have a double chin. It just looks like that on camera."

"Try pulling back your skin with tape. That'll help. How are the kids?"

And so forth.

"What do you think?" I asked Mac at the end.

"Highly educational. I had no idea that feminine coiffure was so complicated. As to Ms. White's heart-rendering statements about J. Calvin Davis, there seems no reason to question any of them. Nor is there the slightest evidence that she was anywhere near the man in his Stuart Diamond persona during the days after his return."

Mac made another trip to the beer tap, a thoughtful look poking its way through his beard.

"Looking at Lynda questioning Ms. White—quite effectively, as one would expect of the seasoned journalist that she is—has given me the notion that perhaps we should look at the Stuart Diamond interview with Fred Gaffe a second time."

"You mean a third time. We also saw it live, remember. What are you thinking?"

"When we saw it live, we had no agenda. And when Lisa Carson showed us the video on the Zoom call, which I then recorded with her permission, we were focused on listening for anything either man might have said that would give us a clue as to why the killer took Fred Gaffe's life a little more than a week later. Am I correct?"

"Sure. But now we know why the Old Gaffer was killed, according to you—he saw the killer throw the gun in the river. What's your point?" Patience is never my long suit, and after a few hours of going nowhere in a slow car it wasn't even my short suit.

"My point is that when we watched the video we were focused on listening, not watching. I know that was true for me. Was it true for you as well? I thought as much. There is a chance—a very small one, I grant you—that there is a visual clue somewhere in that video. And if not in that interview, perhaps in one of the many other recordings made in the course of the work on that ill-fated television program. This is a rare opportunity to go back in time."

"But we were there when it happened! We saw in person whatever the camera recorded."

"We saw, Jefferson, but perhaps we did not observe."

I know that quote. More Sherlock Holmes! I give up.

"All right," I said. "Let's see it again. What could it hurt?"

Mac must have pushed the "record" icon at the beginning of our Zoom session with Carson because the video started with Lipinski in his bolo tie with his arm wrapped around her. He was as charming as I remembered: "This is such bullshit! It should be obvious that—what was his name?—Davis was killed by somebody he ripped off years ago. There's no justification for forcing us to stay here while my restaurant in Santa Fe tanks."

Then followed Mac with his assurance that he was on the case full bore, Carson giving him qualified permission to record the video for non-commercial purposes, the unedited material of Fred Gaffe and Davis-cum-Diamond chatting while Fred put on his mic, and finally the interview in earnest.

"I hear you're quite familiar with the Speakeasy ghost," Davis said.

To my surprise, Mac stopped the replay before the Old Gaffer said a word.

"What—you've heard enough already?"

"No, Jefferson, I have *seen* enough. Or, rather, I have finally observed what I saw all along. The murder weapon! And it confirms the conclusion I was groping toward earlier about the killer of J. Calvin Davis and Fred Gaffe, based on motive and lack of an unimpeachable alibi, before you sidetracked me with your brilliant observations about the Garrisons. Although Ida could have been lying about the effectiveness of her brother's disguise—you are quite correct about that—she was not. No one was."

Then Mac told me whom he had pegged as the double murderer, almost precipitating a fall off the chair on which I sat.

"It only remains for me to check one key fact with the witness," Mac said, "the only true witness in the case."

"What witness?"

"Daphne Saunders, of course."

Chapter Twenty-Nine
Gun Play

By the time Mac reached Daphne, and then Oscar to tell him what he had in mind and set everything up, we had run out of Monday. Since Ohio's stay-at-home order took effect at midnight that day, Mac decided to bring everybody together virtually via Zoom on Tuesday to tell them that he'd solved the case.

By everybody, I mean Lynda, Oscar, Holly Burdette, Daphne Saunders, Charles Bexley, Nicholas Haldane, Mary Landfair, Rowan Landfair, Ida Garrison, Lisa Carson, and Stephen Lipinski. They all had a stake in this, but they weren't all happy about taking part in this rodeo. Several made it clear they wanted Mac to just cut to the bottom line. But they all showed up onscreen anyway.

On the first day of lockdown in our state I was already suffering Zoom fatigue from all the meetings I'd attended in my home office over the past week. I shouldn't complain, though; the videoconferencing technology handed Mac the clue that solved the mystery, and the platform to announce that he had done so.

Lipinski's reaction to the online confab was hard to read, even though he wasn't wearing a mask. "Chief, are you on board with this?" he asked Oscar.

"I'm here," the latter said. I figured that avoiding a "yes" gave him plausible deniability later if the whole business turned into a dumpster fire. Clearly, he still had his doubts.

"Why are all the rest of us here?" Bexley asked. "There are twelve people on my screen, not including me."

Twelve—like a jury! There could have been one more, but Mac overruled Lynda's request that Johanna Rawls be brought into the fray. He argued that the presence of the press would change the entire dynamic. Besides, he was recording it all via Zoom so that Johanna could have every quotable word of it later.

Mac spoke from his man cave, while Lynda and I watched from her office (as opposed to mine, where we might be distracted by the music of birds tweeting outside). The others Zoomed in from all over. Carson and Lipinski, for example, were in the hotel room they were so eager to leave.

"I thought each of you would be interested," Mac responded to Bexley's very reasonable question. "I must ask you to be patient for just a little while longer as I explain my thought process that brings us together today. Central to everything is the fact that the disgraced attorney J. Calvin Davis and the beloved journalist Fred Gaffe were murdered by the same killer for different reasons. For ease of explication, I shall begin with the second murder. Unlike the first, it was carried out with so little thought that the assailant very nearly got away with it.

"Initially I pursued the plausible working hypothesis, so familiar to mystery fiction, that the victim knew the identity of Davis's killer or—if the murders were unrelated—something else that so imperiled the killer that homicide was the only protection. As a result of our inquiries, the details of which I need not bore you with, I became convinced that the fatal knowledge was something that Fred Gaffe saw immediately before he was slain. That is why the killer took the exceptionally risky step of killing him in the closed confines of the Erin Ferry.

"And what Fred saw was the killer tossing the gun that killed J. Calvin Davis into the Ohio River."

"Holy shit!" That was Haldane, showing his religious bent.

"How do you know that?" his partner demanded.

"Would you be surprised to learn that I have the gun?" He held up a Sig Sauer .45. "Recreational divers in the Ohio River are more common than you might think, and they frequently find things even when they are not looking for them. I was astounded to learn, for example, how often automobiles are dumped in the river so that their owners can claim they were stolen and collect the insurance. At any rate, finding a submerged gun not far from where the ferry plies the waters is a difficult but not insurmountable task when one has been commissioned to do so."

"But—"

"Please do not interrupt, Miss Saunders," Mac told Daphne in a stern-professor tone of voice. She looked as pissed as a young woman with shocking pink hair can look, but she shut up. "You will play your part later, I assure you. For now, I request that you remain silent while I say that this gun was purchased in Santa Fe by Stephen Lipinski and that I am confident the ballistics experts at the Ohio Bureau of Criminal Investigation will establish it was the source of the fatal bullets in the Davis shooting. Did you get the idea for disposing of the gun from Oscar's comment to you that it was probably at the bottom of the river, Chef Lipinski?"

Lisa Carson first looked at her husband, then uttered several short words that my mother would never use in her poetry. But Allen Ginsberg would.

Meanwhile, Lipinski regarded Mac the way he might look at an overcooked steak served with a glass of jug wine. "That's nuts, McCabe! First of all, I don't own a gun."

Carson turned away from the camera, toward her husband. "Yes, you do!"

This time, Lipinski's expression as he looked back at her was more like *et tu, Brute?* I was glad he wasn't wearing a mask so that I could see it. "Well, I might as well not have it," he said lamely. "I've hardly ever fired it." *Six times, at least.* "Besides, New Mexico doesn't require gun registration. There's no way you could tell who owned that gun."

"Oscar?" Mac said.

"This is your show," the Chief said. *Translation: Leave me out of this.* He had good reason to take that attitude.

Mac nodded at this reminder of the agreement they reached before the charade began.

"Registration is not required to determine a firearm's ownership," he informed Lipinski. "All that is necessary is an unbroken chain of ownership without a second-hand sale. The National Tracing Center of the Bureau of Alcohol, Tobacco, and Firearms uses the gun's serial number to determine its manufacturer or importer. From that, the NTC can trace the weapon through the wholesale and resale distribution chain to its first retail purchaser. As long as the gun is not resold, the NTC is able to tell the requesting law enforcement agency the owner of the gun."

"They made a mistake," Lipinski mumbled.

Mac ignored that and proceeded with the script.

"You know what happened, Chef, but I will explain for the benefit of the others.

"Daphne Saunders works at the Erin Ferry. The one substantive thing she could tell us about the other ferry passenger on Saturday, the killer, was that he or she wore what she called 'a red mask, a big one.'" He held up the issue of *The Erin Observer & News-Ledger* with Tall Rawls's front-page story, **Searching for Spirits at Erin's Gastropub.** He pointed to the photo of Stephen Lipinski in a white chef's coat and a traditional red chef's scarf. "Is that scarf what you meant by a big red mask, Miss Saunders?"

She nodded. "Pretty sure. It was pulled over his face, but yeah, that looks like it."

"Fred Gaffe was at The Speakeasy the night that photo was taken, Friday the thirteenth. Johanna's story quoted him. So he would have seen Lipinski, the celebrity chef, circulating among the patrons that night. A week and a day later, on the ferry, he saw him again. Fred would have recognized him from the scarlet chef's scarf he wore, conveniently used as a mask without setting off any alarm in this age of COVID, and from his rather solid body type. Lipinski, realizing that the other patron on the ferry may have seen him toss the gun overboard, approached the latter's car. Unburdened by the slightest inclination to reticence at any time, Fred probably hailed him by name. Did he also make it clear that he saw your disposal of the Sig Sauer, Chef?"

"Drop dead."

We'll take that as a "no comment."

His wife looked like she wanted to be anywhere else, like maybe Mars, but said nothing. Her silence made me think she might be getting ready to bail on him.

"Whether he did or did not," Mac continued, "Lipinski had to assume that Fred Gaffe—whose name he may have never known—could implicate him in murder. That would never do. Lipinski decided quickly and acted quickly. He garroted Fred with that signature bolo tie, which was fortuitously concealed by his scarf mask. After I reasoned my way to a near-certainty that Fred was killed because he witnessed the killer getting rid of the murder weapon, that tie presented itself to me as the murder weapon. Lipinski wore it during a Zoom conference I had with his wife, just as he is wearing it now."

"He almost never takes the damned thing off," Carson said in a subzero tone of voice.

"He did that afternoon, with fatal consequences."

"You bastard," Ida Garrison spat at Lipinski.

He turned toward Carson, frantic. "But I was with you during both murders!"

She shrank away. Her body language was loud and clear, but she put it into words anyway: "I'm not going to keep covering for you!"

Lipinski decided quickly and acted quickly. He bolted from the hotel room. Or tried to.

He got as far as the door, which he yanked open. This bothered Mac and me not at all, because we knew that Lt. Col. L. Jack Gibbons was waiting on the other side.

"Stephen Lipinski," I heard Gibbons intone off-screen, "you are under arrest for the murder of John Calvin Davis and Frederic Gaffe. You have the right to remain silent..." And so forth.

"I was not really certain, not one hundred percent, until he ran," Mac mused.

"But you said the gun was recovered and traced to Lipinski," Rowan Landfair objected. His wife, on a separate screen, looked too shocked to say anything at that moment.

"Strictly speaking, Mr. Landfair, I did not say that. Lipinski should have listened more carefully. I began by saying 'Would you be surprised to learn,' and I never actually stated that we found the gun. Later, I instructed Daphne Saunders to 'remain silent *while I say* that this gun was purchased in Santa Fe by Stephen Lipinski,' etc." Mac contends that's not lying, but I think he should have a discussion with his confessor about that.

"As far as I know," he amplified, "the Sig Sauer that killed J. Calvin Davis still resides in the river somewhere between the states of Ohio and Kentucky. I believe that, had I not stopped her, Miss Saunders would have announced that she saw no attempt by a diver to retrieve it."

"Sorry," she said. "I didn't realize you were scamming the killer."

Mac looked pained at that characterization of his trap, but that didn't stop him from expounding further.

"We could have employed divers to attempt a retrieval of the murder weapon, for it is not beyond the bounds of possibility. I feared, however, that Chef Lipinski and his wife would soon lose their patience and leave town. I took a huge gamble that Lipinski acquired the gun legally, and in Santa Fe, and that he could be tricked into a confession by being given the impression that we had the weapon and could tie it to him. And he did confess, in a sense, by his actions."

"I had nothing to do with the murders!" Carson almost shouted. "I'm appalled!"

"But why would Lipinski kill Cal?" Mary Landfair understandably wanted to know.

"In a sense, he did not. He killed Stuart Diamond."

Chapter Thirty
Murder Most Simple

Not counting Lipinski's attempted bolting, here's the only confession you will read in this book:

In violation of the state's stay-at-home order, we assembled a few hours later on the Cody deck to get the rest of the story. But it was just Mac and Kate—with whom we practically live anyway—and Johanna Rawls, who needed to round out her story for the *Online Observer* and the next day's print edition. And we were well distanced beneath our masks. It's a big deck.

"The double identity of Davis-Diamond obscured what was essentially a very simple case of an insanely jealous husband who removed a man he believed to be a rival," Mac said.

"Recall what happened: When we learned the true identity of the victim, numerous credible suspects emerged out of his sordid past. And yet, no one admitted to recognizing J. Calvin Davis beneath his newly grown beard, dyed hair, glasses, and trimmed-down body. *No one.* When his sister asserted that even she would not have known who he was if she had not been prepared, it seemed clear to me that he had either offended someone local in his brief time in Erin this month—which seemed highly dubious—or he was killed by one or more of his associates in the television enterprise.

"Jefferson briefly shattered my confidence in that hypothesis by pointing out that Ida Garrison could have lied on that point to protect someone else. That was, indeed, possible—and yet, why lie and at the same time reveal that she had been in contact with Davis all these years? She could have said that he was unrecognizable to her without telling that uncomfortable truth that would subject her to scorn, if not some legal entanglement."

Mac shook his head. "No, no one in Erin knew that Diamond was Davis, therefore he was not killed for being Davis. It was unlikely that an Erin resident would be moved to murder for any other reason, given his short stay here. My attention, therefore, turned to those involved in the WSTV production. We had proof that Nuno Robles and Kerri Raines spent an innocent evening playing miniature golf at the time of the murder. Stephen Lipinski and Lisa Carson, on the other hand, only alibied each other."

After the arrest, Carson said Lipinski claimed to be out for a walk on the night of Davis's murder and at the liquor store—still open as an essential business!—when he went to the ferry to dump the gun. He brought back a bottle of Bulleit bourbon to support the latter cover story. He also brought back a different rental car, having driven off the ferry and straight to the agency in Kentucky to ditch the tell-tale Camry for another vehicle. Hence the ineffectiveness of Oscar's APB. Carson said she thought the real reason he went out was that she was getting on his nerves. "He was sure as hell getting on mine." Lipinski convinced her they should say they were together during both murders in the hope that they would be cleared as suspects and allowed to leave town.

"We constructed convincing scenarios for how the killer lured Davis to The Speakeasy," Mac said, "yet the truth was the simplest scenario of all: Davis thought he was telling the truth when he said recording would be done that night in the gastropub, for that is what Lipinski told him."

Tall Rawls crossed her long runner's legs and looked up from the reporter's notebook. "How did you figure out the motive?"

"The simple process of elimination. I could conceive of no way in which Lipinski or Carson could profit monetarily from his death. Publicity from the murder of the guest co-host? That strains credibility. In fact, the murder might well prevent the episode from airing. I briefly considered the possibility that was the motive—to prevent the broadcast for some reason I could not fathom. That seemed, however, entirely too drastic, given that there must have been some other way for Lipinski and spouse to sabotage their own production. It might work in fiction, however, and I have made a note of that for future use.

"On to other speculations: Blackmail could have been a motive for either partner. However, considering the brevity of their acquaintance with Davis, he had a rather narrow window for acquiring damaging information.

"What did that leave? A person at the fringes of this case, Tony Ranieri, was on to the right motive—albeit the wrong killer—when he suggested romantic jealousy as the impetus. In retrospect, it is telling that Lipinski suggested to us that perhaps Davis was meeting someone at The Speakeasy for a romantic tryst. That showed that he identified the man he knew as Diamond with such activities."

"Lisa Carson was involved with Davis?"

"She says not," I put in. That came after the Zoom meeting ended.

"I am inclined to believe her," Mac said. "Why lie? The important thing, however, is not the truth but what Lipinski believed. Father Juan, in his interview for *Dining (Way) Out*, talked about the need to trust God. Trust is also an essential element in any successful marriage. Lipinski clearly did not have it. Perhaps Ms. Carson had made some lapse in the past, or perhaps he was deeply wounded by his broken relationship before they met, or perhaps he was simply a deeply insecure person. For whatever reason, Lipinski was controlling and jealous. He phoned Ms. Carson incessantly when she was here in Erin several days in advance of him—staying, mind you, at the same hotel with the man they knew as Stuart Diamond."

"Nuno Robles mentioned Lipinski constantly calling his wife," I informed the others.

"We heard that twice ourselves, Jefferson, on the day Davis interviewed me and the others. And on one of those instances, Lipinski asked where she was and whether Stuart Diamond was with her. We could deduce that from her responses."

Oh.

Mac later speculated that maybe Lipinski found one of those light-up *Strange World of Stuart Diamond* advertising pens in their hotel room and refused to believe that Diamond hadn't left it there during a romantic visit. In reality, Davis probably gave one to everybody. I keep mine as a souvenir.

"Lipinski's behavior seems similar to that of a jealous wife Mitzi Gold is dealing with in her relationship counseling practice," Mac mused. "The woman calls her husband frequently when he is not in her presence and checks his phone to see with whom he is in contact. Do you recall what Ms. Carson told you for your story in the *Observer* about Diamond's true identity, Johanna?"

"She said she worked closely with the guy, but only for a short time."

"The key word there is closely—too closely, Lipinski must have thought."

"Especially since she liked older men," Lynda tossed in. "That's what it said in the *WSTV Magazine* profile about their courtship and marriage. You know, it also said her boyfriend died in a hit-and-run accident a year after she started working with Lipinski. Somebody should look into that."

"Awesome!" Johanna said, scribbling in a notebook.

Mac raised an eyebrow. "Indeed! That was yet another clue, had I but realized it. We must have Oscar alert the police in whatever jurisdiction applies. Well spotted,

Lynda!" My beloved spouse glowed prettily, and I began to wonder how long our guests were going to stay. "At any rate, Lipinski was demonstrably possessive, and by implication untrusting and jealous. Romantic jealousy seemed the most credible motive, reasoning backwards from my conviction that Lipinski was the killer."

"Was it six bullets worth of motive, or do you think Lipinski was trying to emulate the murder of Jackie O'Brien?" Kate wondered.

Mac shrugged. "We will never know unless he confesses, and I doubt that his attorney will allow him to do so. However, I incline toward the latter. The earlier crime must have been much on his mind, and he did raise the possibility of a homicidal specter in a weak attempt to throw us off his scent. In any case, I see now in retrospect that choosing to kill Davis in that place and manner was one of two psychological clues to the murderer I should have picked up on. It showed a flare for drama, and reality television is about drama far more than it is about cooking, home renovations, decorating, wine and spirits, or any other ostensible subject. His wife even referred to Lipinski's 'artistic temperament.'"

"Wow," said Johanna. "What was the other clue?"

What took you so long to ask? He's been waiting.

"Fred Gaffe's murder was planned and executed on the spot. Quick thinking and decisive action are the hallmarks of a successful entrepreneur like Stephen Lipinski."

Before Johanna could fawn any further, my phone rang. Seeing that the caller was Grant Kingsley, I began walking away as I answered. SBU's president, imbued with military training, is a chain-of-command guy who doesn't often contact me directly. Whatever was up had to be big, and probably not good.

"It's Father Joe," he said without preamble. And I already knew before he said the rest: "He's gone."

Chapter Thirty-One
Loose Ends

The Lipinski-Carson marriage is over, but the trial is still pending as I write this. It should be an interesting one. Although the Sig Sauer that killed Cal Davis was never dragged up from the Ohio, the AFT's National Tracing Center did establish that Lipinksi owned such a gun.

Oscar still reminds Mac once a week or so that he was right when he suggested the day Davis's body was found that one of the TV crew was responsible. He may get tired of crowing about that someday, but not soon.

The ghostly manifestations at The Speakeasy have stopped. Whether that's because Sebastian McCabe solved the murder of Jackie O'Brien, or because Father Juan said the Office for the Dead, or because *Dining (Way) Out* came and went, we will never know. But I wouldn't rule out the supernatural explanations.

Nicholas Haldane also went. He sold Charles Bexley his half of The Speakeasy and moved back to Savannah full-time. I gather that the parting of the partners wasn't altogether amicable, but that's none of my business. There's a rumor that Bexley may change the gastropub's name in hopes of a fresh start. Maybe he will rename Poltergeist Porter as well.

Father Pirelli's funeral was live-streamed. I was honored to be one of only ten friends in attendance. Mac played "Amazing Grace" on the bagpipes, which seemed like a final insult to me but apparently was requested by Father

Joe. Go figure. It was surreal for me to look at the great man in his coffin and realize that I would never again see the neatly written "Good job!" or something similarly encouraging on a printout of a speech I'd drafted for him.

And that's not all that's surreal. Everything is these days. Don't tell me it's "the new normal." I'm tiring of hearing that. There's nothing normal about the Age of COVID. Just one small example: So far this summer I've gained almost fifteen pounds from Lynda's fabulous cooking during the lockdown. I call it the COVID-15. To be clear, I know I could have far worse problems.

"As Father Juan and Rabbi Nachman of Breslov both counseled, echoing Holy Writ, we need to not be afraid," Mac said the other day during the virtual cocktail hour that has turned into a regular Friday night event between the Codys and the McCabes.

"I am reminded of what Sherlock Holmes said at the dawn of World War I, which he compared to 'an East Wind': 'It will be cold and bitter, Watson, and a good many of us may wither before it's blast. But it's God's own wind none the less, and a cleaner, better, stronger land will lie in the sunshine when the storm has cleared.'"

"Let's hope so," I said. "It's nice to think that something good will come out of this nightmare someday."

"I'll drink to that," Lynda said.

A Few Words of Thanks

Jeff Cody and I cannot bring this tenth novel (and twelfth volume overall) in the McCabe-Cody series to a close without thanking the team who once again made it possible:

Nuno Robles, my friend and fan from Lisbon, Portugal, who lent his name to one of the characters;

Ann Brauer Andriacco, for suggesting the means in the second murder as well as for general support as we sheltered in place together during the writing;

Kieran McMullen, my friend and sometime co-author, who once again lent his expertise on weapons and police procedure;

Marc Lehmann, conjuror extraordinaire and devotee of these chronicles, for calling my attention to the "Done with Mirrors" magic trick;

Jeff Suess, for proofreading; and

Steve Winter, yet again, for giving the manuscript the incredible benefit of his engineering eye.

Any errors that remain are mine, not theirs.

Publisher Steve Emecz and cover illustrator Brian Belanger are the easiest collaborators any writer was ever so lucky to have. MX Publishing is a social enterprise venture that is both enterprising and venturesome.

About the Author

Dan Andriacco has been reading mysteries since he discovered Sherlock Holmes at the age of nine, and writing them almost as long.

The earlier Sebastian McCabe–Jeff Cody volumes are *No Police Like Holmes*, *Holmes Sweet Holmes*, *The* 1895 *Murder*, *The Disappearance of Mr. James Phillimore*, *Rogues Gallery* (novellas), *Bookmarked for Murder*, *Erin Go Bloody*, *Queen City Corpse*, *Death Masque*, *Too Many Clues*, and *Murderers' Row* (novellas). Dan is the co-author, with Kieran McMullen, of *The Amateur Executioner*, *The Poisoned Penman*, and *The Egyptian Curse* mysteries solved by Enoch Hale with Sherlock Holmes.

Also the author of *Baker Street Beat: An Eclectic Collection of Sherlockian Scribblings*, Dan is a member of the Baker Street Irregulars ("St. Saviour Near King's Cross"), the leader of the Tankerville Club of Cincinnati, and a member of numerous other scion societies of the BSI. Follow Dan's long-running blog at www.danandriacco.com and his Facebook Fan Page, Dan Andriacco Mysteries.

Dr. Dan and his co-conspirator, Ann Brauer Andriacco, have three grown children and six grandchildren. They live in Cincinnati, Ohio, USA, about forty miles downriver from Erin.

Praise for the McCabe–Cody mysteries

For someone like me who loves to travel, secures a front-row seat at our local 4th of July parade, and attends baseball games with butterflies-in-the-stomach excitement (*Murders' Row*), was a delightful read.
     —Mystery writer Kathleen Kaska

"With the McCabe and Cody mysteries, Dan Andriacco is doing for us what Conan Doyle did for the readers of Holmes and Watson in the late XIX century and early XX century: He's writing not only fantastic mystery stories but also creating unique characters that we can relate to, while admiring their adventures. *Too Many Clues* is another fantastic achievement in this series. Wonderful characters, amazing writing. Dan Andriacco is in great form."
     —Nuno Robles, Lisbon, Portugal

"Again, Andriacco displays an encyclopedic memory for his enormous roster of clever and colorful characters. There is never a lull in his writing, and he propels his story to a surprising conclusion for this reader. *Death Masque* is another witty and lively novel by Andriacco."
     —Writer Felicia Carparelli

"Dan Andriacco's *Queen City Corpse* is the latest in his series about Jeff Cody and Sebastian McCabe, who are in Cincinnati for a mystery convention and encounter mystery and murder, and a surprising solution; it's a lively story."
     —Peter Blau in *Scuttlebutt from the Spermaceti Press*

"This *(Queen City Corpse)* is the seventh novel in a deliciously literate, witty series, with ingenious plots and engaging characters. Highly recommended!"
     —*Sherlock Holmes Society of London*

"This (*Erin Go Bloody*) is Dan Andriacco's best book to date! I feel I could actually walk around downtown Erin, Ohio and not get lost. The characters are charming and believable. These are always entertaining reads!"
—Retired Sheriff Kenneth Ramsey, Sr.

"The ingenious twist at the end is an example of Andriacco's masterful ability to pen a page-turner. *Bookmarked for Murder* is a must-read for anyone who loves a classic who-done-it."
—Mystery writer Kathleen Kaska

"You're in the hands of a master of mystery plotting here. *Rogues Gallery* is a delightful read, hard to put down, and highly recommended. And did I say fun?"
—Screenwriter and novelist Bonnie MacBird

(*The Disappearance of Mr. James Phillimore*) "is a fun read in a series that keeps getting better with each new tale."
—Philip K. Jones

The 1895 *Murder* is the most smoothly-plotted and written Cody/McCabe mystery yet. Mr. Andriacco plays fair with the reader, but his clues are deftly hidden, much as Sebastian McCabe hides the secrets to his magic tricks under an entertaining run of palaver."
—*The Well-Read Sherlockian*

"I loved Dan Andriacco's first novel about Sebastian McCabe and Jeff Cody, and I'm delighted to recommend (*Holmes Sweet Holmes*), which has a curiously topical touch."
—Roger Johnson, *Sherlock Holmes Society of London*

"*No Police Like Holmes* is a chocolate bar of a novel— delicious, addictive, and leaves a craving for more."
—*Girl Meets Sherlock*

Also from MX Publishing

Visit www.mxpublishing.com for dozens of other Sherlock Holmes novels, novellas, short story collections, Conan Doyle biographies, Holmes travel books, and more.

MX Publishing is the award-winning, world's largest independent Sherlock Holmes Book publishers with over 150 new authors and 500 new Sherlock Holmes stories in print.

On Facebook:
https://www.facebook.com/BooksSherlockHolmes/

On Twitter
https://twitter.com/mxpublishing

On Instagram
https://www.instagram.com/mxpublishing/